INDIAN COUNTRY

INDIAN COUNTRY

by

John T. Young

IngramElliott

Indian Country

Copyright © 2017 John T. Young

Published by IngramElliott, Inc.
www.ingramelliott.com
9815 J Sam Furr Road, Suite 271, Huntersville, NC 28078

Cover design by: Tammy Rojas
Interior design by: S Squared Design
Original photography by: John T. Young

ISBN paperback
978-0-9981659-4-3
ISBN e-book
978-0-9981659-5-0

Library of Congress Control Number: 2017937105
Subjects: Action and Adventure—Fiction. Thrillers—Fiction.
Suspense—Fiction.

Published in the United States of America
Printed in the United States of America
First Edition: 2017, First International Edition: 2017

Dedication

To all the soldiers who gave their lives in the War on Terror.
To those who are still fighting it.

CHAPTER 1

An FBI report links the Los Zetas Mexican drug cartel to the Bandidos outlaw motorcycle gang.
—FBI National Gang Intelligence Center, 2013

Interstate 25
May 21, 2016

Wayne Kincaid downshifted and throttled back his Harley Street Glide as he took the exit off Interstate 25 to Pecos, New Mexico. He crossed the bridge over I-25, then headed north on Route 50 for a hundred yards before stopping on the right side of the narrow two-lane highway, near a historical marker. Early afternoon on a Saturday, and the road was busy with pickups and campers headed up the Pecos River for the weekend.

Kincaid lowered the kickstand with his boot and got off his motorcycle. He took off his leather jacket, wiped the sweat from his brow, and ran his hand around the edge of his black doo-rag. Kincaid stretched his six-foot-two frame as he walked toward the historical marker. He placed his right foot on a post near the sign, leaned over, and pulled up his jeans to check the top of his boot.

Inside was a Kahr 9mm, seven-round compact semi-automatic he carried in a concealed holster. Keeping his back to the road, he took out the Kahr and pulled the slide back, injecting a round into the chamber. He put the weapon back into its holster and felt in his right pocket for his Emerson

3.25-inch knife. The textured fiberglass handle had a thumb disc mounted on the blade spine for easy opening. He flipped it open to examine it, then closed it and put it back in his pocket.

Kincaid scratched the stubble of his month-old beard and looked at the sign for Glorieta Pass, known as the "Gettysburg of the West," where in 1862 a Confederate army regiment fought the Union army in a futile attempt to break the Union hold on the West. One of his Texas ancestors, Joshua Kincaid, had fought and died in that fight. And now, he mused, another Kincaid was ready for battle in New Mexico.

At 195 pounds, Kincaid was lean and fit. He had left the army more than a decade earlier, following his last tour in Iraq, but he'd stayed in shape. He had a black belt in karate and was trained in the Israeli defensive art of Krav Maga. As an agent for the Drug Enforcement Agency, however, he knew that his most powerful weapon was his mind. If he had to use the Kahr or his knife, he would likely have already lost the battle. It was his ability to think on his feet that had kept him alive through DEA tours in Mexico and South Asia.

Staring across the valley, Kincaid reviewed his cover, which he had rehearsed for the past month. Much of it was based on the truth. He had been a soldier in the Eighty-Second Airborne, but only for three years after he joined the army. He then served in the US Army Special Forces for seven years—including four years in the elite Delta Force—before joining the DEA. His story, however, was that he'd recently retired from the army after serving twenty years in the Eighty-Second. If anyone checked, he had a DD-214, the official army discharge paper, backing up his story. The army records repository in St. Louis, Missouri, would also verify his cover, and the sergeant major of the 504th Parachute Regiment at Fort Bragg had been briefed.

A cover, however, was only as good as the agent selling it.

He had to believe in his story and live it. As Kincaid got back on his Harley and headed west on Route 50 toward Pecos to meet the Bandidos, a rush of adrenaline sent his heart racing. Very few undercover agents had infiltrated the motorcycle gang and lived to tell about it.

Route 50 was a narrow, winding two-lane highway bordered by pine, cedar, and juniper trees, mixed with patches of piñon. To the north, he could see the Sangre de Cristo Mountains, home of the Pecos Wilderness. In the distance, Pecos Baldy rose 12,559 feet above sea level. With a population of 1,440, Pecos was home to mostly Hispanic families, whose modest homes lined the highway for the five-mile ride into the village. He rode past Griego's Market and Liquors, which featured the "best half-pound burger west of the Pecos." Farther down the road he passed the Dairy Queen and a Family Dollar store.

At the intersection of Routes 50 and 63, Kincaid turned right and rode a few blocks to Buck's Tavern, an adobe one-story building with a red Coors sign on top of a ten-foot pole. About two dozen Harleys were lined up on the east side of the building, all backed in and parked forward for a fast exit. Several Bandidos were hanging out front on the two wooden benches flanking the entrance, which consisted of battered oak double doors.

Kincaid parked at the far end of the gravel parking lot and sat for a moment, taking a few deep breaths. Like an actor about to go on stage, he was apprehensive. He thought about his discharge from the army at Fort Bragg ten years earlier. He imagined it happening only a month ago. Turning in his rifle. Getting a final medical exam. Driving out the front gate.

As Kincaid walked in, several Bandidos eyed him warily. Kincaid ignored them, hoping to show confidence but not arrogance. He didn't want to get into a fight, but he had to display just enough swagger to say: *I'm not afraid of you, so don't fuck with me.*

3

Buck's was a Bandidos hangout, and strangers were not welcome. In the next room, an old jukebox blared the Animals' "We Gotta Get Out of This Place." To the left, every one of the half-dozen tables held Bandidos and their girlfriends. A busy waitress delivered pitchers of beer. An elk head with antlers hung over the bar on the right, where five Bandidos leaned over their drinks.

The Bandidos wore their colors on leather jackets with patches showing a Mexican bandit brandishing a pistol and a machete. The patch read *Bandidos Worldwide*, with *1%* on the side. In 1947, when several biker gangs invaded Hollister, California, and caused a riot, a reporter quoted the American Motorcycle Association as saying that 99 percent of its members were law-abiding citizens, implying that the rest— the 1 percent—were outlaws. With about 2,400 members around the world, the Bandidos gang was viewed by the FBI as an organized crime syndicate, second in size only to the Hells Angels.

Kincaid walked up to the bar, and a woman turned and looked him over. Long black hair fell down her shoulders, nearly to the top of her short black miniskirt, which showed off long, muscular legs tucked into calf-high black boots. She was around thirty, half-white, half-Navajo, with mischievous brown eyes and a smile that suggested an invitation to Kincaid. She turned to the hulking bartender. "Hey, Buck," she said. "This man needs a beer."

She gently shoved the man next to her to make room for Kincaid, who returned the smile and sat close to her at the bar. The man, only slightly smaller than the massive bartender and a few years older than Kincaid, with black hair down to his shoulders, a full beard, and tattoos covering both arms, glared at Kincaid, who recognized him as John Henry, president of the New Mexico Bandidos. On the other side of Kincaid was Harry Dowdy, whose gray hair hung down his back in a ponytail. On his jacket was a patch that read *Expect No Mercy*.

"Thanks," Kincaid said to the woman. "What's your name?"

"Linda. Linda Benally. And this big handsome man next to me is John Henry."

Kincaid nodded to Henry, then turned back to Benally. "I'm Wayne," said Kincaid.

Henry stared at Kincaid with undisguised attitude. He drained his glass of beer and shoved it across the bar for a refill. "If you're lost, the bartender can give you directions," said Henry.

"Just passing through," Kincaid said. "What's going on?"

"We're living the dream," Benally said. "Drinking beer and riding our motorcycles."

Henry turned to face Kincaid. "You a cop?" he asked.

"Hell no, man," said Kincaid, as he received a draft beer from the bartender. "Just retired from the army."

Dowdy, who had been listening, moved closer to Kincaid. "What was your unit?"

"504th, Eighty-Second Airborne," said Kincaid.

"So you were over at Fort Campbell?" asked Dowdy.

Kincaid looked at him and shook his head. "Eighty-Second's at Fort Bragg."

Dowdy sipped his beer and said, "What two things fall from the sky?"

Kincaid stared at Dowdy for a few seconds, then grinned. "Bird shit and fools," he said. "Were you airborne?"

Dowdy laughed and slapped Kincaid's back. "I'm Harry. I was in the 101st, back in 'Nam. Just checking. We see a lot of assholes claim they were in the military but never served a day." He looked Henry in the eye and said, "Anybody crazy enough to jump out of airplanes can drink a beer with me."

"You don't look old enough to be retired," Benally said.

"Joined right out of high school, soon as I turned eighteen," said Kincaid.

"So what brings you to Pecos?" Henry asked.

"I bought a Harley when I got discharged at Bragg. Been riding around the country," Kincaid said. He sipped his beer. "No particular place to go. Nothing to do, first time in twenty years. I saw the sign for Pecos, and I thought I'd check it out."

Dowdy smiled at Kincaid. "Used to ask myself: Why would a normal person jump out of a perfectly good airplane?"

"What makes you think I'm normal?" asked Kincaid, who sipped his beer and looked at Dowdy. "Where'd you serve in 'Nam?"

Henry answered for him. "Harry was on Hamburger Hill. I think that screwed up his head. Harry's a little bit crazy."

Dowdy laughed and drained his beer. He opened his eyes wide and tilted his head sideways, looking at Kincaid. "Not just a little bit," he said. "I *am* crazy."

Henry raised his beer in a toast to Dowdy. "Right on, brother," he said. "We're all crazy here."

Kincaid turned to Benally. "How about you? Are you a Bandido?"

Benally laughed. "Just met these guys a few weeks ago."

"You ride a Harley?" asked Kincaid.

"Yeah," she said, smiling. "I love riding my Harley. It has really good vibrations."

Henry and Dowdy laughed and clinked beer glasses with Benally, while Kincaid smiled and raised his glass in a salute.

"When I met Linda, I asked her if she wanted to get laid," Henry said. "She said she would, but she had the clap. I told her, no problem, I did too."

"Lucky for him, I'm a nurse," Benally said. "I gave him some penicillin for his clap. But I don't have a cure for his bullshit."

Benally smiled at Kincaid. In her dark brown eyes, Kincaid saw mischief and defiance. She seemed to be inviting him in, but with a warning that the trip could be dangerous.

"How about you, Wayne?" Dowdy asked. "You got the clap?"

Kincaid drained his beer, wiped his mouth, and said, "Not lately."

He smiled at Benally. Henry, Dowdy, and Benally laughed, and Dowdy put an arm around Kincaid's shoulder.

"You spend time in combat, brother?" asked Dowdy.

Kincaid nodded. "Two tours in Iraq, one in Afghanistan."

"Fucking army," Dowdy said. "You kill any ragheads?"

Kincaid looked down into his beer and said, "A few."

More than a few, Kincaid thought. More than he could remember. Except for the twelve-year-old boy in Mosul, Iraq. That one he couldn't forget. It was one of the reasons he had left the army a month later.

Benally drained her beer and said, "You shoot pool, Wayne?"

He nodded, and she pointed toward the next room, which had two pool tables and a dance floor.

"I have twenty bucks says I can take you," she said.

"You're on," Kincaid said.

As Kincaid racked the balls for a game of eight ball, he casually glanced back at Henry and Dowdy, who were talking quietly. Henry briefly looked at Kincaid and scowled, then turned back to Dowdy.

"Henry doesn't seem too friendly," Kincaid said, lifting the rack and moving aside as Benally prepared to shoot.

"They don't trust outsiders," she said, taking aim. Benally fired a straight shot directly into the tip of the triangle of balls, sending them all over the table. The eleven ball fell into a corner pocket.

"Looks like you got the odds," Kincaid said, as Benally leaned over for another shot. He tried not to look at her legs when her miniskirt hiked up her thighs.

Was that meant to distract me? Kincaid wondered. Whatever her intent, it was working. He might be able to use Benally to work his way in with the Bandidos, but there was a huge risk. If she was Henry's woman, she was dangerous territory. But she didn't act like she was with Henry. So to hell with it. Let it ride.

Benally sunk the three ball in a side pocket, then used a soft touch to nudge the seven ball into a corner pocket.

"You didn't tell me you're a pool shark," Kincaid said.

"Nobody here will take me on anymore," she said. "So I have to look for an easy mark, like you." Benally eased the five ball into another corner pocket, then scratched on the one ball.

"Nice of you to give me a chance," Kincaid said, as he took aim at the two ball. He dropped it into a side pocket, then punched the ten ball down the table. It bounced off the corner pocket and rolled back.

"You hit it too hard," Benally said. "A pool ball's a lot like a woman. You need to go slow, and use a soft touch."

"I never thought of it quite like that," Kincaid said as he rubbed a piece of chalk on his cue tip. "But thanks for the advice."

Benally smiled as she lined up for another shot. "You don't look the kind of man who needs advice about women." She dropped the nine ball into a corner pocket and moved around the table to set up for the one ball.

As she walked close by Kincaid, he said, "There isn't a man alive who doesn't need advice about women."

Benally laughed and sank the one ball, then softly dropped the thirteen ball in. She lined up for a final shot at the eight ball.

"Corner pocket," she said. She gently dropped the eight

ball and turned to Kincaid, holding out her hand. "You owe me twenty bucks."

Kincaid opened his wallet and paid her. "You're ruthless," he said, smiling. "Want to have dinner with me sometime?"

"I guess I should take pity on you," she said, "since you're not a very good pool player."

Benally casually ran her hand down the pool stick as she put it into a rack, then took Kincaid's cell phone and entered her name and number. Kincaid took it and moved toward the exit. As he walked past the bar, he overheard Henry talking to Dowdy.

"Gotta head over to the Pecos Casino tomorrow," Henry said. "After Sanchez gets here."

It wasn't much, but it was a lead. Kincaid quietly left the tavern and got on his Harley.

CHAPTER 2

Samson Cowboy, director of the [Navajo] Division of Public Safety . . . reported there are about 225 documented gangs on the Navajo Reservation. . . . The total number of gang members on the reservation is between 1,500 and 2,000.
—*Navajo Times*, Aug. 6, 2009

Navajo Reservation, New Mexico
May 22, 2016

Arturo Sanchez gripped the armrest on the passenger door of the Cessna 182 and fought to control his nausea as the pilot sharply banked the airplane into the west wind blowing across northern New Mexico. Sanchez tried to focus on the horizon to calm his stomach and quietly prayed that he would not humiliate himself by throwing up.

Over the Navajo reservation, the first light of dawn illuminated the Bisti Badlands. The white rock formations sculpted by the wind for millions of years stood like sentries over what was once the floor of an ocean. Just above the badlands lay Chaco Canyon, where the ancient Anasazi had developed a thriving civilization until they migrated nearly a thousand years ago. The pilot veered south, located Highway 197, just east of Torreon, and dropped abruptly for a landing on the narrow two-lane strip of asphalt. The area was sparsely populated, with only a few scattered Navajo homes contiguous to the highway. No cars were visible in either direction.

Sanchez was arriving in New Mexico after a harrowing trip that had begun on a private airstrip near Juarez, Mexico, and crossed the border into the state halfway between Deming and Lordsburg. The pilot had flown up narrow valleys that skirted Silver City and passed through the Mogollon Mountains of southwestern New Mexico. A full moon allowed the pilot to fly a few hundred feet above the ground to escape radar detection. US Customs and Border Protection deployed its unmanned aircraft system surveillance along the New Mexico border, but it often failed to detect low-flying small aircraft. For Sanchez, the flight had been like riding a roller coaster in the dark for three hours while being buffeted by high winds.

A young Navajo flashed the headlights of his old Ford F-150 and backed up the truck next to the Cessna. As Sanchez got out to greet him, he unsnapped the tab on the holster carrying the Glock 9mm that he wore on his belt, concealed under his black leather sport coat. At forty, Sanchez was still physically fit, a legacy of his time with the Mexican Army Special Forces—a time before he joined the Los Zetas drug cartel. He wore faded Wranglers and lizard-skin cowboy boots, and with his styled haircut and trimmed mustache, he had assumed the entirely convincing look of a successful middle-class New Mexican.

Sanchez had to make sure the Navajo was his contact and not some local trying to rip him off. He stood with his back to the east, presenting a shadow to the Navajo as the sun appeared over the horizon.

Sanchez looked the driver over, then relaxed; he recognized Danny Haskie. In his faded blue jeans, Nikes, western shirt, and backward baseball cap, Haskie looked like a college kid but was really one of the Manhunters, a drug-dealing Navajo gang. He also freelanced as a distributor for the Zetas.

Sanchez looked at Haskie's eyes, searching for the dull glaze of too much crystal meth. Although he made his living selling drugs, Sanchez was too smart to use them and did not trust those who did. He was relieved that Haskie seemed clean. As he often did, Sanchez reflected on the irony of his trade. If Americans didn't buy and use drugs, the Zetas and the other cartels would go out of business. While the American government and news media frequently—and accurately—accused Mexicans of corruption, the drug trade could not flourish without the endemic corruption that existed throughout American society. Many of the Zetas' customers were wealthy Americans who bankrolled the purchase of drugs, using middlemen who took the risks involved in distributing the narcotics. People like Haskie.

"The product's in cardboard boxes," Sanchez said. "Get them loaded quickly."

"Okay, boss," Haskie said.

Haskie packed half a dozen cardboard boxes into the back of the double-cab Ford and covered them with a tarp, which he tied down. Haskie got into the driver's seat, and Sanchez sat next to him after stashing a small travel bag behind the seat.

For his frequent trips to the United States, Sanchez had cultivated a Tex-Mex accent that was common in southeastern New Mexico, complete with his cover as a cattle rancher. Through an intermediary, Sanchez had purchased a ranch about ninety miles northeast of Roswell. He also had an American passport in the name of José Santiago, courtesy of his contact at the US Consulate in El Paso.

Everyone had a price, Sanchez had learned. And everyone feared the Zetas. Los Zetas was the largest criminal syndicate operating in Mexico. Originally made up of thirty-four Mexican Special Forces soldiers, Los Zetas had expanded to include hundreds of former soldiers with advanced military training and weapons. Since their beginning in the late 1990s, when a group of Mexican army commandos deserted and began working for the drug cartels, the Zetas had diversified beyond drugs to extortion, kidnapping, and human trafficking.

The Los Zeta cartel had for years used a drug-trafficking route along Highway 70 in New Mexico; the route ran from Las Cruces through Ruidoso to Roswell, then up to Amarillo, Texas, and Interstate 40. Sanchez had established a safe house on his ranch near Portales, a small university town near the Texas border. He had convinced Portales residents that he was from Laredo, Texas. In a bold move, Sanchez had even joined the Portales chamber of commerce. He had also recruited several Portales Hispanics to distribute his drugs in eastern New Mexico, including on the campus of Eastern New Mexico University in Portales.

Haskie and Sanchez drove east on 197, which ran alongside a dry riverbed, through a narrow valley covered with chamisa plants, sagebrush, buffelgrass, and washed-out arroyos. The valley was bordered by high mesas that formed atop an ancient lava bed, the legacy of volcanos that erupted over the plain millions of years ago. A few horses grazed along the road. Sanchez and Haskie passed a mobile home with a 1960s Chevrolet pickup parked on blocks on one end, next to a stack of firewood. A butane tank rested on the other side, and a satellite antenna faced skyward nearby. An ancient windmill, which supplied water for a stock tank and for the home, turned slowly. No matter how many times he came here, Sanchez, who'd grown up in the lush valleys near Cuernavaca, south of Mexico City, always felt as though he had landed on an alien planet. This area seemed like a desolate third-world country.

He was now in enemy territory, Sanchez reminded himself, and he could trust nobody. His only friend was his Glock. He liked the weapon because it had no safety to worry about, and it seldom jammed. Sanchez carried it loaded with seventeen rounds, one round in the chamber. When he had to use it, the Glock became an extension of his right arm. Point and shoot, no more than ten feet from the target. And he had used it, many times. Los Zetas were infamous for beheading their enemies, but Sanchez preferred to keep his distance. He didn't like to get blood on his clothes.

Cuba, New Mexico
7:00 a.m.

After twenty miles, Haskie turned north on US Highway 550. As they neared Cuba, a predominantly Hispanic village of about six hundred people, the landscape changed from high desert to mountains, with piñon, cedar, and pine trees, elevation 6,900 feet. As the day grew lighter, traffic increased on 550, the main highway between Albuquerque and Farmington, a city of forty thousand located near the four corners of New Mexico, Colorado, Arizona, and Utah.

On the outskirts of Cuba, they passed a New Mexico State Police patrol car parked on the side of the road, gold seals on the driver and passenger doors of the black-and-white Crown Victoria. The state trooper, dressed in a black woolen uniform modeled after that of the gestapo of the 1930s, eyed the Ford as it drove past. The first priority of the state police was highway safety and catching speeders, but most officers were also on the lookout for narcotics traffickers.

"Watch your speed," Sanchez said. "We don't need trouble from the cops."

"*No problema*, boss," said Haskie.

"Are you concerned about the state police?" asked Sanchez.

Haskie laughed. "They used to profile us, until the courts told them to stop. Long as I don't speed, they can't do nothing. If they stop me for something like a broken taillight and ask to search my car, I just say no. Ask him if he has a warrant. You'd be surprised how many idiots just let the cops search their car without a warrant, even when they got dope in their car."

As Haskie drove through Cuba, Sanchez noted El Bruno's Restaurante y Cantina, the Del Prado restaurant and motel, and the center of action in Cuba, a Circle K adjoined to a McDonald's restaurant. Mud-splattered pickup trucks were lined up at the Circle K pumps, and the McDonald's was packed with early morning customers, mainly Navajo and Hispanic men on their way to work in the oil and gas fields.

They passed the defunct Doc's Lounge and turned right on State Road 126, a narrow two-lane highway that wound northeast through the village, past a densely populated neighborhood of mobile homes, most of which had several cords of firewood stacked against the walls. Haskie went up an unmarked paved road and down another bordered by a barbed-wire fence, until they came to a mobile home screened from the road by pine trees. Two Harley 1200T SuperLow Sportsters were parked in front. As the pickup stopped near the entrance, John Henry opened the door and stepped out on the porch. On the left side of the mobile home, Harry Dowdy emerged holding an 810 Remington 12-gauge shotgun. Dowdy racked a shell into the chamber and pointed it at the truck.

"Get out of the truck!" Henry ordered.

Both men stepped slowly out of the pickup. As Sanchez walked toward him, Henry smiled and said, "Welcome to New Mexico, Arturo."

"The land of enchantment," said Sanchez as he shook Henry's hand.

Henry had served six years in the New Mexico state prison for narcotics trafficking. Dowdy had been his cell mate, after he was arrested for bank robbery. Both had sworn they would never return to prison. To satisfy their parole officers, they were on the payroll of a motorcycle repair shop in Española.

In reality, the shop, owned by another Bandido, was a front for their main occupation—distribution of narcotics.

Haskie and Dowdy unloaded the boxes and carried them inside the mobile home, which was littered with empty beer bottles and pizza boxes. Metal chairs surrounded a fold-up card table, and a couch that would have been rejected by Goodwill sat in front of an old 32-inch color TV with rabbit ears. Bandidos camped out here when they had business in the area. Henry placed a box on the kitchen counter and opened it with the large hunting knife that he wore on his belt. He took out a kilo package of white powder and cut into it with his knife.

"What the fuck?" Henry asked as he wet a fingertip and tasted the product. He looked at Sanchez and smiled. "I thought you were bringing us black tar? Man, this is pure white heroin! Where'd you get this?"

"Afghanistan," said Sanchez. "We have some new friends there."

Los Zetas had joined up with Al Qaeda, which had direct access to the poppy fields of Afghanistan and the Taliban network. Since the early 1990s, the Taliban, working with Al Qaeda and Osama bin Laden, had expanded its heroin network from Europe to South and Central America. Sanchez had made a bargain with the devil: Al Qaeda would supply the cartel with a steady supply of heroin. In return, the cartel would assist the Al Qaeda operatives with infiltration routes and safe houses, along with a share of the profits.

Sanchez knew that many Americans were squeamish about using the needles necessary to inject the black tar heroin. The pure white could be snorted or smoked. Once a user was hooked on the white, he could then move on to injections for a quicker high. At eighty thousand dollars a kilo, the hundred kilos in his shipment were worth about eight million dollars on the street. Heroin had made a big comeback in America, and the Zetas intended to reap the rewards.

"Outstanding," Henry said as he resealed the box. "Fucking outstanding!"

After Haskie went outside to the pickup to wait for Sanchez, Henry motioned for Sanchez to sit on the couch. He took three bottles of Budweiser from the refrigerator, handed one each to Sanchez and Dowdy, then sat on one of the metal chairs and sipped his beer. Dowdy sat to the side, watching Sanchez.

"Who's the Indian?" Henry asked.

"His name is Danny Haskie," Sanchez said. "He belongs to the Manhunters, on the reservation. He works for me on occasion."

"I don't like working with Indians," Henry said. "Can't trust 'em."

"Haskie is smart, and he doesn't use drugs," Sanchez said. "We can use him for access to the reservation land. Lot of room out there to hide from the cops."

Henry nodded and took another swallow of beer. He knew he needed to reconcile his dislike for Navajos with his business interests. It was a conflict that stemmed from his youth in Farmington. Henry was the son of an oil-field roughneck who had moved there from Midland, Texas, in the late 1970s, when the oil and natural gas business was booming in the Four Corners area.

Henry's father had instilled a hatred of Navajos in his son. Navajos, his father had told him, were all on welfare, supported by white people who worked hard for a living. That image had been reinforced by many of the Navajos who came into Farmington on the weekends and drank until they passed out in alleys and parks around the downtown area. The drunk Navajos made easy targets for some of the Farmington high school boys, who cruised downtown at night. Rolling drunk Navajos became a rite of passage for some boys, Henry among them.

Henry stood up and clinked his bottle with Sanchez's.

"Guess it's just business," Henry said. "I'll deal with the Indian, but I don't have to like it."

"I appreciate your perspective," Sanchez said.

CHAPTER 3

In the eyes of law enforcement, reservations have become a critical link in the drug underworld. They have . . . facilitated the passage of cocaine and methamphetamine from cities in the West and Midwest into rural America.
—*New York Times*, Feb. 19, 2006

Pecos Casino
May 22, 2016
5:00 p.m.

Sanchez parked his rented Malibu in front of the Pecos Resort and Casino near the ruins of the ancient Pecos Pueblo. The parking lot was nearly full with cars bearing New Mexico license plates. A dozen long-haul tractor-trailers were parked to one side. Most of the customers were strangers, so he would fit in well. Just one more guy trying his luck.

A pair of Kokopelli figures playing flutes decorated the archway entrance of the eight-story sandstone casino designed to recapture the look of the Pecos Pueblo. The casino, Sanchez thought, was the Pueblo's revenge on the white man, who had taken their land but would now lose their money in the casino. Unfortunately, many of the casino's patrons could not afford to gamble and ended up bankrupt. Not his problem. Sanchez regarded gamblers the same way he did narcotics users: both were losers who deserved to be preyed upon.

Sanchez walked through the lobby, which featured

paintings by Georgia O'Keeffe and Ted DeGrazia. No expense spared for the gamblers, he thought, most of whom would have no knowledge of either artist. Sanchez walked through the smoke-filled casino, past rows of slot machines occupied by senior citizens gambling their social security checks and long-haul truck drivers hoping to get lucky during a brief respite from the nearby interstate. Other customers lined up around the blackjack, craps, and roulette tables. Cocktail waitresses circulated through the casino, ensuring that the customers were sufficiently inebriated to want to spend their money.

As Sanchez walked through the casino, Kincaid watched from behind a slot machine, where he had arrived a few hours earlier. Surveillance was the most boring part of his job, but it was often the most productive. The casino, filled with strangers, provided an ideal environment. He could move around the floor, playing different slot machines, and nobody would pay him any attention. As long as he wasn't winning much money, even the team watching the security cameras would overlook him. The challenge was to actually keep an eye on who came through the doors without being too distracted by the incessant ringing and spinning of the machines. Not to mention the attractive waitresses who were constantly parading through the casino.

Sanchez looked vaguely familiar, but Kincaid could not recall where he had seen him. Kincaid noticed him because he did not seem interested in gambling but walked straight across the floor with a purpose. Sanchez walked to the rear of the casino, past two restaurants and a gift shop featuring Navajo and Pueblo pottery and jewelry. Through the glass doors lay a pool and the edge of an eighteen-hole golf course. Kincaid followed Sanchez to the elevator, watched it rise to the top floor, then walked back to the slots to look for Henry.

The elevator deposited Sanchez at the top-floor office of Manny Martinez, who managed the casino. As Sanchez walked into his office, Martinez, an overweight Pueblo in his late forties, came around his desk to shake Sanchez's hand. Martinez had hair down to his collar and a thin mustache. Sanchez noted his suit, which appeared to have come off the rack at Sears. A man who did not dress well was a man who lacked self-respect, Sanchez believed. And a man who lacked self-respect was vulnerable. He would not be able to withstand an interrogation by police.

"Good to see you again, Manny," said Sanchez.

"You, too, Arturo," said Martinez.

Sanchez took a seat on a nearby couch and motioned for Martinez to sit next to him.

"Are we good to go?" asked Sanchez.

Martinez handed a thumb drive to Sanchez. "This gives you instructions for acting as a wire transfer manager," said Martinez. "I've booked you in a room here as Juan Hernandez."

"Excellent," said Sanchez. "Have you told anyone here about me?"

Martinez swallowed quickly, as he experienced a moment of fear. "*Dios mío*, no!"

Sanchez stared at him for several long seconds, looking for signs of deception. Did Martinez wet his lips? Did he maintain steady eye contact? Did he shift in his seat? Sanchez knew that his look could send fear through most men; it was a look he had cultivated and frequently used. Sanchez smiled at Martinez in reassurance.

"I trust you, my friend," said Sanchez. He got up and walked to the bar, where he poured himself a Scotch over ice. He stared out the window, which overlooked the Sangre de Cristo Mountains. The Blood of Christ, as they were named by Spanish explorers, because the setting sun cast a red glow over the mountains.

21

It had been many years, Sanchez mused, since he had been to church. Would he go to hell for his sins? Did he still believe in hell? If God existed, why did he allow the Zetas to commit such atrocities?

Sanchez turned back to Martinez and said, "We will both make a great deal of money with our new arrangement." He walked to the couch and sat down.

Martinez was the weak link in his New Mexico chain, but Sanchez needed to launder money through the casino, since the US Treasury Department's financial investigation teams had grown more efficient in tracing money moved overseas through American banks.

The cartel had been losing money in marijuana sales since several American states had legalized the weed. Farmers in many areas of Mexico were no longer growing the crop because the price for a kilogram of marijuana had dropped. Consequently, Los Zetas were trying to create new markets for heroin. New addicts had to cross the psychological threshold—overcoming the stigma of needle use. Mexican farmers were shifting to poppy cultivation, but there was not enough supply to meet the demand. By importing pure white heroin, which could be snorted, the cartel hoped to create new markets within America's white middle class, including college students.

There was, however, a price to be paid for the new arrangement. The Al Qaeda terrorists facilitating the movement of the heroin wanted access to the human smuggling routes used by the cartel. Sanchez and other Zetas leaders had calculated the risks: If the terrorists caused serious damage in America, it could harm the economy and the very markets the cartel relied on for sales. On the other hand, the heroin provided by Al Qaeda could result in enormous profits.

In the end, the cartel had decided the gains outweighed the risks. Their knowledge of Al Qaeda operations in the United

States could also prove valuable if deals had to be made with the American government. The Al Qaeda operatives were expendable.

John Henry parked his Harley in front of the Pecos Casino and walked through the gaming tables, en route to the same elevator Sanchez had used. As Henry passed through the casino, Kincaid, still playing the slots, recognized him and looked down as Henry walked by. Henry didn't appear to be looking for surveillance, which indicated to Kincaid that he was either complacent or simply untrained. As Henry neared the elevators, Kincaid moved along the bank of slot machines, using them as concealment in case Henry turned around. He didn't.

Kincaid waited until he heard the elevator chimes ring and the doors close, then walked up and observed the light going to the top floor. A sign posted by the elevator said the floor was the site for management offices. It was the same route the Hispanic with the mustache had taken. Kincaid returned to the slot machines. He would drop a few more dollars, then casually leave the building. Kincaid didn't want to risk being seen by Henry; it was enough that he had seen him going to the casino management offices. It was a piece of the puzzle he would fit in eventually.

Henry knocked on the door and Martinez opened it. He walked in, nodding to Sanchez. He helped himself to a beer from the small refrigerator and flopped on an easy chair.

"Have you begun to move the product?" asked Sanchez.

Henry sipped his beer and nodded. "On its way," he said. "I've got people taking it to Albuquerque, Phoenix, Denver, and Dallas."

The Bandidos transported the heroin in nondescript sedans,

mostly Hondas and Toyotas, throughout the United States. They avoided using their motorcycles, which attracted attention from law enforcement. They adapted to their environment. If the distribution area was in a conservative community, they sent members with short hair and no beards. The Bandidos were actively recruiting members who could pass as college students, to expand distribution on college campuses.

"What about Haskie?" asked Henry. "What's your plan for him?"

"Haskie can move a little product on the reservation, and work his way over to Flagstaff and Phoenix," Sanchez said. "There are many Indians in Arizona, so he can blend in. He also has contacts in the Sioux Nation. We can use their reservations in the Dakotas to store the drugs, if we need to create a distribution center for the Midwest. We need to go slow and let Haskie develop his network for us."

Sanchez sipped his Scotch, debating how much more to tell Henry and Martinez. He didn't trust anyone outside of his own cartel, but he would soon need their assistance. "Our new partners from the Middle East want our help moving some people up the pipeline," he said. "They want to use a safe house on the Navajo reservation. Haskie has a place."

Since the attacks on the World Trade Center, the cartel had smuggled scores of operatives from the Middle East across the Mexican border into the United States. One of their primary routes had been from the state of Chihuahua into southern Arizona, where operatives from Al Qaeda had dressed as Mexicans and joined the illegals who were brought in by "coyotes"—Mexican smugglers. Their first destinations in Arizona had been the mosques in Tucson and Phoenix, but federal law enforcement agencies had begun investigating those locations. It was time to diversify.

Henry took a long swallow from his beer and looked out

the window. He was smart enough to know that he might be getting into something that could come back and bite him in the ass.

"We're talking about bringing in terrorists, right?" Henry asked.

"Perhaps," said Sanchez. "Does it matter, as long as you are well paid?"

Henry nodded and said, "What are these people planning to do here in the States?"

"I believe they are looking to make a profit from smuggling drugs into the United States," Sanchez said. "This would be to our mutual benefit."

Henry took a long swallow of beer and leaned against the bar, staring at Sanchez. He knew bullshit when he heard it but decided that he really didn't care, because he hated the US government. If the ragheads exploded a few bombs around federal buildings, it was okay with him. As long as the Bandidos weren't implicated.

"We have a good thing going, Arturo," Henry said. "Don't fuck it up. We don't need the Feds breathing down our neck."

Henry turned to Martinez, who was uncomfortable around the menacing biker. Martinez was scared of Henry but tried never to show it.

"You had any more Italian boys from the east coast nosing around here?" Henry asked.

"No. They tried to make a business arrangement with me, but I told them we weren't interested," Martinez said.

"Make sure you continue to give them that message," Sanchez said. "Those Mafia morons are careless, and they attract attention from the FBI."

The FBI lacked the resources to adequately investigate all the Indian casinos, a weakness that Sanchez sought to exploit. He intended to bring dollars taken from drug profits into the casino and exchange the money for chips, later cashing out the chips for clean cash. Sanchez would set up scores of accounts for fictitious customers and wire less than ten thousand dollars at a time to banks in the Cayman Islands and Belize. The ruse would not withstand close scrutiny, but for some time he could move a steady stream of drug profits out of the country, using the Pecos Casino. The FBI, after all, had more important matters at hand—such as preventing terrorism in America.

Sanchez was also concerned about the Internal Revenue Service. The 1970 Bank Secrecy Act required banks to report any transactions over ten thousand dollars to the IRS to prevent money laundering, but Indian casinos had often been lax in complying with the law. Some reservation leaders viewed their land as sovereign territory and resented any investigations by the federal government.

In 1988, Congress enacted into law the Indian Gaming Regulatory Act, which was passed to regulate gambling on reservations. The casino money provided badly needed cash for many tribes, but it also opened the door to organized crime. Decades earlier, a secret witness had told a US Senate panel that organized-crime families already ran twelve of the ninety Indian gambling operations that he knew about. He said that 50 percent of the operations had some link to organized crime, usually through the purchase of supplies from Mafia-owned companies.

Sanchez finished his drink, stood to leave, and turned to Henry. "I will be in touch very soon. I want to meet some of your colleagues in the Bandidos. And I may need your help transporting some of our friends across the state."

CHAPTER 4

Kokopelli's flute is said to be heard in the spring's breeze, while bringing warmth. It is also said that he was the source of human conception. Legend has it, everyone in the village would sing and dance throughout the night when they heard Kokopelli play his flute. The next morning, every maiden in the village would be with child.
—indigenouspeople.net

Santa Fe, New Mexico
May 22, 2016
Sundown

Kincaid rode his Harley off Interstate 25 on the southern outskirts of Santa Fe and took the Cerrillos Highway exit, turning back north. The sun was dipping below the Santa Fe Mountains, setting the sky ablaze with an orange glow, diffused by cumulus clouds into a kaleidoscope of colors. He headed up Cerrillos, past the New Mexico State Police headquarters and academy, and then west, toward the part of Santa Fe unvisited by tourists.

A mile down the road, he entered the Riverside mobile-home park, a well-kept community with a brick fence around it. Since Santa Fe is one of the most expensive places to live in the Southwest, many middle-income people who work in Santa Fe either live in fringe communities or commute from nearby towns. Rising property taxes that followed the increase in real estate prices often forced long-time residents of Santa Fe to sell their homes and move out of the city. Most residents blamed the increase in prices on people moving from California, the "Californicators" who drove their Mercedes-Benzes and BMWs through Santa Fe to their multimillion-dollar mansions perched on the hillsides surrounding the city.

Kincaid parked his Harley in front of a modest double-wide prefabricated home, which had a small wooden porch with a rail. Parked in front was an older model white Jeep Cherokee with an Indian Health Service decal on the door. Benally's Harley Sportster sat next to the Jeep. Kincaid knocked on the door, and Benally opened it.

"Hello," she said. "Aren't you the guy I beat at pool?"

"I always let a woman win the first game," he said as he walked inside.

Kincaid noted a Ben Franklin stove at the end of the living room. A stack of oak firewood lay next to it. The living room furniture consisted of a brown leather couch and love seat, two lamps on end tables, and a TV resting on an oak veneer stand with a stereo on the bottom half. A Navajo rug hung on one wall, and a two-foot-long Kokopelli figure in a metal frame hung over the couch. Kokopelli was hunchbacked, with feathers protruding from his head, playing a flute.

Benally took his jacket and hung it on a clothes rack, then stepped into the adjacent kitchen, which was separated from the living room by a half wall.

"Want a beer?" she asked as she opened the refrigerator.

"Sure," Kincaid said, sitting on the couch. Benally walked into the room with two Negra Modelos. She handed one to Kincaid and clinked his bottle in a toast.

"Here's to good times on Harleys," Benally said, as she sat across from Kincaid on the loveseat. Her leather miniskirt hiked up, and Kincaid could see her panties: black lace. She was teasing him, and she knew he knew it. No time to show weakness, he thought; a woman had no interest in a desperate man. Although he was a little desperate. It had been a long time.

Kincaid pointed to the Kokopelli figure and asked, "What's the story on the guy with the flute?"

"Indians believe Kokopelli carries unborn children on his back and gives them to women," she said. "He's the god of fertility."

Kincaid sipped his beer and smiled. "Does that have some special meaning for you?"

"Kokopelli's also a trickster," she said. "Always out trying to seduce innocent young women. So I'm wondering, are you one of those Kokopellis?"

Kincaid set down his beer and moved next to her. He gently brushed back her hair and kissed her softly and slowly on the mouth. Benally responded with passion, running her tongue into his mouth and wrapping her arms around his shoulders, pulling him closer. Kincaid ran his hand along her thigh, and she moaned with pleasure. He moved his hand closer to her breasts and started to unbutton her shirt, but she stopped kissing him and sat up, staring into his eyes.

"Do you think you can handle a purely sexual relationship, with no strings attached?" she asked.

Kincaid tried to slow down his breathing as he sat back. "I guess we could do that," he said.

Benally picked up her beer and stood up. She slowly walked around the room, avoiding his gaze.

"I don't want a relationship," she said. "No strings."

"I'm willing to give that a try," Kincaid said.

Benally leaned against the wall and sipped her beer. "You sound a little too eager. Has it been a while?"

Kincaid laughed and said, "Yeah, it has." He stood up and

reached for his jacket. "Maybe we can do this some other time."

Benally put her hand on his arm and said, "Don't go."

She sat on the edge of the couch and smiled at Kincaid. "It's nothing you did," she said. "I have some problems with men."

Kincaid sat back on the couch and said, "I never would have guessed."

"Long story," Benally said. She stood up and walked to the kitchen. "Want something to eat? I've got tamales and some green chili."

"Sounds good," he said.

Kincaid joined her in the kitchen, sitting at a small round table with one-inch tiles that formed a mosaic of a three-story pueblo. A clock made of driftwood hung above the sink. He looked down the narrow hallway that led to the bedrooms and wondered whether he would head that way or leave out the front door after dinner. Probably the latter, he guessed.

Benally put a bowl in the microwave and sat down across from Kincaid. She took another sip of beer and intently looked at him.

"You're obviously a superior man, and I would like to have sex with you," she said. "I just need some time."

"I'm a patient man, Linda," Kincaid said, smiling at her.

Is she just yanking my chain? he wondered. *What kind of game is she playing? Maybe she gets off teasing men. Keep your head straight, Kincaid. She's your only connection to the Bandidos. Don't screw this up.*

The microwave bell went off, and she got up and put the tamales on plates, with the green chili in small bowls. Benally grabbed two more beers from the refrigerator, sat down, unwrapped a tamale, and began to eat it. Kincaid opened his tamale and spread some chili on it.

"I got married on the reservation, when I was only

seventeen," she said. "His name was Virgil. He was a Navajo police officer, over at Shiprock."

Kincaid nodded and continued to eat, saying nothing but paying attention.

"We were only married about four months. I came home one day and found him packing his things. He said he had a good time with me, but he was going back to his wife," she said.

Kincaid stopped eating. "Wasn't that illegal? Having two wives?"

"Yeah," she said. "But he was a Navajo cop. What could I do? Besides, I'm half-white. On the res, that's no better than white. Navajo people don't really trust whites."

Kincaid sipped his beer and looked at her. "Tell me about your parents," he said.

"My mother was a teacher, from Boston," she said. "She was very idealistic. She came out to New Mexico to save the Indians. She met my father at the Diné College in Crownpoint. He was also a teacher."

"Where are they now?" Kincaid asked.

"When I was five years old, a drunk Navajo in a pickup ran into their car outside of Shiprock on Highway 666," she said. "We used to call it the Devil's Highway, until the government changed the name a few years ago."

"I'm sorry," Kincaid said. "Five is pretty young to lose your parents."

"It was hard," she said. "But I was very fortunate to have an uncle. He took me into his home, out on the reservation."

"What about your grandparents, back in Boston?" Kincaid asked.

Benally shrugged and sipped her beer. "I guess they weren't as idealistic as their daughter," she said. "Not much place in Boston society for a Navajo."

31

"Did you see Virgil again?" asked Kincaid.

"Yeah. I caught up to him a few months later. I found out where he lived, and I drove my pickup through the bedroom wall of his trailer. I tried to kill him and his wife," she said. "Lucky for me, they were in the living room. He didn't press charges, and I got over it."

"Remind me never to piss you off," Kincaid said. "I saw the Indian Health Center Jeep outside. You work there?"

Benally wiped her mouth with a napkin and took a sip of beer. "Yes. I'm a nurse practitioner. I make home health care visits on the reservations in northern New Mexico."

"I've heard a nurse practitioner is almost a doctor," he said. "You can even write prescriptions?"

Benally sat back, looking smug. "And you thought I was just some biker groupie, or a bar slut," she said.

Kincaid raised his beer in a toast to her and she clinked her bottle against his. "Touché," he said. "Although I have nothing personal against bar sluts or biker groupies."

"How about you, Wayne? Twenty years in the army is a long time. What are you planning to do now?" she asked.

Kincaid shrugged. "Don't really know. Guess I'll just kick back for a while. Enjoy my freedom. Ride my Harley."

As he looked at Benally, Kincaid reflected on how he had learned to lie and live with those lies every day he worked undercover. In the bar, he had assessed Benally as a potential asset, although she would be an unwitting one; she could never know his real identity, for her safety as well as his own. His mission was to investigate the links between the Bandidos, the cartels, and the Navajo gangs on the reservation. Benally, with her social ties to the Bandidos, plus her access to the reservation, was a gift. By getting closer to her, he could more easily infiltrate the Bandidos. She could be the key to his entire operation.

Could he engage in a purely sexual relationship with her, with no strings attached? Of course. As he watched her, however, he sensed that he would pay a price. She radiated sexuality with an intoxicating intensity, and he was captivated by her personality and good looks. If he got emotionally attached and lost his objectivity, he'd endanger the mission and himself. Or he could add another layer to the emotional shell he wore. His combined twenty years in the army and the DEA had resulted in one failed marriage and a host of disastrous affairs; his undercover work made it difficult to start or maintain any relationship.

"You ever been married?" she asked.

"Once, when I was eighteen," he said. "A girl I dated in high school. After I went into the army, she met a rich kid in college, in law school. She figured he was going to make a good living, and I was just a private in the army."

Benally laughed. "Guess we're not lucky at love."

Kincaid finished his tamale and stood up to leave. He walked into the living room and began to put on his jacket.

"Appreciate the meal," he said. "Maybe I can treat you to dinner sometime."

At the door, Kincaid paused and kissed her on the lips. It was a soft, tender kiss that probed gently, and she responded with passion. Benally took his jacket from him and tossed it on the floor. They backed slowly into the living room, kissing more intensely, then fell onto the couch. Kincaid pulled off her black lace panties while she furiously unbuckled his belt. She lay back as he entered her, hungry for her. She wrapped her legs around him and cried out with pleasure.

"You are one of those Kokopellis," she said.

CHAPTER 5

A Department of Homeland Security (DHS) report published this year revealed that approximately 2,000 police and other law enforcement officials are under investigation for their involvement in organized crime. The DHS is currently investigating public officials who have received bribes to protect criminals, facilitate drug trafficking, escort drug shipments, and traffic the Mexican cartels' drugs.
—InsightCrime.org, Oct. 21, 2014

Drug Enforcement Agency
Albuquerque, New Mexico
May 23, 2016

Bill Roberts drove west on Central Avenue toward downtown Albuquerque, wondering why George Jackson, his boss, wanted him to come to DEA headquarters. Roberts was working undercover at the casinos, and Jackson generally wanted his agents to avoid headquarters as much as possible. As Roberts pulled into the underground parking lot beneath the US federal complex on Gold Avenue and Fifth, he figured he had fucked up his time card or put in for too much overtime. He got out of his gray Malibu and took the elevator up to the fourth floor of the Dennis Chavez Federal Building.

Roberts had a belly that hung a few inches over his cowboy belt. He was out of shape but had stopped caring when he'd hit forty a few years back. His black hair extended a few inches over his ears, and he wore a mustache that was thick but well-groomed. The product of a white father and a Latina mother, Roberts could pass for Hispanic until he tried to speak Spanish, a language at which he was not very proficient. He wore Wranglers, a western shirt, cowboy boots, and mirrored aviators—a cheap pair he'd bought online. The overall effect was of a cop trying to disguise himself. He showed his ID card at the entrance to the DEA offices and walked down the hallway. He knocked on Jackson's door and entered.

George Jackson was special agent in charge of the DEA Albuquerque office. He was a little younger than Roberts, but already bald on top, with a light, well-trimmed beard that showed some gray mixed with the light brown. Jackson's trim build was a product of years of running and watching his diet. His eyes, a pale shade of blue, looked tired. He motioned for Roberts to sit in a chair while he finished signing some papers.

"What's up, George?" Roberts asked as he shifted in the overstuffed leather chair, trying to get comfortable and to show that he was not intimidated by Jackson.

Jackson put down his pen and smiled at Roberts. "Anything new on the Indian casinos?"

Roberts had been tasked with finding some proof that the cartels were laundering money through the casinos. He shook his head. "I don't know where you got your intel," he said. "It may be true, but I'm not getting any closer to proving it."

Jackson leaned back in his chair and folded his hands in his lap. "Tell me how you're going about this."

"I've been going to some of the casinos, hanging out, watching who's coming and going," he said. "I've got those photos of the guys we know about, but I haven't seen any of them."

"What else have you been doing?" Jackson asked.

"I've made friends with a few of the bartenders and waitresses," he said. "Told them I'm interested in scoring some meth or coke."

"Anything come of that?" Jackson asked.

"You know how it is," Roberts said. "Takes time to get people to trust you."

"Yeah," said Jackson. "Think you need some help? I can always bring in another agent."

Roberts took a deep breath and looked hard at Jackson. "You don't think I can handle the job?"

Jackson leaned forward and clasped his hands, resting them on his desk. "It's not that, Bill," he said. "I just want to know if we need more manpower."

Roberts stood up and walked over to the window, which was heavily tinted and designed to stop a bullet. He looked out on Gold Avenue, where some people were walking out of their offices. The working day was almost over for the middle-class office workers who would drive to the suburbs of Albuquerque or Rio Rancho.

"Do you know what it's like, George, to spend fifteen years in the DEA and still be only a GS-12?" Roberts asked.

"If you want to get promoted, you have to get results," Jackson said.

Jackson had been with the DEA for only thirteen years, but he was already a GS-15. Roberts glared at him as he leaned against the wall, folding his arms.

"Got any ideas on how to move this along?" Roberts asked.

"Yeah," Jackson said. "Look up John Clearwater, our contact on the Navajo police narcotics. See if he can give you a lead. We need to make some progress."

Roberts nodded and walked out of the office. Jackson waited until he was down the hallway, then picked up his cell phone and dialed a number.

"He's moving," Jackson said as he walked out of his office and headed for the parking garage.

Kincaid, who was sitting on his Harley in the parking lot of Weekdays Restaurant, just south of DEA headquarters, took the call from Jackson. He put his cell phone in his pocket and strapped on his helmet with the visor down. A few minutes later, Roberts drove out of the parking lot and turned right on Fifth Street, then right again on Central Avenue. Kincaid stayed back, letting several cars get between him and Roberts, who headed east through heavy traffic.

A month earlier at DEA headquarters in Washington, Kincaid had met Jackson, who told him he suspected a leak in his office. Jackson had spent months working off intelligence obtained through an NSA wiretap about an upcoming meeting between Los Zetas and the Bandidos; it was a meeting that never happened. Besides Jackson, only Roberts knew about the operation and the meeting date. Jackson was convinced that Roberts had leaked information about the wiretap to either the Zetas or the Bandidos. Kincaid's instructions were to gather evidence on Roberts and discover his connections in the cartel.

As they approached the left-turn access lane to get onto Interstate 25, Kincaid slowed enough to allow another car to get ahead of him. The access road was a block long, with a stop sign at the end, and traffic was backed up because each car had to wait for a break in the cars exiting the freeway. Kincaid prepared to make a hard decision: wait his turn, or ride around traffic to keep Roberts in sight, exposing himself to the target. Fortunately, he caught a break in traffic and was able to stay behind Roberts, who continued north past the Big I, where Interstates 25 and 40 intersected. Kincaid couldn't get too close to Roberts or the target would spot his lone Harley, but he couldn't stay too far back because Roberts could take an exit and lose him.

Roberts continued north past the Albuquerque city limits, joining the horde of commuters headed back to Santa Fe. After they passed the Bernalillo exit, Kincaid pulled back a little farther. Since Roberts was likely headed for Santa Fe, Kincaid slowed and let two more cars get between them. Kincaid pressed a button that connected his earbud to his cell phone.

"Looks like he's going to Santa Fe," he said.

"I'm headed that way," Jackson said through the Bluetooth in his car.

Normal DEA surveillance would have involved four or five cars, all communicating over two-way secure radios. One would stay close for a while, then back off as another car took over. Kincaid, however, was on his own. The Albuquerque DEA office had a leak, and Jackson was running Kincaid without backup. Kincaid would never set foot in the office, and no other DEA agents there would know about him.

Kincaid liked working alone and away from the office. He could barely sit still for the time it took to write a report, let alone tolerate mingling with people in the office, listening to inane office gossip. Kincaid was a lone wolf. He was a good listener but not a good talker. DEA psychologists called him a "selective extrovert," which meant that he was introverted until he had to deal with people. Then he could turn on his magic and bullshit with the best.

As Roberts and Kincaid approached La Bajada Hill, the elevation rose steeply to almost 8,000 feet. At the crest, the highway dropped sharply to Santa Fe, a mere 7,000 feet. To the north, the Santa Fe Mountains were still capped with snow, and cedar and piñon trees appeared alongside the road. Roberts continued east on I-25 to the St. Francis Drive exit, where he turned off and drove north.

Kincaid now closed the gap, concerned that Roberts could turn off at any street. Drivers here were as crazy as the ones in California, he thought, as he watched several cars abruptly change lanes without signaling. He was aware that most motorcycle accidents were caused by drivers who weren't looking for motorcycles. When the contest was between a man on a motorcycle and a metal car weighing over a ton, the man would always lose.

Roberts crossed Zia Road and continued north to Cerrillos Road, the longest and busiest street in Santa Fe. Here Kincaid was most at risk of losing Roberts, who could quickly turn left or right on any of a dozen narrow, winding streets, all clogged with traffic. The streets of the ancient city had been built for horses and wagons, not cars and trucks.

Roberts turned right on Paseo de Peralta, which looped east around the state capitol. After passing numerous art galleries, he veered left onto Washington Avenue. He found a metered parking space in front of the Bull Ring restaurant, a watering hole popular with Santa Fe's politicians and bureaucrats.

Kincaid spotted a parking lot just ahead on his left. A sign said it was parking for library patrons only, and violators would be towed, but Kincaid figured he could take the chance. He quickly parked his Harley, took off his helmet, and ran fifty meters alongside the building to the corner of Nusbaum and Washington, just in time to see Roberts enter the plaza.

Kincaid saw the large sign for the Bull Ring, but Roberts could be going somewhere else. The plaza had several exits. Kincaid crossed the street, slowed to a walk, and casually peered into the window of a jewelry store as he watched Roberts enter the restaurant, never looking back for surveillance. *He's careless*, Kincaid thought, but Kincaid could not afford to grow complacent. The Zetas could have operatives in the area, working countersurveillance.

After waiting a few minutes, Kincaid trailed after a group of a half dozen people walking in, using them as cover to slip past the hostess. The bar, on the left, was separated from the restaurant by a wall with three large, open arches. Kincaid casually walked past one of the arches and spotted Roberts sitting at a table talking to the Hispanic man Kincaid recognized from the casino. The table was set apart just far enough to offer some privacy, and the noise in the restaurant served to mask any conversation between Sanchez and Roberts.

After a waiter delivered two glasses of beer, Sanchez asked, "Have your friends at DEA said anything about me?"

"Nada," Roberts said. "But my boss is getting impatient. He wants more information about the casinos."

Roberts is nervous, Sanchez thought. *He is not good at concealing his emotions. And if I see this, it is likely that his supervisor also does. Perhaps we need to give him something to make him seem more credible. At the same time, we can damage a competitor.*

"I may be able to help you," Sanchez said. "In a few days, the Sinaloa cartel will be taking a produce truck with a hundred kilos of cocaine through the border crossing at Deming."

Sanchez consulted his phone, then wrote on a pad and slid it across the table to Roberts. "Here is the license plate of the truck, and the time."

Roberts took the paper, looked at it, then put it in his pocket. "I'll see what I can do about it," he said.

In the bar, Kincaid took out his cell phone and held it to his ear, as though he had just received a call. While standing near one of the arches, Kincaid snapped a photo of the two men. The bar was dimly lit, so that even if they had looked in his direction, they would have been unlikely to see him, but the restaurant had enough natural lighting to allow a clear picture. He moved slowly through the crowd and left the restaurant.

Kincaid walked west from the Bull Ring, through a covered passageway that led to Lincoln Avenue, where he stopped to admire a bronze statue of Allan Houser, a Chiricahua Apache sculptor and painter who was born in Oklahoma and lived and died in Santa Fe. Kincaid entered a gallery that featured Houser's works and looked at his art, while also looking through the large glass windows for any surveillance coming from the area of the Bull Ring.

Kincaid was always concerned about being made. If Roberts was dirty, he might have protection, and Kincaid didn't know the identity of the Hispanic Roberts was meeting at the Bull Ring. He was the same man Kincaid had seen at the Pecos Casino, so he could be with one of the cartels. Or, he might be tied to the Bandidos, since John Henry went to the same floor at the casino. Kincaid might be paranoid, but he was right to believe that there were people out to get him. A DEA agent could die a very unpleasant death if captured by drug dealers.

Most of the art in the gallery was in the range of twenty to eighty thousand dollars, a bit much for Kincaid, who enjoyed looking at art but seldom bought anything. After all, where would he put it? He hadn't had a home since leaving high school. He had lived in army barracks or motels most of his adult life.

After a final look out of the window, Kincaid walked south on Lincoln Avenue, stopping to browse in a few shops. He walked past the overhang in front of the historic Governor's Palace, where Native American artists sold their jewelry during the day in tourist season. The sidewalk was packed with Navajos and Pueblos who had laid their artwork on blankets on the sidewalk for display, as scores of shoppers wove along the sidewalk. He walked across Palace Avenue and through Santa Fe Plaza, a small park that had been the destination for supply trains from St. Louis in the nineteenth century. A hundred years before that, it had been the end of El Camino Real, the Spanish Royal Road from Mexico City.

The park was full of Anglo artists selling their arts and crafts. In the center was an obelisk, a four-sided monument with origins in ancient Egypt—a smaller version of the Washington Monument. At its base sat a gray-haired, bearded man playing an accordion. On one side of the obelisk was an inscription that read: *To the heroes who have fallen in the various battles with Indians in the Territory of New Mexico.* Kincaid wondered how the Indians in New Mexico felt about that inscription. He knew that the Pueblo Indians had revolted against the Spanish in 1680 and killed about forty Spaniards while driving several thousand out of New Mexico.

Kincaid walked through the park to East San Francisco Street, where he entered the Five and Dime General Store, which was a Woolworth's until 1997. Kincaid walked down an aisle on the right side of the narrow, rectangular store and casually turned to face the entrance while pretending to shop for tourist items. The store was full of Route 66 memorabilia, including miniature turquoise New Mexico license plates with individual names, coffee cups, T-shirts, and packages of plastic bows and arrows for children.

After a few minutes, satisfied that he was not being watched, Kincaid continued through the store to the south end, where an elevator took him down one floor to Guadalupano Imports, which contained a variety of art, including Mexican pottery and decorative crosses. Kincaid avoided eye contact with the clerk, who looked up as he walked by, then returned to her magazine, quickly writing him off as a customer.

The exit at the back of the store led to Water Street. Kincaid walked out and turned left, headed for the Old Santa Fe Trail, one block east. As he passed by shops and galleries, he paused briefly at Santa Fe Native Design Jewelry & Pottery, where he used his peripheral vision to scan the sidewalk behind him. His last stop on Water Street was a corner store that featured baskets of turquoise stones, with racks of colorful shirts hung on overhead racks. Kincaid walked through the cluttered display and emerged onto the Old Santa Fe Trail, turning back north.

On the right was his destination, the La Fonda Hotel. If he was being followed, there would likely be one operative coming down the street to parallel him from his last location in the plaza. Kincaid was looking for anyone paying attention to him—or trying hard not to be paying attention.

He determined finally that he did not have surveillance and crossed the street to a side door of the La Fonda Hotel, a Santa Fe landmark. When the Spaniards founded Santa Fe in 1607, the hotel was one of the first businesses established. During the nineteenth century, trappers, soldiers, gold miners, and gamblers all stayed at the La Fonda. It's now a favorite destination for tourists. And its numerous exits make it a good meeting place for DEA agents.

Kincaid walked across to the bar, where he sat facing the lobby that swarmed with tourists. The bar was dark mahogany, with wooden beams across the ceiling. A mural of an ancient cliff dwelling wrapped around a pillar, and a buffet with appetizers sat at one end of the room.

Kincaid ordered a beer and watched TV for half an hour, until his cell phone buzzed with a text message from Jackson. Kincaid walked to the rear of the lobby and up the stairs to the third floor, along a gold carpet with red-and-blue southwestern designs. Each room had carved oak doors, and Native American art hung throughout the hallways. Kincaid walked to a room and knocked. Jackson opened the door and let him in.

"Good to see you again, Wayne," Jackson said as he shook his hand. "Did you get anything on Roberts?"

Kincaid nodded and flopped in a chair.

43

"Something's not right," he said, pulling out his cell phone to show Jackson the photo. "He was meeting this guy at the Bull Ring. I don't know who he is, but I saw him in the Pecos Casino yesterday. I think he took the elevator to the management offices. John Henry took the elevator to the same floor, same time."

"I'll be a son of a bitch," Jackson said as he looked at the photo. "I've seen this guy somewhere. I just can't place him. But we think that casino is linked to the Zetas. This guy could be the connection. And it looks like the Bandidos are tied in too."

"Want me to email this to you?" Kincaid asked.

"Yeah," said Jackson, who sat in an opposite chair. He clasped his hands behind his head and stared up at the ceiling, trying to make sense of it all. "I'll run it by the analysts at EPIC." The El Paso Intelligence Center, or EPIC, is the DEA's fusion center at Fort Bliss, Texas, where scores of analysts from the DEA, FBI, Customs, and local police agencies accumulate information on narcotics dealers.

"I'm tempted to confront Roberts right now and shake him up," said Jackson. "But I want to know what the hell he's doing in Santa Fe talking to this guy."

"We've got nothing solid on Roberts, right?" Kincaid asked.

Jackson stood up and folded his arms, then walked around the room staring down at the floor. He looked out the window at the Old Santa Fe Trail, where the street was crowded with government workers headed for happy hour, mixed with tourists exploring the myriad art galleries and jewelry stores.

"It's all circumstantial," Jackson said. "Just rumors and secondhand gossip from informants. We know he has a gambling problem, and he's always in debt. We know he's made several trips to Belize. We suspect he has a bank account there."

"What's his connection with the cartel?" Kincaid asked.

"I think he tipped off the cartel about a meeting they were

going to have with the Bandidos," Jackson said. "We knew the location and bugged it, but the meeting never happened."

Jackson shook his head and took a small bottle of Scotch from the minibar and poured himself a drink. He sat down and sipped the Scotch. "We think Roberts got in too deep with his gambling, so the cartel made him an offer, to pay off his debts. The real question now is, what the hell is the cartel planning here? And what do they expect from Roberts? We just don't know enough."

"You want me to keep surveillance on Roberts?" Kincaid asked.

"For now, let's focus on the Bandidos," Jackson said. "Any progress?"

"I may have a way to get closer to them," Kincaid said.

Jackson nodded and motioned for Kincaid to continue.

"I met a Navajo nurse practitioner who hangs out with some of them," Kincaid said, "including John Henry."

"No shit?" Jackson asked, leaning forward.

"Yeah," Kincaid said. "I went out to that bar in Pecos you told me about. Henry acted like he would just as soon shoot me as talk, but this nurse practitioner, Linda, knows him. She was friendly. Gave me a chance to meet Henry."

Jackson nodded and leaned back in his chair. "Go easy with these guys, Wayne. Don't push it. If they make you, they'll cut you up into little pieces with a chainsaw."

"Henry's the key," Kincaid said. "If I can get close to him, he may lead me right to the cartel."

Jackson stared at Kincaid and said, "I can't give you backup. Nobody here I can trust."

Kincaid stood up and walked to the door, then turned to Jackson. "I think I'm headed over to the Navajo reservation tomorrow."

"Going with your new lady friend?" Jackson asked.

"I think it's time I see Indian Country," Kincaid said, then he opened the door and left.

Kincaid walked out of the La Fonda onto San Francisco Street and wove through the crowds of tourists in Cathedral Place, then back to his Harley. It was another surveillance detection route, something he did every time he was on an operation.

An SDR is a basic maneuver used by virtually all intelligence agents and police detectives to determine whether or not they're being followed. Most of the time, it's done while driving. A series of turns through both commercial and residential areas allows the driver to note any cars that he could spot in different locations. If the driver spots the same car over time and distance, it's a good sign he has surveillance.

Before entering a new area, Kincaid would use Google Earth to check out the best routes. By changing environments and turning corners, he could look for surveillance without being too obvious about it. Even on his own time, he walked or drove SDRs, often without planning. It was habit, his way of staying alive.

He was relieved to see that he had not received a ticket on his Harley, or worse, been towed. He rode his bike back through the lot, north on Otero to Marcy Street, then south on Paseo de Peralta. As he passed several art galleries and the rotunda, where the state legislature met, it occurred to Kincaid that Santa Fe would be a good place to visit as a tourist.

Unfortunately, he never had time for vacations. By law, he was supposed to receive a month of vacation time each year, plus all the federal holidays. In reality, he was too busy to use his vacation time, and he didn't really care. To him, undercover work was his life. The adrenaline rush of matching wits with the opposition was addictive.

Kincaid turned west on Cerrillos Road, then south on

St. Francis Drive to his apartment complex. The two-story complex had an adobe facade, as well as a pool and an exercise room. Kincaid headed up to his second-floor apartment. The one-bedroom dwelling boasted basic furnishings—all courtesy of the DEA. Two chairs were placed at a breakfast nook. A TV rested on a wooden table. Kincaid took a beer from the refrigerator and turned on his stereo. He put in a CD of "Ride of the Valkyries" and sat on the balcony, watching the sun set over the Santa Fe Mountains.

The apartment was no different from a dozen others he had occupied while working undercover. The complex was loaded with attractive single females, but he could not risk exposing his cover by getting involved with anyone. The apartment was not even rented in his name but to a front corporation used by the DEA.

Why did he live this way? Did all his effort really amount to anything? He knew he couldn't fit into a normal job sitting behind a desk. Sometimes he felt he had been born a century too late; he identified more with his nineteenth-century cowboy ancestors, who raised cattle, rode horses, and didn't have to deal with paperwork or bureaucrats.

As Kincaid sipped his beer and listened to Wagner, he grew nostalgic, thinking about his short-lived marriage to Robyn Stewart, whom he'd met at Boerne High School, just west of San Antonio. She was a cheerleader, tall with long blond hair and blue eyes; he was on the football team. Her father was a Baptist preacher, and his was a cattle rancher. It was lust at first sight. He smiled recalling her refusal to have sex until after they were married. All those long, frustrating evenings making out in his old Bronco. After driving him to the edge of madness, she would finally give him a hand job. It was sex the Baptist way.

After graduation, he joined the army. A superb athlete, Kincaid craved the physical challenge, his sense of adventure untainted by the reality of combat. They were married after his advanced infantry training and airborne school at Fort Benning. By then, she was a freshman at the University of Texas at San Antonio. They agreed she should complete her first year of college before joining him at Fort Bragg, where he was newly assigned to the Eighty-Second Airborne.

Kincaid thought he would surprise her by coming home early a few days before Thanksgiving. He still remembered digging for his key as he approached the apartment. He entered quietly, planning to tap her on the shoulder and take her in his arms. Once inside, he heard moaning from the bedroom. He opened the door and saw her making love to another man. Robyn looked up, pushed the man aside, and pulled up the sheet.

"Wayne! I thought you were coming home tomorrow," she said, torn between indignation and shame.

Kincaid stood frozen in the doorway, barely able to comprehend the scene. Robyn's lover cautiously got out of bed and reached for his pants. Kincaid turned his gaze from Robyn to the student and struggled to control his temper. His first instinct was to beat the shit out of the man, but Kincaid was afraid that he wouldn't be able to control himself and would end up killing him. He quickly decided that it wasn't worth it.

"Get your clothes and get the hell out of here," Kincaid said quietly.

The man stumbled out of the room, clutching his pants and shirts. Robyn wrapped the sheet around herself and stood up, still keeping her distance.

"Who is he?" Kincaid asked.

"He goes to the law school," she said. "We just met a few weeks ago. I'm really sorry."

"Do you love him?" he asked.

Robyn paused and looked down, then slowly raised her

head. "I don't think I was ready for marriage, Wayne," she said. "I'm too young. I like being in college."

"A lot better than being a soldier's wife, I guess," Kincaid said.

Kincaid left the apartment without saying another word. He filed for divorce the next day in Bexar County Court, the day before Thanksgiving. Robyn didn't challenge it, and he never saw her again. Kincaid joined the ranks of the many divorced paratroopers in the Eighty-Second. With his buddies, he prowled the bars in Fayetteville, drinking too much, sometimes getting into fights. He never married again. Kincaid told himself it was because he could never meet the right woman, that he was always deployed somewhere. Over the years, he'd had a series of relationships that never lasted more than a few months, mostly with divorced women who had been married to other soldiers.

And now, here he was, thirty-eight years old and ready to use Linda Benally to get in with the Bandidos. What was he going to do about her? How would she react if she found out what he was really after? And what if he ended up wanting her for more than her connections? He was beginning to think that his attraction to Benally was more than just physical, and that could be dangerous—for both of them.

CHAPTER 6

Navajo elder Jay Tsosie winces when he recalls those torturous classroom drills from his childhood. . . . When caught whispering Navajo to classmates, Tsosie felt the wrath of an often sadistic English-only system: Teachers washed his mouth with soap and forced him to kneel on pencils and hold two heavy soda bottles in his outstretched arms. "Some days," Tsosie said, "I had to write on the blackboard 100 times: 'I will not speak Navajo.' "
—*Los Angeles Times*, Oct. 24, 2014

Navajo Reservation
May 26, 2016

As Linda Benally drove west of Albuquerque on Interstate 40 in her Indian Health Service Jeep, Kincaid looked out to the north at Mount Taylor, which rose more than 11,000 feet and was still capped with snow. The area around the mountain, an active volcano several million years ago during the Pliocene era, was surrounded by volcanic debris. Mount Taylor itself, however, was largely forested, rising like a blue cone above the desert below. It was home to large elk herds, mule deer, black bears, and mountain lions.

"That's quite a mountain," he said. "Ever been there?"

"Yes. That's Mount Taylor, one of our four sacred mountains," Benally said. "It's the southern boundary of the Navajo land."

"Pretty hard country to make a living," Kincaid said, as he noted the barren landscape around the mountain.

"Navajos are a tough people," she said. "My ancestors survived the Long Walk, right through this area."

"The Long Walk?" Kincaid asked.

"When Kit Carson and the American army went to war with the Navajo people—1864," she said. "Carson burned their crops, killed their livestock, and rounded up about eight thousand Navajos. They marched them over three hundred miles, over to Bosque Redondo, on the eastern side of New Mexico."

Benally went on to explain how the Navajos had migrated from Canada to New Mexico around 1500 BCE. After obtaining horses from the Spanish in the 1600s, the Navajos evolved into mounted marauders, alternately raiding or trading with other tribes. In 1863, the US government dispatched Kit Carson to control the Navajos, who were already fighting the migration of white settlers into New Mexico. The Navajos had bows and arrows; the cavalry had guns. In less than a year, Carson defeated them.

"I think I heard about that in one of my history classes," Kincaid said.

"The Navajos made it back home in 1868, after they signed a treaty," Benally said. "The government thought they were giving us worthless land, but it turned out the Navajo land has big deposits of uranium, coal, and natural gas."

About twenty miles west of Grants, Benally turned north on Highway 371, toward Crownpoint. The road passed through a landscape that seemed impossible to cultivate and unlikely to sustain livestock. Scattered clumps of sagebrush clung to sheets of red sandstone, with lone mesquite trees that appeared to reach out in a desperate search for water.

"You have a lot of territory to cover out here," Kincaid said.

"We're stretched pretty thin," she said. "The Navajo reservation is the biggest in the country."

"So what kind of problems do you see out here?" he asked.

"A lot of diabetes, heart problems," she said. "But the biggest problem is alcohol. A lot of Navajos drink too much, get the DTs."

"DTs?" he asked.

"Delirium tremens," she said. "It's a form of alcohol withdrawal. If an alcoholic goes one or two days without a drink, he can start to have nightmares, get confused, even have hallucinations. He may imagine insects, snakes, or rats crawling over his body. About half of what I do on the res involves treatment for alcoholism."

"What do you do for them?" Kincaid asked.

"Usually, I give them doses of benzodiazepines," she said. "I wish I could get them to stop drinking."

"I thought alcohol was illegal on the reservation," Kincaid said.

"It is. But people here have cars, so they drive to Gallup or Farmington," she said. "No way the police can stop that."

Benally turned her Jeep left off Highway 371 and parked in front of the Indian Health Service headquarters at Crownpoint. The brown brick one-story complex served a population of more than thirty thousand Navajos in western New Mexico and eastern Arizona. The center had a twenty-bed hospital with several physicians and nurse practitioners. Out front were three flags: the United States, the state of New Mexico, and the Navajo Nation. Kincaid saw a young Navajo woman emerge from a pickup truck with a baby on a traditional Navajo cradle board, a ponderosa pine frame with buckskin laces looped through it.

As Benally and Kincaid got out of the Jeep, Danny Haskie

emerged from the entrance. He slowly walked over to Linda, shooting a wary glance at Kincaid.

"What's up, Linda?" he asked.

"Going to work," she said. "You should try it sometime."

Haskie smiled and nodded his head toward Kincaid.

"New boyfriend?" he asked.

"Wayne, this is Danny. He's my cousin. Danny, this is Wayne," she said.

Kincaid extended his right hand, but Haskie ignored him and glared at Benally.

"How come you always date white guys?" Haskie asked. "What's wrong with your own people?"

Benally laughed and turned Haskie's backward baseball cap to the front.

"I tried that once, remember? Not a good experience," she said.

Haskie shrugged, turned his cap backward again, and began walking toward his pickup. As he neared his truck, he turned back toward her and smiled.

"I know some guys who would like to meet you," he said. "If you get tired of white men."

Kincaid watched Haskie drive away and turned to Benally. "I don't think he likes me," he said as they walked to the entrance of the health service building.

"It's not just you, Wayne," she said. "Danny doesn't trust any white people."

"What does he do for a living?" Kincaid asked.

Benally turned and watched Haskie's pickup turn a corner, heading north on 371. She remembered teaching him to drive when he was ten years old, at her uncle's ranch northeast of Crownpoint. Several years earlier, she had taught him to ride a horse, bareback.

"He's in a gang called the Manhunters," she said. "They deal drugs on the res."

"No future in that," Kincaid said as they walked through the entrance to the health center.

"I'm not making excuses for Danny," she said. "But there aren't many jobs on the res."

Benally pointed toward a door for employees and told Kincaid, "I have to pick up some case files. Wait here a few minutes?"

"Sure," he said. "I'll just stop in the restroom."

As Kincaid walked straight down the hall toward the men's room, the several dozen Navajos waiting in the lobby stared at him; he was the only Anglo in the room. After Kincaid relieved himself, he washed up at the sink and looked in the mirror.

Once more into the breach, he thought, as he took a deep breath and let it out slowly. Linda could be the key to unraveling the cartel's distribution network in the Southwest. Getting close to the Bandidos, through her, had been his priority. But now, another approach was possible, through her cousin and the Manhunters. Kincaid felt like he was on a raft, flowing down a river with no way to steer. He knew he had to let the flow carry him, to be patient, to be the innocuous gray man. Working as a narc was not like a chess game; it was more like playing pinball—and sometimes he was the ball.

Benally emerged from her office, carrying a briefcase full of files. They walked back to her Jeep.

"Busy day for you?" Kincaid asked.

"Just the usual. Take blood pressure on a few patients, write some prescriptions," she said. "Sure you don't mind coming along?"

"Like Danny, I'm unemployed," he said, climbing into the passenger seat.

"Maybe he can find some work for you," she said, laughing as she headed for the highway.

"I think a white guy like me would be a little conspicuous on the res." Kincaid laughed.

The desert floor was sparsely covered with sagebrush and cedar shrubs. Kincaid saw a lone coyote walking along the road, seemingly oblivious to the Jeep.

"That coyote doesn't seem afraid of us," Kincaid said.

"Maybe it's not just a coyote," Benally said.

Kincaid raised an eyebrow and smiled at her. He raised his hands in question.

"The Navajo people believe in Skinwalkers," she said. "They're witches who wear the hide or skin of the animal identity they want to assume."

"You believe in that?" Kincaid asked.

Benally was silent for a few moments. She clenched her teeth as she thought how to respond to Kincaid. "I have a bachelor's and a master's degree from the University of New Mexico. I've lived in what you consider the rational world. But I know that some people on the res have experienced things that can't be explained in rational terms."

"Could you give me an example?"

"I told you about my ex-husband, Virgil," she said. "He cheated on me and lied to me, but something he once told me seemed true. Or at least he thought it was true. One night, after we were married, he came home really scared. He said he had been on patrol down south of Shiprock, driving along about sixty miles an hour, when this dark creature, wearing some kind of ghost mask, starting running alongside, trying to get into his car."

"Some creature was running at sixty miles an hour? Are you sure Virgil wasn't high on something?"

"No. Virgil was a pretty good cop," she said. "He said this creature followed alongside his car for about half a mile, banging on his window, trying to get in. It scared the living hell out of him."

"Did anybody else see this creature?"

"Virgil told me he talked to two state police officers a few weeks later. They'd had the same kind of encounters, but they kept quiet about it. If they told that story to other cops, they'd probably send them to a shrink."

"I know New Mexico has a history of UFO sightings," Kincaid said. "But this is the first time I've heard about Skinwalkers. Maybe they're aliens."

Linda smiled and turned briefly to face Kincaid. "I don't really believe in Skinwalkers. Navajos are superstitious, and I think the legends become exaggerated with time. Just like the Christian Bible. Do you really think Jesus walked on water and raised Lazarus from the dead? Or are these stories just metaphors for some real things that happened? But if the Navajos believe these things with Skinwalkers happen, it can affect how they live."

Kincaid stared at her for a few seconds, then gazed over the landscape. Benally turned north on Highway 7900. The pavement gave way to a gravel road. They passed a chalk-white cliff and drove through a narrow valley bordered by red sandstone.

"I try to keep an open mind," Kincaid said. "Tell me more."

Benally smiled and gathered her thoughts. She was silent for a few moments. "The Navajos believe that Skinwalkers have the power to steal the skin—or body—of a person. If you look into the eyes of a Skinwalker, they can enter your body. Skinwalkers avoid bright light, and their eyes glow like an animal's when in human form," she said. "Skinwalkers are witches. They can make people hurt themselves. They can even jump over cliffs."

Here we go again, Kincaid thought. *Just when you think you meet a good-looking woman who might be normal, she turns out to be a wacko.*

Benally caught his look and burst out laughing. "You think I'm nuts, don't you?"

Kincaid smiled and said, "I'm a little confused by all of this."

"One thing I forgot to mention," she said. "Skinwalkers can read minds."

Kincaid shrugged. "Just hope you aren't one."

At the top of the cliff, Benally drove a few miles farther, then turned down a dirt road. They passed a herd of a dozen horses, who stopped their grazing to look up at them.

"Where we headed?" asked Kincaid.

"I thought we would drop by and see my uncle. He's getting old, and I like to check on him, because he lives alone, since my aunt died a few years ago."

"How old is he?" asked Kincaid.

"About seventy-five. We're not really sure, because he never got a birth certificate until a couple of years after he was born," Benally said.

In the distance, Kincaid saw an old one-story brown adobe home, next to an ancient hogan, a conical structure built with adobe and logs. Nearby was a small open-sided shed, and a wood-fenced corral with two horses. Parked close, a 1980s Ford pickup featured bald tires, a rusted body, and a cracked windshield. Two rusted barrels looked like they were used for burning trash. The home was surrounded by a dozen cedar shrubs, separated by large clumps of sagebrush.

"This is where you lived, after your parents died?"

"Yes," she said. "Until I went away to college."

Benally parked in front, and she and Kincaid walked to the front door. She knocked once, then opened the door and walked in. "Herman, you in here?"

Herman Benally was sitting in front of the TV, watching an old John Wayne movie, *She Wore a Yellow Ribbon*, on the DVD player. He slowly raised his stocky frame and turned to greet Linda as she walked in with Kincaid at her heels. Most of Herman's hair was gone, and his hearing and vision were fading. His mind, however, was still intact, and he scrutinized Kincaid like a hawk looking at its prey.

"Hello, Linda," he said.

She hugged him, then turned toward Kincaid.

"Herman, I want you to meet a friend," she said. "This is Wayne Kincaid."

"Pleasure to meet you, Mr. Benally," said Kincaid as they shook hands.

"Call me Herman."

Kincaid noticed a plaque with the US Marine Corps insignia hanging on the wall. Next to it was a framed photo of half a dozen young Navajos in uniform, including a young Herman Benally. "Were you in the Marines, Herman?"

Herman nodded. "I was in the infantry."

Linda walked over to the refrigerator to get some Cokes, while Herman motioned for Kincaid to sit on the couch, and he sat back in his old La-Z-Boy chair. Like Linda's home, Herman's had a Franklin wood-burning stove. The floor was covered with faded linoleum, and the room smelled of cigarettes and old dirt.

Linda handed out the Cokes, then sat next to Kincaid and sniffed the air. "You been smoking again, Herman?"

"I'm seventy-five years old," he said. "What difference does it make?"

Linda looked at the TV, where John Wayne prepared to lead a cavalry patrol to fight Indians.

"I never could understand why you like John Wayne," she said. "He was always killing our people, in the movies."

Herman laughed and said, "John Wayne was a real man. Not like those pretty boys they got now in Hollywood."

"Spoken like a true Marine," Kincaid said, raising his Coke in a salute.

"Were you in the Marines?" Herman asked.

"I was a paratrooper, Eighty-Second Airborne," Kincaid said. "Just retired from the army."

Herman nodded, then raised his Coke and said, "Here's to fallen warriors."

Kincaid leaned over and clinked his can with Herman's. "To fallen warriors," he said.

Herman studied Linda and Kincaid. He turned to Linda and smiled. "Is he your man?" he asked.

Linda laughed. "None of your business, Herman," she said.

"You should hang on to him," Herman said. "He's a warrior."

Kincaid leaned back in his chair and smiled. He tipped his Coke toward Herman in acknowledgment. "Where did you serve, Herman?"

Herman looked up at the photo. He stared at it for several moments. Kincaid raised an eyebrow at Linda, wondering if he had opened a wrong door.

"I was in the First Marine Division," Herman said. "I went to Da Nang, Vietnam, in 1965. I was in recon. We used to sneak up to North Vietnam and call in air strikes. Sometimes we had to call in a helicopter to get out."

Herman stared out of a window for a few seconds, then pointed to the picture on the wall. "See those young Marines? All of us joined, in 1965. We all grew up together. I'm the only one still alive," he said. Herman stared at the photo, then turned his gaze back to Kincaid. "It's been a long time since I talked about the war." He looked away and was silent for several moments. "I remember getting off the bus at the Marine depot in San Diego. The drill instructors screamed at us." Herman was quiet again, then returned his gaze to Kincaid. "Sometimes on recon, we had to lie in the mud for hours."

"I've spent a lot of time lying in the mud," Kincaid said.

Herman smiled and nodded. "My father was also in the First Marine Division, during World War II," Herman said. "On Guadalcanal. Then Tarawa, and Okinawa. He was a code talker. The Japs never could break our code. They never heard Navajo before, and there weren't any books on it, back then."

"A lot of Navajos join the Marines," Linda said, looking at Wayne. "Navajos are warriors."

"What are you doing now, Wayne, since you retired?" Herman asked.

Before Kincaid answered, he paused. It was normal lying to strangers in order to protect his cover, but lying to Herman made him feel uneasy. Here was a man who deserved his respect. He was also a man, Kincaid suspected, who was not easily fooled.

"I'm still trying to figure that out," Kincaid said. "I've been in the army all of my adult life, and I don't know anything else."

Herman nodded, then asked, "Did you serve in Iraq?"

"Yes, sir," said Kincaid. "Two tours there with the Eighty-Second."

Herman stared at Kincaid for a few seconds, then smiled as if he had just developed an insight into Kincaid's character.

"Are you part Indian?" Herman asked Kincaid.

"My great-great-grandmother was a Comanche, in Texas," Kincaid said. "But I don't look like an Indian. How did you know?"

"Being Indian is more than how you look," Herman said. "It's something inside. I could sense it."

Kincaid felt as though he was in a trance, unable to divert

his eyes from Herman. Linda nudged him on the shoulder.

"Hey, you want to see the horses?" she asked.

Not wanting to be rude, Kincaid looked at Herman, but Herman turned back to the TV and said, "I want to see the rest of this movie."

As Benally and Kincaid walked toward the corral, she turned to him and smiled. "I think Herman likes you," she said.

"I feel like I've been interrogated," he said.

"He can be pretty intense," she said, "for an old man."

"He has a way of looking right through you," Kincaid said.

"You have blond hair and blue eyes," she said. "I never would have guessed that you're part Indian."

Kincaid shrugged. "I just consider myself an American."

"There's something you should know about Herman," she said. "He's a Hitali, a medicine man."

They reached the corral, and the two Appaloosa horses walked toward them. Benally reached over and petted one of them on the neck and scratched him behind an ear.

"What does that mean," asked Kincaid, "medicine man?"

"It's not the same as a doctor, in your world," she said. "A medicine man is one who tries to restore harmony. A person becomes ill because he is out of harmony with his environment, or he has been in contact with evil spirits, like a Skinwalker, or a witch."

Kincaid reached over the fence and rubbed the nose of the other horse. *Here we go again with the superstition*, he thought.

"How does a medicine man restore harmony?" he asked.

"The Diné, the Navajo people, believe that everything in the universe is alive and has spiritual powers," she said. "The universe was shaped by powerful deities who are still alive and influence events in this world. The Hitali is like a liaison between man and the deities."

Benally turned and pointed at the old hogan. "See that hogan? That's where Herman performs healing ceremonies," she said. "Like the Enemy Way rite, which is an exorcism to remove ghosts, violence, and negativity that can bring disease and do harm to a person."

"Sounds complicated," Kincaid said. "Where did he learn all that?"

"A medicine man has to be an apprentice to another medicine man," she said. "I think Herman began after he got back from the war. My aunt told me he had a difficult time getting over his combat in Vietnam." Benally turned to Kincaid and smiled. "I know this all seems strange to you. Try to understand, a medicine man is honored and respected among the Navajos."

Kincaid looked over at the hogan. "Would he mind if I looked inside? I've never seen a hogan before," he said.

Benally nodded and walked with him to the hogan, which was roughly fifteen feet in diameter and built with logs. The roof was covered with thatch and mud, with a hole in the center to allow smoke to escape. The entrance faced east. She pulled back the wooden door. Inside, Kincaid saw layers of old carpet and animal skins covering the floor, except for a patch of sand. In the center was a small circle framed by stones, where a fire was built during a ceremony. The hole in the center of the roof allowed meager light into the room. As he looked around, Kincaid felt a chill, as though something had just passed through him. He stepped back outside.

"Maybe I can ask Herman to perform a ceremony for you," she said, "if you feel the need to get rid of your ghosts or negative feelings."

"I don't think I could handle it," Kincaid said. "Just a moment in there and I felt pretty weird."

Benally pointed toward the horses and said, "Want to go

for a ride? The Appaloosas need some exercise."

"Yeah, I'd enjoy that," Kincaid said.

Benally smiled as she opened the tack room at the end of the shed and handed Kincaid a saddle and bridle.

"You take Peanuts," she said, pointing toward the larger of the two horses, "and I'll take Popcorn."

Kincaid laughed. "Are we going to ride 'em or eat 'em?"

Benally placed her saddle and blanket over the top rail and opened the gate, as the horses began neighing and moving closer; they were eager to get out of the corral. Benally and Kincaid stepped through the gate. Kincaid patted Peanuts on the neck and reassured him. Peanuts reluctantly took the bit into his mouth, and Kincaid placed the bridle over his ears and tied the strap beneath. They led the horses to the fence and tied them to the rail while they put on the blankets and saddles. Kincaid tied the front and back cinches, then gently poked Peanuts in the side so he would let out his breath and cinched the saddle one notch tighter.

"I can see you've done this before," Benally said.

Kincaid put his left foot in the stirrup and mounted Peanuts, who backed up a few feet.

"I grew up on a ranch near San Antonio," he said.

Benally mounted Popcorn and walked him through the gate. Popcorn champed at the bit, eager to take off, as was Peanuts. The horses began at a fast trot, then loped across the pasture, scattering a small herd of sheep. They followed a thin trail through cedar and piñon trees interspersed with berry-laden juniper shrubs. They skirted the edge of a prairie-dog town, whose sentinels barked a warning, sending scores of the tan rodents into their holes.

As they rode off, Kincaid looked back and saw the silhouette of a man in a baseball cap on horseback, high up on a ridge. As Kincaid watched, the man moved back out of sight.

Kincaid and Benally followed the trail for several miles through a narrow valley bordered by red rock cliffs. The trail then descended into a vast plain that was surrounded by the Chuska Mountains to the west, the San Juan Mountains to the north, and the San Pedro Mountains to the east. The plain seemed to stretch to the horizon. They stopped to take in the view.

"Are we near anything?" asked Kincaid.

"We're just about fifteen miles south of Chaco Canyon," Benally replied. "Over a thousand years ago, it was the culture center of the Anasazi people. My people, the Navajo, call them the ancient ones."

"What happened to them?" asked Kincaid.

"Nobody knows for sure," she said. "Some say the rains stopped, and the people had to leave."

They rode down the trail and came to the edge of a small lake fed by a stream coming in from the east. Across the lake, a small herd of elk grazed. Several of them looked up, then began walking away. Kincaid and Benally got off their horses and walked around the lake. In the distance, a coyote trotted casually through the sagebrush, probably looking for a jackrabbit. Kincaid saw a hawk flying low overhead. Cumulus clouds were forming to the west, and a cool breeze passed across the lake.

"When I was at the University of New Mexico, I took a course in anthropology," Benally said. "We talked about this area. The weird thing is, they didn't find any bones or human remains in Chaco Canyon, just some old ruins of kivas."

"What's a kiva?" asked Kincaid.

"It was a structure, where they cooked and ate, slept, made clothing," she said. "And made love."

Kincaid leaned over and slowly kissed her on the lips. She responded, and ran her fingers over his arms and shoulders, then pulled back and smiled.

"I know a place nearby, with a pond and a tree," she said. "Are you interested in seeing it?"

Kincaid smiled and climbed on his horse. "Show me the way," he said.

Benally and Kincaid rode back up through the cliffs, then followed another trail to the north for a mile, to a small pond, about fifty feet long and twenty feet wide. The pond was fed by an underground spring that emerged from a cleft in the rocks. A single cottonwood tree provided shade on one side of the pond. Benally and Kincaid tied their horses next to the tree.

"Feel like swimming?" she asked.

"I didn't bring a bathing suit," Kincaid said, smiling.

Benally began taking off her clothes. "Neither did I."

After stripping, Benally jumped into the water and turned to watch Kincaid, who took off his shirt, his boots, and then his Levi's. Taking off his underwear, he noticed his growing erection. As he entered the water, Benally laughed.

"Do I turn you on, Wayne?"

Kincaid swam to her and kissed her. "Just a little."

Benally reached down and grabbed his penis. "That's more than just a little."

Kincaid kissed her slowly on the lips, then picked Benally up and sat her on a sandstone ledge on the edge of the pond. He licked her nipples, then moved down to her stomach. He slowly probed her with his tongue, and she lay back on the rock and moaned as she stared at the cumulus clouds overhead. After a few minutes, Kincaid thrust himself inside of her, and she wrapped her legs around him, sitting on the ledge while he remained halfway in the water.

Lying behind a cedar shrub on a cliff above the pond, Haskie watched his cousin make love to Kincaid. He'd been planning to visit Herman until he saw Kincaid was there; instead, he rode up to the top of a mesa, where he could observe Kincaid and Benally from a distance.

He would never admit it to Linda, but he didn't really hate all white people. Just the men who took advantage of her. He had been alarmed when Benally started hanging out at the Bandidos bar in Pecos. Although he was younger, Haskie viewed himself as the man in the family, and it was his obligation to protect her. He wondered about Kincaid. What kind of man was he? What was he doing here?

Everyone had secrets, Haskie knew. A few months earlier, he was stopped by the Navajo tribal police while driving with a load of marijuana. He was arrested and brought to police headquarters at Shiprock. After he was booked, however, he was not thrown into jail to wait for arraignment. Instead, he was taken to an office and introduced to a Navajo police detective, John Clearwater.

Clearwater, who had served two tours in Iraq with the US Marines during the battles for Fallujah, knew Haskie's uncle Herman, who had asked him to look out for his nephew. Clearwater told Haskie he had two choices: take his chances in court, with the possibility of serving three to five years in state prison, or become an informant. Haskie didn't take long to choose the latter option. Clearwater wanted to stop the distribution and use of drugs on the reservation. The gangs were growing, and their influence was becoming more pervasive. It wasn't just the drug use; the numbers of rapes, robberies, and assaults had increased along with growth of the gangs.

Haskie wondered if Kincaid was involved in narcotics trafficking. He didn't have a job, after all. He made a mental note to report on Kincaid to John Clearwater at their next meeting. He took his Canon out of his backpack and aimed the 300-millimeter telephoto lens at the pond.

When Kincaid and Benally returned to Herman's place, he was sitting in a chair next to the front door of his home, smoking a cigarette. They halted the horses near him.

"How was your ride?" Herman asked, with a slight twinkle in his eye.

"We had a great time, Herman," Linda said as she dismounted. Kincaid also got off his horse, and Linda led them to the corral. Kincaid noticed that she avoided eye contact with Herman. He felt like a high school kid bringing his date home late.

"Take a seat, Wayne," Herman said, pointing to another chair. He opened a cooler and took out a can of Coke, which he offered to Kincaid.

Kincaid sat down and opened the can. "Thanks for letting us ride your horses," he said.

"Anytime you like, Wayne," he said. "They need the exercise. I'm getting too old to ride."

They watched as Linda took off the saddles and bridles, then began to brush the horses while they drank water from a trough.

"I was thinking about you, Wayne, retiring from the army. When I got back home after Vietnam, I had a hard time getting settled," Herman said, still watching Linda and the horses. "I had bad dreams for a long time."

Herman drank from his Coke and stared off at the mountains. "I'll always be a Marine. It was fifty years ago, but sometimes it seems like yesterday. One time on patrol, we had to hide from a whole battalion of North Vietnamese soldiers out looking for us," he said. "So we cut bamboo straws and lay down in a rice paddy, breathing through the straws. The soldiers walked right near us. We had to stay hidden for almost an hour. After I got home, I dreamed about that rice paddy. In my dream, I couldn't breathe and started to choke. But I couldn't move, because of the soldiers. I had that dream for years."

Kincaid nodded at Herman. He understood how he felt, but he said nothing.

"Did you see much combat, Wayne?" he asked.

"We were mostly hunting insurgents," Kincaid said. "Not a lot of major battles, like you guys had."

"Do you dream about it?" asked Herman.

Kincaid sipped his Coke and nodded. "Sometimes. It's been a few years since I was over there, so not as much."

Kincaid was a good liar, but he sensed that Herman did not believe him. He still had dreams about the night his Delta team raided a house in Mosul, looking for an Al Qaeda battalion chief. He remembered the boy rushing out with his AK-47. The boy had opened fire at him, so he had no choice but to shoot him. Three shots to the chest, and the threat was over. Kincaid and his men frequently had to make quick decisions. Shoot or don't shoot. Who lives and who dies? How could he ever forget it?

Herman lit another cigarette and puffed on it, slowly exhaling the smoke.

"You never really get over combat," Herman said. "You just learn how to get on with your life."

Kincaid lifted his can and tapped it against Herman's.

"Thanks," he said.

Herman slowly stood up and prepared to go inside his home, then turned to Kincaid.

"I'm a Navajo medicine man," he said. "But sometimes I treat white folks. The Enemy Way ceremony is one Navajos use for soldiers who were in combat. If you ever need me, I'm here for you."

"I appreciate that, Herman," Kincaid said. Then he walked slowly over to the corral and picked up a brush to help Benally.

CHAPTER 7

These men don't become Bandidos because they are simply motorcycle enthusiasts. They become Bandidos because they love being known as the badasses. And when you get a bunch of men like that together in one club, you better watch out, because there's no telling what can happen.
—Texas law enforcement officer, *Texas Monthly*, April 2007

Pecos National Wilderness
May 26, 2016
Sundown

Kincaid had returned with Benally to Santa Fe in late afternoon. He'd been tempted to stay the night at her place, but he didn't want to wear out his welcome. He had another reason for leaving: Benally had told him the Bandidos were having a party on the Pecos River that night. Kincaid didn't tell her he was going to it, but he had to start working his way inside the gang.

As the light faded over the Santa Fe Mountains, Kincaid rode his Harley up Highway 63, through the village of Pecos, past a gray retaining wall with the words *NO FEAR WITH JESUS* written in large white letters. A block later, he saw St. Anthony's Catholic Church. Across the street was a statue so unusual that Kincaid turned his Harley around and went back to look at it.

An angel with widespread blue wings, dressed in blue

armor and a gold helmet, held a bloody sword over a crouched, subdued figure of Satan, with red wings and small curled horns protruding from his scalp. The statue was placed directly in front of the Pecos Independent School District. *Subtle*, Kincaid mused as he turned back to the highway. Pecos was a very religious place—except for Buck's Tavern and its customers.

Kincaid followed the narrow, winding road for ten miles, to the Windy Bridge picnic area. It was dark by the time he arrived. He turned left off the highway and parked in the gravel lot situated next to the picnic site, which was located amid seventy- to one-hundred-foot-tall pine trees.

The Pecos River, which had run on the right side of the highway, flowed under a bridge and emerged on the left side, just past the picnic area. Several dozen Bandidos were gathered around picnic tables, drinking beer and grilling burgers and hot dogs. Kincaid walked up to Henry and Dowdy, who were sitting on a picnic table.

"Could you spare a beer?" Kincaid asked Henry.

Henry glared at Kincaid. "How'd you know where to find us?"

"The bartender at Buck's told me you guys were up here," Kincaid said.

Dowdy shrugged, reached in a cooler, and handed Kincaid a Budweiser. "First you take our woman, and now you take our beer," he said, smiling. Kincaid sat next to Dowdy.

Henry stood and walked around the table to the cooler. He took a Bud and opened it, drinking most of the bottle in one swallow. Kincaid put down his beer and stood up as Henry moved closer.

"What are you doing here?" Henry asked.

"I like to ride," Kincaid said. "I was hoping I could hang out with the Bandidos for a while."

Henry turned to Dowdy. "Did you check him out?" he asked.

"I called up an old buddy who knows some people in the Eighty-Second," Dowdy said, turning to Kincaid. "They never heard of you." He walked up close to Kincaid, staring at him.

Kincaid tensed, getting ready to fight or get the hell out of there.

"So I called the sergeant major at the 504th," Dowdy went on. "I told him I was looking for an old friend, Wayne Kincaid. He said you retired and left a few months ago."

Kincaid tried not to show his relief. "Must have talked to Sincada," he said.

"I talked to some asshole," Dowdy said. "Most sergeant majors sound the same."

Henry walked closer to Kincaid. "You don't just show up and join the Bandidos. You gotta prove yourself."

"You ever see our membership card?" asked Dowdy.

Kincaid shook his head no, and Dowdy handed him a card. Kincaid turned on the flashlight on his phone and looked at it. Across the top, the card read, *We are the people your parents warned you about.* In the center: *Bandido by profession, Biker by trade, Lover by choice. You have just had the honor of meeting Harry Dowdy.* In the lower left corner were the initials FTW.

Kincaid looked up at Dowdy. "FTW?"

"Fuck the world," Dowdy said with a flat stare.

Kincaid nodded. "Not sure I want to join," he said. "Just thought I'd ride with you for a while and see how it goes."

Dowdy laughed. "It's not like in the old days, when I joined after Vietnam," he said. "We used to ride all day and party all night. We'd head out to the woods, where the cops wouldn't hassle us. Lots of booze and dope. Lots of girls."

Henry drained his beer and threw it into the river; he was getting drunk. "We're the last free Americans," he said. "We don't need the fucking government telling us what to do." He opened another beer and walked around Kincaid, circling him like a wolf closing in on his prey. He stopped up close and looked at Kincaid. Light from a fire cast shadows across his face. "Maybe you could be a prospect. But there's something you have to understand. We get a lot of bad rap in the media. We're not criminals. Most of our people have regular jobs."

Kincaid nodded. "I'm not looking for trouble. I just want to ride my Harley and drink beer," he said. "And get laid now and then."

Henry sat his beer on the table and turned to Kincaid. "That's another thing. You took my woman."

"I didn't know she belonged to anyone," Kincaid said.

"We don't steal women from each other. If you want to see Linda, you're gonna have to get my permission," Henry said, as he moved closer to Kincaid.

Kincaid sighed and turned to look at Dowdy, then lashed out with a karate kick to Henry's solar plexus. Henry threw up his beer as he fell to his knees.

"You either fight," Kincaid said, "or you talk."

Henry continued to vomit. Other Bandidos ran up, prepared to attack Kincaid, who tried to appear indifferent. *Show no fear, even if they kick your ass.* One Bandido was pulling a chain from around his waist.

Dowdy waved them off. "It is what it is," he said.

Dowdy slapped Kincaid on the back, then helped Henry sit up on the table. Henry caught his breath and glared at Kincaid. Dowdy opened another beer for Henry and gave it to him. Henry took a long swallow, then laughed, along with Dowdy.

"You don't believe in a fair fight, do you, Kincaid?" Henry said, still trying to catch his breath.

"Hell no," said Kincaid. "I fight to win."

Henry took a deep breath and stroked his beard, then looked at Dowdy, who shrugged. "What the hell, Kincaid," Henry said. "You can have Linda. She don't mean nothing."

"Might as well take her; we've all had our turn," Dowdy said, laughing. "Our motto is, find 'em, fuck 'em, and forget 'em."

"If you guys have all had her, maybe I better get checked for the clap," Kincaid said.

Dowdy laughed and toasted Kincaid with his beer. He waved his arm around, pointing to the other Bandidos eating, laughing, and drinking. Several of them had women with them, one of whom danced around a small campfire. A Bandido began to clap in time to her dance, as a boom box blared "Born to Be Wild."

"See those women? They all carry cards that say 'Property of the Bandidos,' " Dowdy said. "This is a man's world."

Henry stared at Kincaid, who still wasn't sure he should have kicked Henry. Kincaid had spent a lot of time on Harleys, riding with some vets who had their own club near Fort Bragg. If Henry was like most bikers, he would respect a man who knows how to fight.

"You can smoke a little weed, but no hard drugs," Henry said. "No chemicals, no needles. You okay with that?"

Kincaid nodded and drank from his beer. "I've always been a juicer," Kincaid said. "No room in the Eighty-Second for dopers. They can get you killed in combat."

"Amen to that, brother," Dowdy said. "We didn't put up with that shit in the 101st."

Kincaid noticed the tattoos covering Henry's arms. One forearm had *HONOR* and the other *LOYALTY.*

"Nice tattoos," Kincaid said. "Where'd you get those?"

Henry flexed his muscles and looked at Kincaid, smiling. "Prison. Santa Fe," he said.

Dowdy laughed and said, "John likes motorcycles so much, he stole a couple."

"That's where I met Harry," Henry said.

Kincaid turned to Dowdy and said, "What were you in for?"

"Armed robbery," Dowdy said. "I needed cash, so I robbed a bank over in Albuquerque. Fucking clerk put a dye pack in the bag, and it exploded. Then the cops showed up."

Kincaid sipped his beer and sat on the picnic table next to Henry. "Must have been tough in prison," Kincaid said. "Without women."

Henry laughed as he exchanged looks with Dowdy.

"Don't get the wrong idea, Kincaid," Dowdy said. "Me and Henry ain't faggots."

"So you went without?" Kincaid asked.

Henry and Dowdy both laughed and clinked their beers. Henry sipped his beer and smiled at Kincaid.

"In prison, there's two kinds of men," Henry said. "Givers and takers. Me and Harry were givers."

Kincaid nodded. His experience and training had taught him not to be judgmental. If you want to cultivate a source, you have to show empathy. *You and me, we're the same. I understand you—or at least I pretend.*

Dowdy laughed. "We like women better. But it's like the song says, 'if you can't be with the one you love, love the one you're with.'"

While Henry staggered behind some bushes to take a leak, Dowdy said, "We're headed up to Red River tomorrow. Want to ride with us?"

"Sure," Kincaid said. "What's going on up there?"

"It's Memorial Day weekend," Dowdy said. "Red River has a rally for bikers. Last year about twenty thousand showed up."

"All Bandidos?" Kincaid asked.

"Nah. We expect maybe three or four hundred of us," Dowdy said. "Some Hells Angels, and other clubs. Mostly just middle-aged weekend dudes, like lawyers and doctors, out pretending to be bad."

"I need a place to crash," Kincaid said. "Any motels around here?"

Dowdy pointed toward a van. "We got some extra sleeping bags in there," he said. "You can borrow one."

Kincaid nodded and took a sleeping bag from the van. He walked down the river about fifty yards, away from the noise, and laid the bag on a patch of soft grass near the river. He collapsed on the bag, looking up at the stars. Kincaid took several deep, slow breaths as he tried to collect his thoughts. He had taken an enormous risk fighting Henry; he could easily have ended up badly beaten, or dead. But he was now inside the Bandidos. The invitation from Dowdy to ride to Red River was a huge step toward acceptance. He just had to be patient and watch for opportunities.

Lying in the sleeping bag, he could see the stars. A horned owl floated through the trees, searching for its prey, and coyotes howled in the distance. He thought about Linda Benally and making love to her in the pond, as the Bandidos continued to play their music and drink.

Lying prone under some bushes near the Pecos River, Haskie slowly backed up, preparing to leave. He had followed Kincaid to the party from a distance in his pickup, which he parked under some trees near the highway. He'd then crept along the river, going under the bridge and close to the party.

Haskie was upset at the way the Bandidos had talked about Linda, but he was outraged at Kincaid's response; Kincaid seemed to agree with the Bandidos that Linda was nothing more than a biker slut. *Something she should know about*, he thought as he headed toward his truck.

Haskie didn't know who Kincaid was or what he was doing

with the Bandidos. But he was sure he didn't want the bastard screwing his cousin. What white man was going to treat a Navajo woman with respect, let alone marry her? He had a duty to protect his cousin. Hell, Kincaid probably was a doper. Why would any decent man hang with the Bandidos? He was trouble, and he needed to go.

CHAPTER 8

> *Returning veterans used their severance pay to buy*
> *motorcycles and party in taverns. . . . Conventional*
> *activities offered no acceptable alternatives and these men*
> *were threatened with a loss of identity, companionship,*
> *and security as military involvement ceased.*
> —James F. Quinn, *Deviant Behavior*, vol. 26, no. 5,
> September–October 2010

Angel Fire, New Mexico
May 27, 2016

Kincaid rode with the Bandidos east on Interstate 25 to Las Vegas, a largely Hispanic town located on the edge of the eastern plains of New Mexico, at the foot of the Sangre de Cristo Mountains. When the railroad arrived in 1879, Las Vegas was a major stopping point between Independence, Missouri, and San Francisco. The trains brought not only prosperity to Las Vegas but also outlaws and thieves.

When Kincaid had studied history at Texas A&M, he learned that Jesse James, Billy the Kid, and Doc Holliday had all visited Las Vegas. And now, he mused, the Bandidos were passing through, followed by several local police patrol cars.

As they rode through the city, their Harleys shattering the peace and attracting attention from residents, Kincaid noticed a sign for the New Mexico Behavioral Health Institute, the state's psychiatric hospital. It would have been an appropriate stop for the Bandidos, he thought—or for him. He had to be a little bit crazy to try to infiltrate the Bandidos. They headed north to Angel Fire, a small resort town that catered to skiers.

At Angel Fire, instead of continuing right to Red River, Henry led his band of fifty Bandidos left, to the Vietnam Veterans Memorial State Park. As they arrived in the parking lot, Kincaid noted the Peace and Brotherhood Chapel, which resembled a large white sail, perched on a hillside overlooking the Moreno Valley. To one side was a UH-1D Huey helicopter, shipped back from Vietnam after being badly damaged in battle, and donated to the park.

Kincaid parked next to Dowdy and asked, "What are we doing here?"

"Got to pay our respects," Dowdy said quietly. "It's Memorial Day weekend. A lot of the Bandidos are vets. I'm the only one left from Vietnam. Other guys served in Iraq or Afghanistan."

As Kincaid walked up the path with Dowdy, he noted how physically fit most of the Bandidos were. Take away their beards and long hair, and they still looked like soldiers. Maybe, he thought, that was one reason Dowdy had accepted him. In a garden of flowers, they walked past a bronze statue of a soldier holding an M-16 and kneeling over a map. Just outside the memorial was a black POW-MIA flag. Inside was a sculpture of a pair of bound hands rising from an American flag, a symbol of American prisoners of war never accounted for by the Vietnamese government.

Dowdy stood silently in front of the bronzed hands for a few moments. He turned to Kincaid and said, "I had some good buddies captured in 'Nam. We never heard what happened to them."

"You lose a lot of friends over there?" Kincaid asked.

"Too damned many," Dowdy said. "And all for nothing. It don't mean nothing."

As he looked out over the valley, Dowdy reflected on his service in Vietnam. He still remembered the first time he stepped off the jet at Tan Son Nhut Airport near Saigon. The heat and humidity were so overwhelming that he immediately wanted to go back inside the jet, to feel that air conditioning. But there was no going back; he was there for a year.

He remembered slogging through jungle mud and being rained on. It always seemed to rain. And there were the mosquitos. Every day and every night, sucking his blood. Monday was the day for swallowing the malaria pill. It turned his skin yellow and gave him diarrhea, but it saved him from malaria.

Dowdy recalled his first encounter with a Vietcong soldier, while on point, leading a patrol. He had rounded a trail and almost walked into the Vietcong, who was equally startled. In sheer panic, Dowdy had emptied an entire magazine from his M-16 but missed the Vietcong, who ran away in terror. Most of the time, the enemy remained in shadows, firing quickly in ambush, then melting into the jungle or down tunnels.

The only real set battle Dowdy fought in was in May 1969, at Hamburger Hill, or Ap Bia Mountain. Dowdy was one of the troopers of the 101st Airborne Division's Third Brigade. After the Americans suffered one hundred killed and more than four hundred wounded, the hill was abandoned to the enemy soon after it was taken. It was one of the most significant battles of the war. Americans, already opposed to the war, were outraged at the loss of lives and the lack of a clear strategy. Why spend so much blood to take a hill and then walk away from it? President Nixon responded with orders to end major combat operations in Vietnam.

For Dowdy, the battle changed how he viewed the military

and the war. He adopted the slogan of many vets: "It don't mean a thing." As an eighteen-year-old enlistee from Houston, Dowdy had volunteered because he considered it his patriotic duty. After Hamburger Hill, however, he began to smoke marijuana and use cocaine when he was off patrol in base camp. After returning from Vietnam, he grew a beard and started riding with bikers. He later joined the Bandidos. Dowdy lived the Bandido motto: "Fuck the World!"

As other Bandidos moved into the chapel, Dowdy motioned for Kincaid to walk outside with him. They walked toward the end of the path and looked out over the valley dotted with cabins built for skiers.

"I remember coming back through the airport in San Francisco, after my tour in 'Nam," Dowdy said. "Bunch of hippies screaming at us. Calling us killers. One bitch spit on me."

"You guys got a raw deal," Kincaid said. "Things are different now. At the airports, they have welcome-home committees, people shaking your hand."

Dowdy continued walking and asked, "What about you, Wayne? You think you can ever fit into a regular job? Have a normal life, after what you've been through?"

"I really don't know," Kincaid said. "I'm still trying to figure that out."

"Well, until you do, you can hang with us," Dowdy said. "We're all brothers here. You cut one of us, we all bleed."

Red River
5:00 p.m.

After the Bandidos crossed Bobcat Creek on Highway 518, they had a panoramic view of the Red River valley. Alongside the river, a herd of elk grazed in a lush green meadow. The town, with fewer than five hundred permanent residents, straddled the narrow river. Once a mining town, Red River had become a tourist destination.

Thousands of motorcycles had already filled Main Street— Harleys, Honda Gold Wings, Yamaha Road Stars, and a dozen other makes. Most of them were touring bikes, with saddlebags and windshields. Hundreds of motorcycles were parked in rows in the center of Main Street, while others lined up on the sides. On the outskirts of the town, a large banner that said "Welcome Riders" was strung across the road. The rally was good business for Red River.

As the Bandidos rode into town, Kincaid noted the vendors. Hot Leather featured jackets, leggings, and other biker paraphernalia, while others offered a variety of food, including barbeque, hot dogs, and hamburgers. A country and western band was playing from a stand on one side of the street. Several couples danced in the street, while scores of bikers walked down the street drinking beer. About fifty police officers from state and local departments were scattered among the crowd, alert for trouble but not expecting much. The bikers usually remained on good behavior during the rally as part of an unwritten agreement with the Red River Chamber of Commerce.

Henry parked in front of the Alpine Lodge, and his Bandidos joined him, parking wherever they could on the crowded street.

"We got some rooms here," Dowdy said as he got off his bike. "I'm sharing a room with Henry, but you can throw your sleeping bag on the floor if you want."

"Thanks," Kincaid said. He noticed several women walking around in shorts and T-shirts that did little to conceal their breasts. Many of them had tattoos. One smiled at him as she walked by.

Dowdy laughed as he observed the women. "Lots of good times in Red River," he said.

Dowdy and Kincaid took their overnight bags from the van and checked in at the front desk. The lobby, crowded with guests, had a fireplace with several easy chairs in front of it. Dowdy walked up the stairs to his room, followed by Kincaid. The room had two queen beds, a couch and chair, and a small writing table with an Internet connection. Dowdy tossed his small overnight bag on the bed and walked into the bathroom.

"Got to take a leak," he said.

After Dowdy closed the door, Kincaid took a pen from his pocket, slid back the pocket clip, and laid it on the table, next to another pen and a pad of paper with the hotel logo. The pen contained a voice-activated recorder, with a one-gig memory and 140 hours of recording time provided by a rechargeable battery. When Dowdy emerged from the bathroom, Kincaid was leaning against the desk, with his arms folded.

"Let's go grab some beers," Dowdy said.

Kincaid walked with Dowdy down the street to the Motherlode Saloon, where two women paraded along the bar in an impromptu leather-and-lace "fashion show." They were wearing very little leather or lace, and the bikers were cheering them on and demanding they take off what little they were wearing. Kincaid and Dowdy ordered beers and watched.

As Kincaid casually looked around the bar, he saw several Bandidos with bottom rockers on the jackets from Texas and Colorado. The rockers showed the club name and location. They were mingling with New Mexico Bandidos. It was a reunion for bikers, including Henry, who sat at a corner table talking to two Bandidos, one from Texas and another from Colorado. Half a dozen members of the Phoenix chapter of the Hells Angels were drinking at the bar.

"You guys get along okay with the Bandidos from other states?" Kincaid asked.

"Yeah, man," Dowdy said. "We're all brothers. We have to watch out for some of the other gangs, though. We had some trouble with the Cossacks over in Waco."

"I heard about that," Kincaid said. The Cossacks, a gang based in northern Texas, had worn the Texas rocker bar on their vests without the permission of the Bandidos, who viewed themselves as the premier motorcycle club in Texas. A meeting in Waco in 2015 between the Cossacks and Bandidos ended in a shoot-out that left nine bikers dead, eighteen injured, and over 170 arrested.

Arturo Sanchez, dressed in a black leather biker's jacket, jeans, and cowboy boots, walked into the bar and scanned the crowd. He saw Henry talking to the other Bandidos and had started moving to join him when he noticed Dowdy talking to a man Sanchez hadn't seen before. He was curious about the man, so he walked up to their table instead.

"Hello, Harry," Sanchez said.

"Hey, José, pull up a chair and have a beer," Dowdy said.

Sanchez sat and signaled to the waitress. "Who's your friend?" he asked as he looked at the other man.

"Wayne Kincaid," Kincaid said as he extended his hand to Sanchez, who replied, "José Santiago. It's a pleasure to meet you."

"José rides with us sometimes," Dowdy said. "When he's not tending to his cattle."

"You live around here, José?" Kincaid asked.

"I have a ranch near Portales," Sanchez said. "But I like to get out on the road on my Harley. What do you do, Wayne?"

"Just retired from the army," Kincaid said. "Right now, I'm just riding my Harley."

"That must be nice, not to have to work," Sanchez said. "Something I look forward to."

As Santiago talked, Kincaid felt himself being watched carefully. Kincaid made good eye contact but did not want to seem confrontational. Did he look nervous? No. He was calm and self-assured. Hopefully not too much. He didn't want to take any chance at being made as a cop.

"What kind of cattle do you raise, José?" Kincaid asked.

"Mostly Black Angus," he said. "I used to raise Herefords, but they have a tendency to get pink eye. Too much trouble."

Santiago had provided a good answer, Kincaid noted. But it was the kind of information he could have obtained from the Internet. He seemed a little too polished for a rancher. His hands weren't callused, and his fingernails looked manicured. Why had Santiago met up with Roberts at the Bull Ring in Santa Fe? And what in hell was he doing hanging out with the Bandidos? Kincaid knew from DEA reports that a few Mexican dealers dropped loads of marijuana from small airplanes in southeastern New Mexico. Some ranchers were paid by the cartels for allowing them to use their land as drop points. It seemed likely that Santiago was such a rancher.

After the waitress delivered a beer to Santiago, he laid a twenty-dollar bill on the table and stood up. "If you'll excuse me, I need to say hello to some friends," he said, then walked over to Henry and two other Bandidos.

Kincaid looked at Dowdy and said, "Santiago an old friend of yours?"

"We see him now and then," Dowdy said. "I really don't know him that well."

Having made it this far, Kincaid knew he shouldn't rock the boat, but patience was not one of his virtues. He decided it was time to test the waters.

"He looks like a soldier," Kincaid said. "Or maybe he's a cop?"

Dowdy looked over at Santiago, then back at Kincaid. "I'm pretty sure he's not a cop," Dowdy said.

"You said you didn't know him that well," Kincaid said. "How can you be sure?"

Dowdy sipped his beer and studied Kincaid. "How do I know you're not a cop?"

"I've got a DD-214 that says what I did in the army," Kincaid said. "And you checked me out. What kind of proof does Santiago have?"

"I know things about him," Dowdy said.

"Anything you can tell me?" Kincaid asked.

"Maybe when I know you better," Dowdy said. "Maybe if you decide to join the Bandidos."

Kincaid signaled the waitress and ordered another round. He drained his glass and set it on the table, then looked at Dowdy.

"I've been thinking about that," Kincaid said. "So I started doing some research. A lot of people say the Bandidos are criminals. Dealing drugs, running prostitutes. Any truth to that?"

"Well, hell," Dowdy said. "We're a big organization. There's probably some Bandidos doing that sort of thing. That bother you?"

"Live and let live, that's my motto," Kincaid said. "I just don't want to end up in jail."

Dowdy clinked his beer glass to Kincaid's and said, "Amen to that, brother. Been there. Don't plan to go back."

One of the women dancing on the bar had removed her top and was waving it at the crowd of bikers, who were clapping their hands and cheering.

"Pretty good show," Kincaid said.

"It was even better last year," Dowdy said. "A Bandido ate a dancer's pussy right there on the pool table."

"You've gotta be shitting me," Kincaid said.

"Nope. Got some pictures to prove it," Dowdy said.

Alpine Lodge
11:00 p.m.

As Kincaid and Dowdy walked up the stairs, they met Henry, Santiago, and the Bandidos from Texas and Colorado walking down.

"Going to bed early, old man?" Henry asked.

"Like Clint Eastwood once said, a man's got to know his limitations," Dowdy said.

"Good night, Harry," Santiago said. "You too, Kincaid."

"See you guys in the morning," Kincaid said. Henry had not introduced the Bandidos from Colorado and Texas.

After Kincaid and Dowdy entered the room, Dowdy rushed to the bathroom, where he noisily emptied his bladder. Kincaid took his pen from the table, pushed the clip back, and put it into his pocket. He was curious to know what the four men had discussed, but it would have to wait until he got back to his apartment.

CHAPTER 9

There is something in corruption which, like a jaundiced eye, transfers the color of itself to the object that it looks upon, and sees everything stained and impure.
—Thomas Paine, *The American Crisis*, 1776

Farmington, New Mexico
May 31, 2016
9:00 a.m.

Detective John Clearwater drove his Tahoe north on Highway 491 toward the town of Shiprock. He passed Shiprock Mountain, called the "Rock with Wings" because it was a symbol of a legend about a giant bird that brought the Navajo people to the site long ago.

As he viewed the mountain, Clearwater saw nothing more than a beautiful mound of red dirt and rock. He wasn't superstitious, but he appreciated nature. Like many Navajos, he was bound to the land by an inherent sense of the spiritual world, in a way he would not be able to express in words. In part because of his intrinsic bond with the land, Clearwater was often discouraged by many young Navajos, who seemed to have abandoned their traditions and succumbed to drug and alcohol abuse. As a Navajo police detective, he fought those who sought to desecrate his land and his people—especially the narcotics traffickers.

Clearwater turned east and followed Highway 64 toward

Farmington. The highway ran alongside the San Juan River, with farms lined up along the river, feeding off the irrigation. It was a highway to be avoided at night, especially on weekends. Clearwater and other local cops called it "slaughterhouse alley," because so many accidents involving drunk driving occurred on it. In Farmington, he drove to the city parks and recreation area, where he parked under several towering elm trees.

A few minutes later, Haskie pulled alongside in his Ford pickup, his driver's side next to Clearwater's.

"Got your email," Clearwater said. "What's up?"

Haskie handed Clearwater a photo of Kincaid. "You know this dude?" Haskie asked.

Clearwater looked at the photo and shook his head. "Nope. Who is he?"

"Wayne Kincaid. He's hooked up with John Henry and the Bandidos," Haskie said.

"How do you know that?" asked Clearwater.

"I followed him over near Pecos," Haskie said. "He went to a Bandido party. I snuck up close and listened. Looks like he joined up."

Clearwater nodded and looked more closely at Kincaid's photo.

"So why should I care?" asked Clearwater.

"From what I could hear, he's a big-time player, maybe with the Bandidos in Houston," Haskie said.

"Who does he know?" Clearwater asked.

"Didn't catch any names," Haskie said. "Just some talk about dope with John Henry."

"What else you got for me?" Clearwater asked.

Haskie shrugged. "They don't tell me much," he said. "I get a call from Henry, and go out and pick up some weed sometimes. Nothing lately."

Clearwater stared at Haskie for half a minute in an effort

to intimidate him. He didn't trust him or any other informant. They always held back some information, but that was the game. Clearwater knew that Haskie had access to the Bandidos, but he was looking for bigger fish. Rumors were circulating that the Zeta cartel was doing business in New Mexico, and for now, Haskie was his best source.

"You hear anything about the Zetas?" Clearwater asked.

Haskie swallowed, his mouth growing dry. "No, man," he said. "Don't want nothing to do with those guys."

"Keep your ears open," Clearwater said, and he handed Haskie an envelope with five twenty-dollar bills.

After Clearwater drove away, Haskie opened the envelope and counted the money, then tossed it on the seat. It was nothing compared to what he was getting from the Zetas. Several months ago, Sanchez had visited Haskie at a hotel in Farmington. It had been a job interview, and Haskie had passed. The result was a five-thousand-dollar-a-month retainer, in cash, placed in a mailbox in Farmington every month.

So Haskie had no misgivings about not telling Clearwater that he had become a heroin distributor for the cartel, with a territory that covered not only the Navajo Nation in New Mexico and Arizona, but major cities from Phoenix to Albuquerque. Haskie knew that Sanchez also had a business arrangement with John Henry and the Bandidos, but they were, as Sanchez put it, "a high-risk organization." They attracted too much attention from the cops. Nobody would pay much attention to a kid like Haskie. The way Sanchez had explained it to Haskie, he was an investment in the future of the cartel.

As Haskie drove away, he recalled his meeting with Sanchez at the Holiday Inn Express in Farmington. Sanchez had spent hours training him on cartel tradecraft, which was, in reality, strategy taught to the Mexican Army Special Forces by US Special Forces: how to look for surveillance, pick up a source in a car for a meeting, and drive around during the meeting. Sanchez also taught him the importance of cover, communications, and how to remain anonymous. Be the gray man, and don't attract attention from the cops; never argue with cops.

Haskie laughed to himself as he thought of his relationship with Clearwater, who had been concerned that Haskie was too obvious dealing drugs on the reservation. Clearwater had arranged for Haskie's arrest so he could recruit him, because Haskie knew people in the gangs all over the reservation. The arrangement offered Haskie more freedom, but unknown to Clearwater, it also indirectly provided information to Sanchez and the Zeta cartel about what the cops knew and whom they were investigating. All Haskie had to do was play dumb. He was young, but he was not dumb.

Haskie took a circuitous route through Farmington to see if he was being followed. He drove past the Copper Penny, for years an "Indian bar," until a new owner converted it to a country and western hangout. In recent decades, the city had tried to clean up downtown, following a long period of racial tensions between whites and Navajos.

On South Miller Avenue, Haskie pulled over and stopped at Boyd Park. Located on the edge of the Animas River, the park had become to Haskie a shrine of sorts. He turned off the ignition, rolled down the windows, and listened to the water rush by.

He recalled waking up in his parents' pickup when a cop had tapped the window with a nightstick one night in early January, eight years before. After Haskie showed his identification, the cop walked him to the edge of the river, where an ambulance had stopped. Other officers and paramedics were still checking the bodies of Ray and Jane Haskie, who had frozen to death after passing out drunk on the bank of the river. Too cold and numb with shock to speak or cry, Haskie just nodded when asked if the bodies were his parents.

For several years, his parents had taken him with them to Farmington, where they would get drunk with friends and leave him in the pickup to fend for himself. Sometimes he walked to the nearby Farmington Indian Center on Elm Street to get a free dinner of Navajo tacos. One thick tortilla with beans, onion, and beef would sustain him through the night. In the morning, if he couldn't find his parents, he would drive to the Four Winds Addiction Recovery Center, located at the top of a mesa on Mission Avenue, where they'd often wind up. After years of arrests, the city jail was overwhelmed with intoxicated Navajos, so the police stopped arresting them for being drunk in public and simply dropped them off at the recovery center.

After his parents died, Haskie tried living with his uncle, but Herman was too strict. Haskie had to go to school and not stay out late. He didn't like rules, so he left and found a new home in Shiprock with the Manhunters, who introduced him to the world of narcotics trafficking. Early on, Haskie decided he would not use the hard drugs he sold; he saw what they did to the gang members who used. Their minds became numb, their paranoia increased, and their bodies were wrecked. Haskie smoked a little weed now and then to be sociable, but was content to sell drugs, not use them. And he would never drink.

Monsignor Patrick Smith Park
Santa Fe
10:00 a.m.

Kincaid slowly cruised his Harley down Alameda Street, a popular spot in Santa Fe for joggers and walkers. He parked and walked east to Monsignor Patrick Smith Park, where he left the walking path and made his way through a clump of cedar to a picnic bench nestled in a small pocket of mesquite trees. He found Special Agent George Jackson sitting at the table with two cups of Starbucks. Kincaid sat down and took one of the cups.

"No cream, one Splenda, right?" Jackson asked.

Kincaid nodded and sipped the coffee. "What's up?" he asked.

Jackson laid a photo of Santiago on the table. It was similar to the one Kincaid had shot at the Bull Ring, but the background was obviously somewhere in Mexico. Kincaid studied the photo, then laid it down on the table.

"The same guy I saw with Roberts, right?" he asked.

"I ran the photo through EPIC," Jackson said. "Turns out, his name is Arturo Sanchez."

"He's with the Zetas, isn't he?" Kincaid asked.

"Yeah," Jackson said. "He's a major player. A ruthless son of a bitch."

"I met him at the Red River rally," Kincaid said. "He told me his name was José Santiago. Said he has a ranch near Portales."

"Now you tell me?" Jackson asked.

"I wanted to be sure we're talking about the same guy," Kincaid said. "I was there with the Bandidos. I was drinking in a bar with Harry Dowdy, and Santiago—sorry, Sanchez walked in and sat down at our table. He seemed like he was checking me out."

Jackson took a long drink of coffee and thought for a few moments. "This whole thing is getting complicated. And dangerous, for you. Who else did Sanchez talk to there?" Jackson asked.

"After he talked to me and Dowdy, he met with John Henry

93

and two Bandidos from Colorado and Texas," Kincaid said. "When I got back to the room, all four of them were leaving together."

"Any idea what they talked about?" Jackson asked.

Kincaid took out his recorder pen and showed it to Jackson. "I left this on in the room where they met," he said. "When I got back to my apartment last night, I uploaded it to my computer."

"Are you going to keep me in suspense all fucking day?" Jackson asked.

Kincaid chuckled. "From what I could tell, Sanchez has a deal with the Bandidos to transport heroin around the country," Kincaid said. "The Zetas have a new source for pure white. He didn't talk about who it is, but it sounds like a new supply line. He's going to bring it in to New Mexico, and the Bandidos will handle the distribution throughout the country."

"Son of a bitch!" Jackson exclaimed, slapping his hand on the table. "We have to find out where that shit's coming from!"

"Anything new with Roberts?" Kincaid asked.

"The day after you saw Roberts meeting with Sanchez, he came to me with information about the Sinaloa cartel," Jackson said. "He said an informant told him they were bringing some coke across the border in Deming that night."

"Was the information good?" Kincaid asked.

"Yeah," Jackson said. "We made the bust."

"But you're suspicious about the timing, right?" Kincaid asked.

"I don't believe in coincidences," Jackson said. "Roberts is lazy. He's never given us anything like this. So I think Sanchez tipped him off, to get me off his back."

"And Sanchez fucks over Sinaloa," Kincaid said.

"One thing for sure, Roberts is in way over his head," Jackson said. "The dumbshit will be lucky to come out of this alive."

"I've read some EPIC intel reports about the Zetas working with the jihadists," Kincaid said. "You think that's where the dope's coming from?"

"Could be," Jackson said. "We have to find out. How are you doing with your Navajo contact on the res?"

Indian Health Service
Crownpoint
11:00 a.m.

Linda Benally was catching up on some paperwork when Haskie walked in.

"Got a minute?" he asked.

"Of course," Benally said, as she came around the desk to hug him. "What's new with you, Danny?"

Haskie flopped on a chair and put his feet on the coffee table. Benally sat next to him and turned to face him.

"You still seeing that Kincaid guy?" he asked.

"Yeah," she said. "What about him?"

Haskie looked away and avoided eye contact. "Maybe I shouldn't tell you this," he said. "It's probably none of my business."

"You're right," she said. "It's none of your business. But I've got a feeling you're going to tell me anyway."

"I knew the Bandidos were having a party over north of Pecos a few nights ago," he said. "So I went and took a look, after dark. I saw Kincaid there."

"Did he see you?" she asked.

"Nah," he said. "I snuck up behind some bushes and listened to him and John Henry."

Benally stood up and walked behind her desk, where she took a Diet Pepsi from a cooler and opened it. She glared at her cousin.

95

"What were you up to, spying on Wayne?" she asked.

Haskie ignored the question and looked at her directly. "John Henry told Kincaid he could have you," he said. "Henry said all the Bandidos already had sex with you, so they didn't want you anymore. Kincaid laughed and said maybe he better get checked for the clap."

Benally slammed her Pepsi down on the desk and walked slowly over to Haskie. She leaned down, her face inches from his.

"Kincaid said that?" she asked.

Haskie nodded and slumped in the chair. "I figured you ought to know what kind of guy he is."

"That motherfucker!" Benally picked up her purse and fled the office, heading for her truck.

Haskie smiled and picked up her Pepsi.

Benally drove twenty miles an hour over the speed limit down Highway 371. She was going to confront Kincaid and demand an explanation. By the time she reached I-40, however, she realized she didn't know where he lived. She stopped on the shoulder, took out her cell phone, and started to dial, then tossed the phone on the seat. She didn't want to talk on the phone; she wanted to look into his eyes. Then punch him in the mouth.

Rio Grande Nature Center State Park
Albuquerque
2:00 p.m.

Agent Bill Roberts drove his Chevy north on Rio Grande Boulevard to Candelaria Road and turned west, toward the river. The area was a checkerboard of low-income homes occupied by Latinos and expensive, upscale residences bought by Anglos intent on redeveloping the older parts of Albuquerque. It was a trendy area, with joggers on the sidewalks and Range Rovers and BMWs parked in some driveways. Roberts left his car in the parking lot of the Rio Grande Nature Center State Park.

Roberts walked through the park's dense grove of towering oak trees mixed with juniper and mesquite, to a metal bench under a sixty-foot oak tree. John Clearwater sat on the bench, reading the *Albuquerque Journal.* Clearwater had entered the park from the west side of the Rio Grande River, crossing a wooden bridge that led to a jogging path and bike trail that followed the river. He had avoided arriving at the site from the same direction to minimize the chance they would be seen together and blow Roberts's cover.

"Anything good in the newspaper?" Roberts asked, sitting next to him on the bench.

"Same old shit," Clearwater said. "Some gangbanger on Central went crazy last night. Started shooting his .45 at some other gangbanger. He missed him and hit a college girl who was just out for the night. Killed her."

"Ain't that a bitch," Roberts said, not really caring one way or the other. "So, what's up, John?"

Clearwater laid the newspaper on the bench and took out one of Haskie's photos of Kincaid. "Ever seen this guy?"

Roberts studied the photo before handing it back. "Nah," Roberts said. "Who is he?"

"His name's Wayne Kincaid. My source on the res tells me he just hooked up with the Bandidos," Clearwater said. "He may be one of the Bandidos from over in Houston."

"Those motherfuckers," Roberts said. "Can I keep this photo, so I can show it to the guys at work?"

"Sure. I've got copies," Clearwater said, handing the photo back to Roberts. "You think Kincaid could be DEA, or some other narcotics outfit?"

Roberts laughed. "If he was DEA, I would know about it," he said. "Besides, I don't think anyone has the balls to try to infiltrate the Bandidos."

Clearwater stared at Roberts without revealing his emotions. He found Roberts cocky and arrogant, with little justification.

"I'm not so sure," Clearwater said. "I think it could be done."

"Who is this source you have on the res?" Roberts asked.

Clearwater stared at Roberts for a moment, then said, "You know I can't tell you that."

Roberts shrugged. "Maybe I know him," he said. "Couldn't hurt to compare notes."

"No can do," Clearwater said. "Gotta protect my sources."

Roberts put the photo in his pocket and stood up. "I better get going. Don't want to be seen talking to a cop," he said.

"Stay in touch," Clearwater said, as he resumed reading the newspaper.

Roberts forced himself to walk slowly until he was out of sight of Clearwater, then hustled back to his car. He got in and began to think. Who was Kincaid, and why was he showing up now, with everything going down? Did Jackson suspect him? Had he brought in Kincaid to check up on him? For the past several months, Jackson had been more aloof around him. Something had changed. Roberts's guilt was transforming into paranoia—enhanced by an occasional cocaine habit. He had to get the hell out of the country. He wanted to leave today, but Roberts knew he had to clear up any loose ends with Sanchez so the Zetas wouldn't be on his trail.

Roberts raced to his apartment. He opened his closet door and checked his "go bag": toiletries and spare clothes, several thousand dollars in cash, and his passport. He turned on his laptop and started searching for flights to Mexico City, then booked a nonstop flight on Aero Mexico for late Saturday. Once in Mexico, he would use another US passport, with another name. He would use it to fly to Belize, clear out his bank account, and disappear. In the meantime, he would check into a cheap motel, just in case.

The Zetas had been generous with Roberts for the past two years, paying him well for information on the DEA's investigations. Sanchez had first approached him when Roberts was losing badly one night at the Pecos Casino; he was down several thousand at the craps table and had begun using his credit card. He had no idea that Sanchez had been scoping him for months.

"You look like you need a drink," Sanchez said.

Sanchez introduced himself as José Santiago, from Portales. He said he had never played craps and asked Roberts for some advice, offering to spot him a line of credit. Roberts proceeded to lose more money, and by the time he learned Santiago's real identity, it was too late. They owned him.

CHAPTER 10

There is ample and compelling evidence that the Texas-Mexico border is not secure. . . . An unsecure border with Mexico is the state's most significant vulnerability as it provides criminals and would-be terrorists from around the world a reliable means to enter Texas and the nation undetected.
—Texas Department of Public Safety report, February 2015

Juarez, Mexico
Paso del Norte Bridge
June 1, 2016

Sanchez waited in line in his Chevrolet passenger van at the Paso del Norte Bridge, one of three international ports of entry for El Paso. Just a few steps away from the bridge in Juarez was the Kentucky Club, a bar made famous in the 1960s by celebrities such as Marilyn Monroe, Steve McQueen, and Clark Gable. Gringos could stop by the Kentucky Club, have a few margaritas, and stumble back to El Paso across the bridge. Since drug violence had overwhelmed Juarez, however, few celebrities visited anymore. And not many young Americans made their way across the border to drink or visit the whorehouses.

Sanchez took out his American passport and New Mexico driver's license. The van was a rental, for which he had purchased Mexican auto insurance. He had carefully sanitized it, removing his weapons and ammunition, then had it detailed before arriving at the border, so the dogs would not detect any scent of gunpowder.

He smiled at the Mexican customs officer, who checked his passport and driver's license, as well as his proof of insurance.

"What is the purpose of your visit to Mexico, señor?" the officer asked.

"I'm doing some shopping for my wife," Sanchez said.

The officer handed his documents back to Sanchez and waved him on. Entering Mexico was easy, Sanchez knew. Getting out could be difficult, unless one had the right paperwork.

Sanchez turned right off Avenida de Los Aztecas, to a barrio in the Libertad neighborhood of Juarez. Although he was a member of Los Zetas, he had to be careful when driving the streets of Juarez. The Sinaloa cartel, the single largest and most powerful drug-trafficking organization in the Western hemisphere, fought the Zetas for turf in Juarez. And the Juarez cartel, one of the oldest surviving drug-trafficking organizations in Mexico, had aligned with the Zetas to fight Sinaloa.

The Zetas had evolved from the older Gulf cartel when over thirty soldiers of the Mexican Special Forces deserted and ramped up the violence in Mexico with their military training and penchant for audacious acts such as beheadings and petrol bomb attacks. One of those soldiers had been Sanchez's commanding officer, who had in turn recruited Sanchez. The Los Zetas paid better than the Mexican army.

As Sanchez drove through Juarez, widely regarded as the most dangerous city in the world, he thought that the city resembled a police state. Streets were crawling with police officers outfitted like soldiers. With eyes shielded by dark sunglasses and faces masked like bank robbers, the officers pointed machine guns from their truck beds, covering every direction.

Sanchez was on alert as he drove his Chevrolet down

Cinabrio Street, watching the kids playing soccer on the side of the road. Like many Juarez streets, Cinabrio had potholes and crumbling shoulders, with garbage and litter in the ditches. Any stack of garbage, Sanchez knew, could contain an IED. His Zeta compadres had been learning how to make these bombs from their new Al Qaeda associates.

Sanchez arrived at a walled compound and stopped to unlock the gate, drove inside, then got out to lock the gate behind him. He parked his car in front of the purple, one-story adobe house, which was surrounded by dirt and gravel; not many Juarez homes in this area had lawns. The house had bars on every window, and all the shades were closed. Sanchez unlocked the front door and walked inside, straining to see in the darkened room.

Khalid Hamza was smoking a cigarette and sitting at a faded kitchen table, its wood surface scarred by cigarette butts. Hamza, in his early forties, was fit, with a lean build. His short brown hair was flecked with gray, and he had blue eyes, a legacy of his Kurdish mother. Another Iraqi, Adnan Kadar, stood across the room, holding a shotgun on Sanchez. Kadar, a large, stocky Iraqi a few years younger than Hamza, showed little emotion; he could shoot Sanchez and not lose any sleep over it. Hamza waved at Kadar to lower his weapon and extended his hand to Sanchez.

"It's good to see you again," Hamza said.

"Any problems getting here?" Sanchez asked as he opened the refrigerator and found a can of Pepsi.

"No," Hamza said. "But it was a good idea to spend some time in Havana practicing our Spanish, before arriving at Mexico City. The Cuban passports your friends provided made it easier with customs."

Sanchez drank his Pepsi and sat at the table. "Is your Spanish good enough to pass for Cuban?"

Hamza smiled and said, "Not really. My cover is that I immigrated to Cuba from Lebanon. I'm in the import/export business."

"There is a lot of truth in that, my friend," Sanchez said. "My associates were very pleased by the quality of the product you sent our way."

A freighter with Liberian registration had docked at Tampico, Mexico, where a container of heroin was loaded onto a tractor-trailer, which was then packed with produce and driven west to Zacatecas, then north through Chihuahua to Juarez. It was one of several pipelines Al Qaeda had established in Mexico, in partnership with the Zetas cartel. Driving heroin through Mexico was not a problem, as long as you knew which cops to bribe. This was not a major obstacle for the Zetas, who controlled the Gulf portion of Mexico through fear and bribery. Most Mexican cops knew that if you crossed the Zetas, they would not only kill you but your entire family.

Sanchez nodded his head toward Kadar and looked around the room. "How many men did you bring?"

"Only four," he said. "They have all learned enough Spanish to get by, if they also claim to be immigrants from Lebanon."

"Enough to accomplish whatever it is you intend to do?" Sanchez asked.

"*Inshallah*," Hamza said. "If Allah wills."

Sanchez watched as Hamza puffed on his cigarette and exhaled. Sanchez had met Hamza only once before in Havana and was still not sure he could trust him. It was the first time Hamza had traveled outside the Middle East, and he was moving through a strange new world. In many ways, Sanchez knew, the desert landscape, the heat, and the rampant poverty of Juarez would remind Hamza of his home in Mosul, Iraq.

"As I told you during our initial meeting in Havana, we will need some help crossing the border into New Mexico,"

Hamza said. "And we need a safe place to stay on the Navajo reservation."

"I can get you across the border," Sanchez said. "I will have someone meet you in the city of Las Cruces, and from there, you will be driven to the reservation, where I have a place for you."

"Excellent," Hamza said. "And what about the weapons I requested?"

"I can get the AK-47s and an RPG," Sanchez said. "What will you do with them?"

"You don't need to know the details," Hamza said. "But we intend to bring jihad to America. The Americans have spread terror throughout my country, so it is time to let them know what it is like, in their country."

Sanchez nodded and thought, *These crazy bastards are going to get themselves killed.* But their lives were of no consequence to him. His job was to make sure their operation could not be tied back to the cartel and to keep the flow of heroin coming into Mexico from South Asia. He took a map from a drawer under the kitchen counter and spread it across the table, motioning for Hamza to come closer.

"Here is where we are," Sanchez said, pointing at a spot on the map, where he drew a small circle. He used a blue dry-erase marker to draw a line east to Highway 45. He continued with the line directly north to the El Paso border crossing. He drew a circle around the Paso del Norte Bridge.

"I will take you directly across the main border checkpoint in a few days," he said. "You will travel in my Chevrolet van."

Hamza, looking puzzled, stared at Sanchez. "I thought we would be sneaking across the Rio Grande, like the wetbacks," he said.

Sanchez laughed. "No need for that," he said. "I know a US Border Patrol agent who will be on duty at this time. And you have legitimate passports, with visas approved by the American consulate in El Paso."

"Our passports are Cuban," Hamza said. "How will that help us?"

Sanchez opened his briefcase and extracted a manila envelope, which held five Mexican passports. He handed one to Hamza.

"You are now Juan Ramirez, from Monterrey," he said. "You are a businessman who supplies coat hangers to American clothes manufacturers. You and your four associates are on a business trip that includes a convention in Las Vegas."

"How did you obtain such documents?" Hamza asked.

"Everyone has a price, my friend," Sanchez said.

CHAPTER 11

The course of true love never did run smooth.
    —William Shakespeare, *A Midsummer Night's Dream*

Linda Benally's home
Santa Fe
June 1, 2016

Just after sunset, Kincaid parked his Harley in front of Benally's home and knocked on the door. He waited a few seconds, then knocked again. The door flew open, and Benally stood in the entrance, her arms folded and eyes flashing.

"What the hell do you want?" she asked.

Kincaid's mouth dropped. He had expected to be greeted with a kiss, followed by dinner and a night of making love.

"I thought we had plans for dinner," he said, backing away a few inches, confused.

"Did you get checked for the clap yet?" she asked, her voice low and tense.

"What the hell are you talking about, Linda?"

Benally stepped out onto the small porch, forcing Kincaid back further and down one step. "I heard John Henry gave me to you," she said. "Like I'm some damned kind of Bandidos property."

"Who told you that?" he asked.

"Someone who was there, at the party in Pecos," she said. "Do you deny it?"

Kincaid sighed and shook his head. "Henry was drunk and pissed off. It doesn't mean anything."

"So why did you say you were going to get checked for the clap?" she asked.

"It was a joke," he said. "I'd just had a fight with Henry, and I was trying to calm things down."

"Why did you fight?" she asked.

"He was mad because you were dating me," Kincaid said. "I kicked him in the gut, and he puked up some beer."

"And you got away with that?" she asked.

"Bandidos like to fight," he said. "I had to earn their respect."

"So now you're good buddies with the Bandidos. Maybe you can start dealing dope, like they do," she said. "Since you don't have a job, I guess you have to find some way to make a living."

Kincaid was startled to find himself tempted to tell her who he was. For the first time in years, it mattered what a woman thought of him. He wanted to tell her he was one of the good guys, that she had it all wrong. That he was not just another dope-dealing biker. But he knew he couldn't, for her own safety and for his.

Benally started to go back inside, then turned to face Kincaid. "Not that I give a damn what you think, but I never had sex with John Henry or any other Bandido," she said. "I like men, and I enjoy teasing them, but I'm very selective about who I fuck. You're the first man I've had sex with in two years." She went inside and slammed the door, locking it behind her.

Kincaid slowly walked down the porch steps, shaking his head. He put on his helmet, started his Harley, and raced down I-25 toward Pecos, venting his anger with speed.

Another relationship lost because his damned job wouldn't allow him to trust anyone. Or maybe there was something about him that women could sense. Don't get too close to this one. He can't handle a real relationship because something died inside long ago. He'll love you, then he'll leave. And he had always left. Maybe it was the job. But maybe it was him.

Benally sat on the floor and cradled her head in her hands. It had been two years since she had ended her affair with Andrew Rogers, a young doctor from Philadelphia who had worked a year at the Crownpoint clinic. Rogers, like Linda's own mother, had been an idealist who wanted to help the Navajos on the reservation. Benally had the impression that he was going to propose to her, but that dream was quickly shattered when he said he had a fiancée in Philadelphia. He cared about Linda, but he didn't think she would fit in with his world back east. It slowly dawned on her that he had just wanted her for sex. Maybe Kincaid was no different.

Buck's Tavern
7:00 p.m.

Kincaid parked in front of Buck's and went inside, where he found Henry, Dowdy, and a dozen other Bandidos drinking beer. The jukebox was playing "Mustang Sally." Kincaid approached the bar and nodded to Dowdy.

"What's up, man?" Dowdy asked, looking around. "Where's your old lady?"

Kincaid shrugged. "She wanted to be alone," he said, taking the beer Buck offered.

"When you figure out women, let me know," Dowdy said. "I never could."

Kincaid clinked his beer bottle to Dowdy's and said, "I'm sure as hell no expert."

"You look a little down, brother," Dowdy said. "Maybe what you need is a good ride. We're headed up to Taos tomorrow. Wanna ride with us?"

"Sounds like a good idea," Kincaid said. "I could use a change of scenery."

A couple of Bandidos who had too much to drink started singing along with the jukebox. For a few moments, Kincaid put aside his thoughts about work and relaxed. To hell with Linda. He had enough to worry about. Kincaid had always enjoyed the camaraderie of other soldiers and DEA agents, so he could fit in with the Bandidos. He had spent many nights in honky-tonk bars, drinking beer, sometimes singing. He was a lousy singer, but he made up for it with enthusiasm. What the hell—if you were working undercover, you had to enjoy yourself sometimes. He ordered another beer, which he drank as he walked toward the restroom to take a leak.

When he came out, Kincaid noticed Henry talking on his cell phone, walking out a side door that led to the parking lot. Nobody was paying attention to Kincaid, who quietly followed Henry outside. He stepped to one side, back in the shadows, as Henry finished his call and got in a white Ford ten-passenger van with tinted windows. Henry started the van and drove around the front, headed toward the highway.

Kincaid moved to the parking lot, got on his Harley, and followed with his headlight off. There was no other traffic, and Kincaid didn't want to attract Henry's attention. There was a half-moon, and Kincaid knew the road.

On the south end of town, Henry pulled into Griego's to get some gas. Kincaid pulled off on the other side of the road, where he parked in the shadow of an auto-parts store and watched. After Henry started the pump, he went inside to buy some snacks and coffee. Kincaid didn't know where Henry was headed, but he knew it was going to be damned difficult to follow him at night without being noticed. How good was Henry at surveillance detection?

Kincaid waited until Henry was filling a cup with coffee

and his back was turned to the street. He walked up behind the van, pulling his knife out. Using the blunt end of the knife, he cracked the right rear taillight, just enough so that it emitted white light through the red lens. He then quickly faded back into the shadows and returned to his Harley.

Kincaid had filled his six-gallon tank before he went to Buck's, and he could make about forty miles to the gallon. But was it enough to take him to where Henry was going? Where the hell *was* he going? His cover might be blown if Henry saw him, but at some point, he had to start taking chances.

Henry came out of Griego's slowly, looked around, and got into the van. He had received the call from Sanchez, who told him to head to Mesilla Park, near Las Cruces. He would pick up five Al Qaeda operatives and transport them to the Navajo reservation. Henry started the van, drank some coffee, then pulled back onto the road. Years of running dope across state lines had made him cautious; now he was paranoid. Getting busted for possession of dope was bad enough, but if he was caught transporting terrorists, that was federal time; he would never get out of prison. And damned if he was going back to prison. Not ever. Henry looked in his side and rearview mirrors as he drove south down Route 50 toward I-25.

Kincaid waited until Henry's van was half a mile down the road before following him. He could easily discern the white pinpoint light from the broken taillight. He left off his headlight for the short drive to the interstate, hoping he wasn't spotted by local cops. Working undercover, he didn't usually carry a badge and would not be able to break cover in any case; deputy sheriffs and city cops weren't always good at keeping secrets. Fortunately, he passed only one car. After Henry turned onto the Interstate, Kincaid turned on his headlight and followed.

Henry kept within the speed limit of seventy-five miles an hour. Kincaid stayed about a half a mile back, keeping his eye on the white pinpoint from the taillight. There was more traffic on the interstate, and Kincaid was able to keep several cars between him and Henry.

Kincaid's main concern was that some overzealous New Mexico state police officer would stop Henry for the broken light. The state police were trained to use traffic violations or broken taillights as a reason to stop a vehicle they suspected could be transporting drugs. A cargo van made a good police target. If Henry got stopped for the broken light, he would probably suspect something was up. Like most dope dealers, Kincaid thought, Henry was probably paranoid.

Kincaid closed the gap as Henry approached the Santa Fe exits. He needed to see if Henry turned off, and it was good practice not to remain in one fixed position. Anyone trained in surveillance detection could eventually spot the same headlight when it remained at the same distance over several miles. Move up closer for a few miles, then back off when driving over a long, flat stretch of highway.

Henry soon passed Santa Fe and followed the interstate south toward Albuquerque. Following him in Albuquerque would be a challenge. Kincaid didn't know the city well, and Henry could easily lose him in any number of neighborhoods or barrios where Kincaid's Harley would stand out, both for its appearance and its noise.

It was now past nine p.m., and Kincaid was getting cold. He zipped up his leather jacket to his neck, cursing himself for not bringing his gloves. He had planned on spending the night with Linda, not riding across New Mexico—which could be just a waste of time. He had no idea where Henry was going, or if he would learn anything when he arrived.

He began to imagine Benally in that black leather miniskirt

and those black lace panties—her long hair falling across his face as she straddled him in her bed. Kincaid shook his head to clear it. *Stop that, idiot. Get your mind back on business before you run off the road or lose sight of Henry.*

The southbound traffic to Albuquerque was heavy, and Kincaid had no trouble keeping a few cars between him and Henry. As they approached the Bernalillo exit, Kincaid again closed the gap, watching for Henry to turn off, but he kept going toward Albuquerque. A few minutes later, they neared the first city exit, and Kincaid closed within a few hundred meters. From this point, Henry could exit about every mile.

Kincaid could feel the stress mounting as he concentrated on Henry's van, trying not to get too close. He had once followed a car from Los Angeles to Bakersfield, about a four-hour drive, before losing the target because he was caught at a stoplight after getting off the freeway. He had spent hours searching the streets before returning to headquarters. Kincaid still remembered the looks from his fellow agents. He did not want to fail again.

Henry didn't get off in Albuquerque at all. About ten miles south of the city, Kincaid began to worry about his gas mileage. He had just over half a tank left, and he didn't know where Henry was going. If Kincaid had to stop for gas, the game was over. After Belen, the traffic thinned out, so Kincaid fell back even farther, keeping the white taillight in sight. He flexed his fingers, trying to keep them warm. It wasn't working, as the temperature continued to drop to around sixty degrees.

Kincaid hoped Henry would stop in Socorro, a small city on the interstate that had a long strip of gas stations, restaurants, and motels. He could gas up, get a cup of coffee, and maybe even buy a cheap pair of gloves at a convenience store. To Kincaid's relief, Henry did turn off at Socorro and stopped at the Exxon station just off the exit. Kincaid rode in the left lane, using a large delivery truck as cover as he passed the Exxon. The Harley made a loud, distinctive sound, and he was concerned about being seen and heard by Henry. Kincaid stopped at a Chevron station in the next block and pulled up to a pump. He jogged into the station and bought a trail-mix bar and a cup of coffee. There weren't any gloves for sale.

A Sonic drive-in sat between the Exxon and Chevron stations; Kincaid hadn't eaten since noon, and his mouth watered at the thought of a green chili cheeseburger. No time. Kincaid rode around to the south end of the Chevron and waited for Henry to drive by, which he did a few minutes later. Henry continued south on California Street and got back on the interstate. Kincaid's hands were getting cold again as the temperature continued to drop.

An hour later, they entered the city limits of Las Cruces, a city of over a hundred thousand. Henry cut through the city to Mesilla, an old suburb. He made a right on Calle del Sur, a narrow lane barely wide enough for two cars. It was after midnight now, and there was no traffic. Kincaid stayed as far back as he could. He turned off his headlight as he followed Henry down the street, which was bordered by pecan orchards with farmhouses in between. They crossed over several wide irrigation ditches.

After a few miles, Henry turned left onto a dirt road and drove past a pecan orchard that dead-ended at an adobe farmhouse shielded from the road by a small grove of pecan trees. Kincaid stayed back, parking in another grove across the road and back two hundred meters, near an irrigation ditch. He took a pair of binoculars from his saddlebag and moved up along the ditch, watching as Henry approached the house. The door opened, and Henry went inside. No lights came on in the house.

Hamza and the other four Al Qaeda operatives were standing throughout the room. Hamza had a 9mm Glock, provided by Sanchez, pointed at Henry. A couple of fluorescent lanterns provided a dim light. From the shadows, the other men also pointed Glocks at Henry.

"Who is the leader of the Bandidos?" Hamza asked.

"Sonny Barger," Henry said, with reluctance. It was the verbal bona fides provided by Sanchez, who knew it would piss off Henry to name the founder of the Hells Angels. But it was safe because it was something an ordinary member of the Bandidos would never say—or an undercover cop. Hamza motioned for his men to lower their weapons.

Hamza and Kadar were accompanied by three men who all appeared to be under forty: Jabril Salim, a short, wiry man with dark hair and skin; Ahmed Mansur, an Iraqi army deserter from Mosul, and Mohammed al-Badri, a tall, slender fighter from Samarra. Al-Badri had helped his cousin, Haythim al-Badri, blow up the Golden Mosque in Samarra in 2006. Destruction of the Shia mosque had triggered a virtual civil war in Iraq between Sunnis and Shia that took several years to quell.

Henry looked around at the Al Qaeda operatives, thinking he had just walked into a den of rattlesnakes. The Iraqis had the look of men who had faced death too many times. They seemed alert but indifferent to their fates. All of them had shaved their beards before leaving Cuba, to avoid attention from the authorities in Mexico and the United States. Unknown to Henry, they had all made martyrdom videos before leaving Iraq. They were dead men walking. Hamza lowered his weapon and offered his hand to Henry, who cautiously shook it.

"I am Khalid Hamza," he said.

"John Henry."

Hamza pointed to Kadar. "This is Adnan Kadar, my second-in-command."

Kadar did not offer to shake his hand, nor did Henry care. "We better get some sleep," Henry said. "Long day tomorrow."

Outside, Kincaid waited for half an hour, then decided to find a motel and grab a few hours of sleep. He would return before dawn to resume surveillance.

He pulled into a convenience store, where he bought some trail-mix bars, beef jerky, water, and a pair of work gloves to keep his hands warm on the motorcycle. He then rode to a nearby Days Inn and got a room. He set the alarm on his cell phone for four a.m. and also left a wake-up call with the front desk. Too tired to take a shower, he collapsed on the bed and was asleep within a minute.

CHAPTER 12

Abdul Qadeer Khan, the Pakistani scientist accused of selling nuclear secrets, was today freed from five years of house arrest. . . . Khan, lionized as the "father" of Pakistan's atomic bomb, confessed in 2004 to selling nuclear secrets to Iran, North Korea and Libya.
—*Guardian*, Feb. 6, 2009

Islamabad, Pakistan
June 2, 2016

Hasan Rahim drove his Toyota Camry off Pir Sohawa Road and parked near the entrance of the Islamabad Zoo. Rahim got out of his car and took a deep breath as he gazed up at the Margalla Hills, a sight that never failed to inspire him. A light drizzle had fallen earlier, but the sun had emerged through the low-hanging clouds to alleviate the chill. Rahim, who wore tan slacks and a blue blazer, stopped at a stand near the entrance and bought a cone of chocolate ice cream. He licked it as he walked past the large green sign that read *Children's Play Land*. A statue of a pink flamingo rested behind the sign.

Very casually, Rahim walked through the zoo, stopping to examine the elephants, the African lions, and the monkeys. As he turned to look at the animals, he could also look for surveillance without appearing to do so. He was startled by an Anglo woman, apparently European or American, who was allowing a giraffe to lick her face. No self-respecting Pakistani woman would allow a filthy animal to degrade her in such a fashion. Rahim continued past the giraffe and wandered to a bench under a tree. Rahim sat and continued to lick his ice cream, his signal that he believed it was safe to meet. After a few minutes, Mohammed Khan sat next to him and opened a newspaper.

"I see you are still addicted to chocolate," Khan said.

"I've tried to break the habit, but it's no use," Rahim said. "I am a confirmed chocoholic."

Khan perused his newspaper while both men casually looked for signs that they were being watched. A woman with two young children walked by but paid no attention to two middle-aged men sitting on a bench. Rahim finished off his chocolate ice cream and wiped his mouth with a napkin. After several minutes, Rahim, a colonel with Pakistan's Inter-Services Intelligence, or ISI, felt confident they were in the clear.

"I understand that the package is on its way to America," Rahim said. "Are there any problems?"

Khan stopped reading his newspaper and turned to Rahim. It would be odd if he tried to talk while reading the paper, in case anyone was watching. "Our only concern is the radiation-detection device they now use in American ports."

"Our scientists have told me that it does not work very well," Rahim said. "Furthermore, the customs officers check only about three percent of all shipping containers." Rahim paused and turned toward Khan, leaning his arm on the bench.

"What if the Americans find our package?" he asked.

"The driver has been told he is picking up a cargo of illegal weapons," Khan said. "And the container manifest is listed for a company in Mozambique. The owner of that company is now on a permanent vacation."

Khan was a cousin of Abdul Qadeer Khan, the Pakistani nuclear scientist who developed Pakistan's nuclear weapons.

Abdul Khan had created a network of former Pakistani military officers and nuclear scientists who continued to aid the proliferation of nuclear materials, even after the death of Osama bin Laden. Rahim was one of those officers, and he continued to promote bin Laden's vision of an Islamic caliphate.

Bin Laden had viewed Abdul Khan as the key to obtaining an atomic bomb and fulfilling his dream of a war of the apocalypse. Both men believed that the ends justified the means. While bin Laden moved heroin from Afghanistan to Europe, Khan created a nuclear black market, selling uranium enrichment technology to Iran, Libya, and North Korea.

In 2004, after the United States provided Pakistan with evidence, Khan confessed to having sold nuclear secrets to Iran, North Korea, and Libya. Pakistan's president, General Pervez Musharraf, pardoned Khan but placed him under house arrest. The government relaxed the restrictions in 2009 and released him, which encouraged the Al Qaeda sympathizers, the scientists and soldiers who supported bin Laden—including Rahim.

If bin Laden achieved his goal, untold millions would die, but the caliphate would be reborn, and sharia law would replace both democratic institutions and communist regimes. To accomplish this goal, however, he first had to bring America to its knees: to disable its economy and demolish its will to fight. To that end, he had intended to smuggle several nuclear bombs into the United States and set them off. If several million Americans died, the country would lose its will to retaliate, especially if they did not know where to retaliate.

After bin Laden's death in 2011, Rahim and his colleagues continued to promote the research by militant Islamic scientists who were secretly building several highly enriched uranium atomic bombs similar in yield to those that were dropped on Hiroshima. Bin Laden would die before he realized his dream of a nuclear holocaust in America, but his ideas lived on through

Al Qaeda, and many members of the ISI continued supporting their efforts.

"Can we trust our Al Qaeda associates to carry out this task?" Khan asked.

"Their leader, Khalid Hamza, is prepared to be a martyr," Rahim said.

"Why is he helping us?" Khan asked.

"He is motivated by revenge," Rahim said. "The Americans put him in prison in Iraq, and he lost his wife and children because of it."

"I understand that you have an asset in the FBI, in the southwestern state of New Mexico," Khan said.

Rahim stared hard at Khan, surprised that he knew about the asset. "That is a closely guarded secret," Rahim said. "Where did you hear about him?"

"I have good sources," Khan said. "It is my business to stay informed. But do not worry. I realize his importance. I understand how much time and work you have put into this project."

"Since you are aware of our FBI asset, I assume you know about our new relationship with the Zeta cartel," Rahim said.

Khan nodded and said, "Why are we involved with the Zetas?"

"We need them to get our people and weapons into America," Rahim said.

"Do you have a reliable contact with them?" Khan asked.

"His name is Arturo Sanchez," Rahim said. "I have met him several times in New Mexico. I introduced him to our FBI asset. Sanchez also has an asset in the DEA."

"That is very useful to us. I hope we can trust him," Khan said. "Our entire operation depends on it."

"*Inshallah.* Tell me about the shipping arrangements," Rahim said.

⌒

A 500-foot-long merchant ship, the *Seahawk*, had stopped a week earlier at the port of Mabuto in Mozambique. Mabuto was a deepwater port close to Johannesburg, with direct rail and road connections to many of southern Africa's largest cities. Because of its high shipping traffic, customs officers at Maputo were busy and not often diligent about checking manifests or cargo.

A few days before the ship's arrival, another cargo vessel, the *Duchess*, had arrived from Dubai, where it had picked up a metal container from a warehouse owned by Abdul Khan. That container, which concealed a weapons-grade 16-kiloton uranium bomb, was labeled *Agricultural Machinery*, with an origination point listed as Malaysia. Lined with lead to prevent radiation leakage and detection, the container was placed aboard the *Seahawk*, after an envelope containing a few thousand rand was given by the ship's captain to the customs officer. The customs officer signed off on a new manifest that showed the container originated in Cyprus.

The *Seahawk* was registered in Liberia and owned by a corporation based in Cyprus. The ship's manifest said it contained cargo from Germany, Turkey, Egypt, and Mozambique: tractor parts, furniture, textiles, Persian rugs, and a thousand other products.

US Customs required all shippers to declare their containers' contents twenty-four hours before being loaded onto a freighter bound for a US port. The captain of the *Seahawk* wasn't overly concerned, however, because the shippers didn't usually know what was put in the containers before they arrived at the ship. It would be like the US postal service trying to find out what was in every letter before it was mailed.

The captain was aware of a US law that required all cargo

containers be scanned with imaging equipment and a radiation-detection device. But he also knew that the devices were used sporadically. Khan had reassured him that the scanners would not likely be able to detect a nuclear device shipped in a lead-lined container.

CHAPTER 13

Islamic extremists embedded in the United States—
posing as Hispanic nationals—are partnering with
violent Mexican drug gangs to finance terror networks
in the Middle East, according to a Drug Enforcement
Administration report.
—*Washington Times,* August 8, 2007

Mesilla, New Mexico
June 2, 2016

Hamza arose just before dawn and rousted the other Al Qaeda members for morning prayers. They walked out the back door to the east side of the adobe house and laid prayer rugs on the ground. Hamza and his men kneeled on the rugs toward the east, the direction of Mecca, and began their ritual, the Salat.

All praise is for Allah
Who gave us life
After having taken it from us
And unto Him is the Resurrection.

As the Muslims prostrated themselves and prayed, Henry observed from a side door, a cup of coffee in his hand. After they finished, Henry approached Hamza and stared at him.

"Don't you think that's a little conspicuous?" he asked.

"Not many Muslims in New Mexico. Somebody could see this and call the cops. Why do you do it?"

Hamza sighed, as though he were speaking to an ignorant child. "We do this five times a day, when possible. We call this the *Salat al-Fajr*, the morning prayer. It is a feeling of tranquility in your heart and understanding the Quran better, feeling closer to Allah at a time of isolation from others."

"I don't get it," Henry said. "If you guys are so religious, how come you deal drugs and blow people up?"

"The Holy Quran commands us to convert the infidel," Hamza said. "Allah understands that we must use methods that are sometimes harsh, but if we do not try to spread his message to the world, we will be condemned to hell."

You will have one helluva time converting me, you bastard, Henry thought, as he turned back into the house. The other men followed him back inside and began packing their bags with new REI hiking shirts and pants purchased by Sanchez in Las Cruces. They still wore their western business suits because they had to pass one final Border Patrol checkpoint north of Las Cruces. Two of the men began conversing in Arabic.

"Speak in Spanish!" Hamza commanded. "Nothing but Spanish or English from now on."

As dawn filtered over the horizon, the Al Qaeda operatives climbed back into the van, four of them sitting on the two rows in back, with Hamza in the front passenger seat. As Henry closed the back door, he noticed the hole in the right rear taillight and bent over to inspect it. The hole seemed too small and precise to have been made by road debris. Henry walked around the van, looking at the surrounding neighborhood.

"Anything wrong?" Hamza asked, as he got out of the van.

Henry shrugged. "Not sure. Found a hole in the taillight. Wasn't there when I left Pecos."

"Were you followed?" Hamza asked quietly, as Henry stood by his window.

"Don't think so," Henry said. "But you never can tell."

Kincaid froze in his position behind the pecan trees as Henry looked in his direction. He was over two hundred meters away and concealed by the top mound of an irrigation ditch, but he felt as though Henry was looking right at him. From his position, with pecan trees blocking his view, Kincaid could not get a clear photo of the men getting into the van, nor could he identify their nationality. He assumed they were members of the Zeta cartel. He had not seen the men praying behind the house.

Henry got into the driver's seat and drove out of the compound to Calle del Sur. Kincaid watched the van leave, then started his Harley and followed. He stayed back until the van headed up closer to Avenida de Mesilla. Then Kincaid raced his Harley down the street and stopped at the corner, peeking out from behind the concealment of a corner house. He observed the van moving north and followed, staying several cars behind it. Once they were on the interstate, Kincaid kept four to five cars between him and the van.

Daylight was easier for Kincaid. At least his hands wouldn't freeze, with his new gloves. Early June in New Mexico meant cool nights and warm, sunny days. The traffic on I-25 was heavy through Las Cruces, but thinner once they were past the city limits. After only four hours' sleep at the Days Inn, Kincaid was still tired, but at least he'd had a chance to grab a cup of coffee, and he had his trail-mix bars and a bag of beef jerky stuffed in his jacket pockets.

As he rode north on the interstate, Kincaid took in the view of the Organ Mountains, which seemed to touch an overhang of cumulus clouds ten miles east of the city. The igneous rock was similar in appearance to a cluster of organ pipes. He noticed a sign for Highway 70, which ran through the mountains to the White Sands Missile Range, just south of where America had first tested the atomic bomb in 1945. Kincaid had a sudden epiphany. What if a terrorist organization smuggled an atomic bomb into the United States? Was it even possible, with all the safeguards Homeland Security had put in place? Could, say, Al Qaeda operatives just drive across the border in a truck loaded with an atomic weapon? Kincaid was aware that the United States had some corrupt Border Patrol guards who were susceptible to bribery and threats of violence to their relatives, some of whom lived in Mexico. But still, even if it were possible to bring in an atomic weapon, Kincaid thought, terrorists would be aiming for a large city like Los Angeles or New York. He couldn't envision Al Qaeda wasting time in New Mexico.

Just north of Las Cruces, all traffic was diverted to the side through a Border Patrol checkpoint. The officers usually just glanced at the drivers and waved them through, but Kincaid saw them taking more time with Henry's van. Two officers were checking the passengers' identification. After a few minutes, Henry was allowed to head back onto the interstate. Kincaid, with only a few cars between him and Henry's van, was waved through by the Border Patrol. The officers seldom stopped Anglo-Americans. Kincaid accelerated to catch up to Henry, then stayed back, keeping several cars between them.

Kincaid was puzzled about Henry's passengers. Who were they and where had they come from? He had assumed they were illegals, probably drug dealers from one of the cartels in Mexico. But how could they have crossed through the Border Patrol checkpoint? They must have credible identification.

Kincaid still did not know if his effort would result in anything useful. He had not had time to consult with George Jackson in Albuquerque before beginning this surveillance, and he didn't want to call him until he had something to say. Kincaid believed in the value of human intelligence. What the NSA did was vital, but electronic intelligence only provided pieces of the puzzle. An intercepted phone conversation could provide valuable leads, but in part due to press coverage, the more intelligent Al Qaeda leaders had figured out what the NSA was doing and curtailed their use of phones. Satellites could show policy makers who was going into the tent, but not what the terrorists inside the tent were planning.

As for DEA agents, they had to form relationships with drug dealers in order to make a buy. Sometimes, they turned the dealers into informants to get closer to more important targets. It just took a little patience. Everybody needed something. Usually, it was money, sometimes revenge, or a need for adventure. Kincaid's job was to identify those needs and make friends with those people. You had to be a good listener, and you had to show empathy. Even to the scum who dealt drugs.

Kincaid loved the feeling of freedom as he rode across the country on the Harley—even more because the twenty-one-thousand-dollar bike had been confiscated by the DEA during a drug raid. It had a radio with stereo speakers and Mustang saddlebags, and it was black, his favorite color.

Get your motor running, head out on the highway.
Looking for adventure, and whatever comes my way.

No office, no bureaucrats. It was freedom. His ancestors had their horses, but he had his Harley. And to think he was being paid to do this.

He continued following Henry up I-25, and about an hour past Socorro, the van slowed as it approached the exit for Los Lunas, a city of about fifteen thousand people located just south of Albuquerque. Kincaid throttled back, letting a few cars get in front of him as he followed the van off the exit ramp and toward a small shopping center that had two gas stations, a Valero and a Shell, right across from each other. Kincaid needed gas and food but didn't want to risk coming so close to the van, which now had extra pairs of eyes and ears.

He headed across the freeway, to another small plaza with a Phillips 66 station, where he quickly filled up his tank and grabbed a couple hot dogs. He then rode around to the back of the station so he had a view down to the Valero station across the freeway. He pulled a set of binoculars from his saddlebag and looked toward the van as he ate. Henry was filling up the gas tank, but he was parked under an overhang, so Kincaid couldn't get a clear view of his passengers through the heavily tinted windows. He could see a few men moving toward the Valero, probably to use the restroom. The van had a sliding side door on the side he couldn't see.

Finally Henry guided the van back onto the interstate, heading north toward Albuquerque; Kincaid followed about a half mile back. Traffic got heavier as they approached the city, and Kincaid had to get closer, as the van could take any one of a dozen exits. But Henry did not get off in Albuquerque, and continued up I-25 to the Bernalillo exit, Highway 550.

Kincaid was baffled. He had expected Henry to arrive at some urban safe house in Albuquerque. If his passengers were cartel members, why in hell was he taking them out to Indian Country?

Port of Houston
Houston, Texas

The Port of Houston is one of America's busiest, generating more than eleven billion dollars a year in revenue and employing, directly or indirectly, more than a quarter million people in Texas. Harry Dowdy drove his Mack truck down San Jacinto Boulevard toward the Boggy Basin wharf, amazed by the amount of traffic. Trucks were shuttling back and forth with cargo, cranes were moving cargo containers from ships to trucks, and everywhere, it seemed, Port of Houston police and security officers were checking shipping manifests, inspecting trucks, and asking questions.

As he pulled in line behind other trucks at the wharf, Dowdy presented his papers to a US Customs officer, who looked them over, then checked Dowdy's commercial driver's license. Dowdy had tied his hair back in a ponytail and wore a long-sleeved shirt to cover his tattoos.

"What cargo are you picking up?" asked the customs officer, checking to see if Dowdy actually knew what was on the manifest.

"Agricultural machinery," Dowdy said.

"What is this company, Southwest Imports?" the officer asked.

"Mostly farm equipment, I guess," Dowdy said. "Don't know much about it."

Dowdy was told to pick up his cargo and claim ignorance if customs found anything illegal. John Henry had been clear: you just drive a truck. If police tried to contact Southwest Imports, a company registered in Dallas, Texas, they would get an answering machine. The calls were forwarded through routers that went first to Paris, then to Islamabad. The office of Southwest Imports was a private mailbox service that provided an actual street address in Dallas, not just a P.O. Box. Dowdy's cover was that of an independent truck driver who'd gotten this job through an email contact. He had saved the fictitious email in his cell phone. A native of Houston, he actually had a Texas commercial truck driver's license.

The container, which was indeed labeled *Agricultural*

Machinery, was unloaded from the ship and passed through the radiation-detection scanner, a tall, two-sided orange metal frame on wheels, with a small booth manned by an operator on one side. The scanner did not detect anything. The container was then loaded onto the flatbed trailer attached to Dowdy's truck, and he drove out of the shipyard, back down San Jacinto Boulevard. Looking back through his side mirror, Dowdy breathed a huge sigh of relief.

Dowdy, who believed he was carrying a load of illegal weapons, possibly C-4 explosives, headed north on Sam Houston Parkway to I-10, where he headed west. About twenty minutes past the outskirts of Houston, Dowdy turned north on Highway 99 and headed into a rural area, taking an unmarked dirt road that led to an old farmhouse. He drove around the house and pulled into a metal granary large enough to conceal the truck. As Dowdy stepped out of the cab, he was greeted by Mike Akins, a member of the Houston Bandidos.

"Good to see you, brother," Dowdy said as he gave Akins a bear hug.

"You too, bro," Akins said. Like many Bandidos, Akins had done time in prison and had the bulging muscles that came from spending a lot of time lifting weights. His beard matched the long blond hair pulled back in a ponytail, and tattoos covered both arms. He signaled with his arms to guide another Bandido, who was backing up a rented sixteen-foot panel truck to the rear of the trailer.

"What's in the truck?" Akins asked.

"Don't really know," Dowdy said. "Some kind of weapons, I guess. Henry told me not to ask a lot of questions."

"This for those ragheads I heard about?" Akins asked as he opened the door to the trailer.

"I reckon," Dowdy said, stepping into the container. He started pushing out smaller boxes of actual tractor parts before he came to the metal crate. Also marked *Agricultural Machinery*, it was about five feet long, three feet wide, and three feet high, with an electronic combination lock on the lid. Dowdy tried to lift it, then stepped back.

"Son of a bitch is heavy," Dowdy said. "Better get the forklift."

Akins picked up the crate with a forklift and transferred it to the rental truck. The crate weighed nearly a thousand pounds. Dowdy and two other Bandidos covered it with boxed merchandise from the shipping container. He then closed the rear door of the truck and clamped a heavy padlock on it.

"What do we do with this crap?" Akins asked, pointing to the container, which was still half full of merchandise.

"Leave it here for now," Dowdy said. "Maybe later you can sell it."

As Dowdy prepared to get into the rental truck, Akins asked, "What the hell is going on with these ragheads, Harry?"

Dowdy paused and leaned against the door. "I think these crazy bastards are planning some kind of jihad bullshit in New Mexico," he said. "John Henry's a little worried about it, but Sanchez is paying us a shitload of money to move this crate, and we've got a new pipeline for some good white stuff from Afghanistan."

"Where there's dope, there's hope," Akins said, laughing.

Dowdy drove out of the granary and back to I-10. Maybe he would stop in San Antonio for lunch at the Cracker Barrel, he thought, and get a good chicken-fried steak with mashed potatoes and gravy. And a piece of apple pie topped with ice cream. Dowdy was careful to keep within the speed limit, staying in the right lane. He had a long drive across Texas.

CHAPTER 14

On a clear, dry early spring day hiking the Bisti is like a trip to Mars without boarding a spaceship.
—*Durango Herald*, March 7, 2014

Highway 550
Lybrook, New Mexico
June 2, 2016
5:00 p.m.

Kincaid followed Henry's van up Highway 550 through Cuba and past Lybrook, a Navajo area that, although scarred by gas wells and access roads, still featured a picturesque landscape born in the Cretaceous Period, about one hundred million years ago. The cliffs lining the highway had four distinct layers of sandstone, shale, and coal that were covered in a thick layer of caprock, with juniper and cedar shrubs covering the tops of the mesas. The elevation was over 7,000 feet.

Henry turned west off State Road 7900, a gravel road that wound through an area populated by oil wells. Kincaid stayed back over a mile. A few miles west lay the Bisti Badlands, with its mystical, bizarre rock formations of jumbled sandstone.

The van stopped in front of a dilapidated ranch home that had a corral with half a dozen horses. A windmill turned slowly, producing a meager flow of water into a tank in the corral, which abutted a shed containing saddles and bridles on one side and stacks of hay on the other. Kincaid parked his

Harley behind a ridge overlooking the home. He took out his binoculars and a small camera bag and climbed to the top of the ridge, using a large cedar tree as cover.

Henry led the Al Qaeda operatives into the home, where they immediately began changing out of their suits and into their outdoor clothes. The living room had a folding table that seated four, with a couch and chairs lining the wall. A color TV rested on a wooden crate near the wall opposite the dining room table. An old, large painting of Custer's last stand hung on the wall over the couch. The painting showed an Indian removing the scalp of a soldier and Custer firing his revolver as a dozen Indians descended upon him.

"You okay with this?" Henry asked Hamza, who was opening doors and inspecting the kitchen.

"It seems adequate," Hamza said. "But where are the weapons I requested?"

"Sanchez should be along with those pretty soon," Henry said.

Hamza continued walking around the room, opening a closet and checking the door to a bedroom.

"What is this place?" he asked.

"An old ranch," Henry said. "Navajos used to live here, I guess. One of Sanchez's men, Danny Haskie, owns it."

Hamza stepped outside; Henry followed. Hamza walked around, looking at the horizon in all directions. He was intrigued by the rock formations, which began less than a mile to the southwest of the ranch. He turned to Henry and said, "What is that place, with the strange rocks?"

"The Bisti Badlands," Henry said. "Lots of strange rocks. Some people say it's haunted by the ghosts of dead Indians."

Kincaid was puzzled by the man who appeared to be the leader of the group of strangers. He looked familiar, but he was too far away to be certain. He still assumed Henry had brought some Mexicans across the border. Kincaid backed down from the ridge and began moving closer, through an arroyo that was over ten feet deep.

As Kincaid got closer, Sanchez and Haskie arrived in Haskie's Ford pickup. What was Haskie doing there? Did the Manhunters have something to do with this? What was the connection between the Zeta cartel and the Bandidos? Was it all about drugs? Or something else? What in hell was going on here?

They got out of the truck, and Haskie pulled back a tarp, revealing a crate of AK-47s and ammunition, and another crate containing an RPG and several rounds for it. The foreign-looking men began to remove the weapons from the pickup. Kincaid climbed up to the top of the arroyo and found a space behind a piñon tree, where he resumed his surveillance with binoculars. He was now within a hundred yards of the ranch house.

Haskie walked to the corral, where he opened a storage bin filled with oats and began to feed the horses. He'd inherited the place from his parents. Like many Navajos, Haskie loved horses. This was his retreat from the world of drug dealing and the Manhunters. Before arriving at the house, Sanchez had told him he was bringing in some Al Qaeda operatives, but he did not say why they were here. He had been reluctant to allow terrorists to use the site for a safe house, but Sanchez had paid him a nice bonus. Haskie was starting to feel that he might need to get away from Sanchez and his operation.

Hamza inspected the weapons, then turned to Sanchez. "What about the shipment from Houston?"

"Our Bandido friends are handling that for us," Sanchez said.

"How soon can we expect it?" Hamza asked.

"In a few days," Sanchez said. "I will let you know."

"What is our cover for being here?" Hamza asked.

Sanchez returned to the pickup and withdrew a large black case, which he opened. Inside were several 35mm Nikons, along with a video camcorder.

"You are now a freelance photo crew from Mexico," he said. "You are doing a documentary on ancient Navajo trading posts."

Sanchez handed Hamza press credentials for all five men. Hamza smiled and said, "I have always wanted to be a journalist."

"I doubt that you will need to use these," Sanchez said. "But it's always good to be prepared."

Sanchez motioned for Hamza to walk inside the house and closed the door. Sanchez took two soft drinks from the refrigerator, handed one to Hamza, and sat down on the couch. Sanchez sipped his drink and stared at Hamza.

"I wish to clarify our agreement," Sanchez said. "I have not asked you what you plan to do with the weapons in that crate, let alone what is arriving from Houston, but I imagine it will attract a great deal of attention. I also assume that you may not survive."

Hamza nodded agreement. "*Inshallah*. I do not expect to live forever."

"Frankly, I do not really care if you strike a blow at the Americans," he said. "But I want your assurance that the supply of heroin will continue, whether or not you are still on this earth."

"You have my word," Hamza said. "We have given this

matter much thought. We have decided it is to our advantage to import more heroin into the United States. The more America has to spend money and resources on its addicts, the weaker it becomes. And American dollars can be used to buy more weapons."

"Then we have a shared interest," Sanchez said. "Our main connection in New Mexico to the heroin supply is the Pakistani. Have you met him?"

"Yes. He has the blessing of our leaders," Hamza said. "His activities within the FBI are crucial to our movement. I assume that you can be trusted to keep his identity secret. My colleagues in Pakistan have invested a great deal of time and money in him."

Sanchez stood up and moved toward the door. "Of course," he said. "We both need a source within the FBI. I have been dealing with him for the past year, since we made our agreement. I know how to handle him."

Sanchez and Hamza walked outside and watched as the men inspected the weapons. They began to break down the AK-47s and clean them on an old picnic table on the porch.

Henry approached Sanchez and motioned for him to walk around the house and away from the operatives.

"What the fuck's going on?" Henry asked.

"I don't know what they are planning," Sanchez said. "Whatever it is, we need to stay away from the reservation for the time being. We do not want the police to connect us to these people."

"If these crazy bastards start shooting people, it's gonna hurt our business," Henry said.

"For a short time," Sanchez said. "Once they get themselves killed, things will calm down. Our pipeline will remain in place. The advantages of this source of heroin far outweigh the problems we expect."

"I hope you know what you're doing," Henry said.

"Trust me, my friend," Sanchez said. "I have good connections with the people in South Asia."

From behind his tree, Kincaid focused his binoculars on the leader of the mysterious men. Who was he? A member of the Zeta cartel? What in hell was he doing here? Kincaid reached in his bag for his Canon. He took several photos of all the men at the house. At one hundred yards and in the fading sunlight, he had trouble getting accurate details of their faces.

Suddenly, the leader turned to face in his direction, and recognition staggered Kincaid. *Hamza.* He took a dozen shots of the clean-shaven face as his days in Iraq came rushing back to him. How the hell had Hamza gotten out of prison? Was he still Al Qaeda? What was he doing with the Zetas?

Kincaid moved slowly back down into the arroyo. He had to report this to Jackson. As Kincaid made his way back to his Harley, he had a foreboding that all hell was about to break loose.

CHAPTER 15

We love death. The US loves life. That is the difference between us two.
—Osama bin Laden, interview with Hamid Mir, Pakistani journalist, after 9/11

Balad Air Base
Iraq
May 15, 2004

Kincaid put on his helmet as he walked out of the Joint Special Operations Command (JSOC) briefing room toward the flight line at Balad, Iraq. Three Black Hawk helicopters were warming up, their rotors shattering the night with a steady roar. Kincaid, a sergeant first class, led one of three squads of US Army Delta Force soldiers, all wearing body armor and helmets with night-vision goggles and carrying 9mm submachine guns. Their faces were obscured with green, brown, and tan camouflage. Most of the men wore beards. They appeared like ghostly silhouettes, moving slowly through the orange dust and dim light. It was just before midnight: time to go hunting for Al Qaeda.

Kincaid had a Glock 9mm pistol in a holster on his right leg; a Ka-Bar combat knife was in a sheath strapped across his chest. He carried the HK MP5A3 submachine gun, because it was reliable, compact, and accurate. Kincaid stood by the Black Hawk, waiting for his men to climb aboard. He would be the last on and first out of the door, rappelling down a rope to the target, a residence on the outskirts of Mosul.

As soon as he climbed aboard the Black Hawk, it lifted off. Kincaid plugged a cord into his helmet that allowed him to communicate with the pilots, and looked down over the airfield. The runway lights were extinguished at night to make it difficult for insurgents trying to zero in for mortar attacks on the daily flights of C-17 jets that landed at Balad. He breathed in the warm air, trying not to choke on the orange dust that hovered over the base. The helicopters rose several thousand feet and headed northwest toward Mosul: Indian Country.

Since Vietnam, American soldiers have regarded any combat zone as Indian Country, a symbolic reference to the US Army's battles against Native Americans in the nineteenth century. A descendant of ranchers who settled in Texas in the late 1840s and fought Comanches, Kincaid wondered how Americans would later view the soldiers who served in Iraq and Afghanistan. Would they regard the soldiers as patriots? As expendable pawns? Would they think much at all about them?

Kincaid thought about leaving the army. He had joined when he was eighteen, and volunteered for the infantry, airborne, Rangers, and later, Special Forces. After three years in the Seventh Special Forces Group at Fort Bragg, he was selected for Delta Force, a clandestine counterterrorism unit that worked closely with the CIA. Kincaid had learned CIA tradecraft—how to handle agents, detect and conduct surveillance, set up dead drops, and use safe signals.

In October 2001, Kincaid had been one of over a hundred Special Forces troops who parachuted into northern Afghanistan to make contact with the Northern Alliance, a loose coalition of Afghans who were opposed to the Taliban. He had carried five hundred thousand dollars in cash in a backpack, with vague instructions about spreading the money to local leaders in hopes of gaining their support. A month after the 9/11 attacks, America had scrambled to retaliate against Al Qaeda; the Special Forces soldiers, along with CIA's paramilitary operatives, were the first to fight.

With soldiers from the Northern Alliance, Kincaid rode Afghan ponies that quickly took him over rough terrain where no roads existed. It was easy to adapt to the outdoor life on horseback in Afghanistan. It was exhilarating and dangerous; the adrenaline rush he experienced on missions was addictive, and he had never felt more alive. He drank chai tea and shared bread with Afghan warriors living in caves. He slept on the ground, going weeks without a shower. He grew a beard and let his hair grow long. He killed several Taliban fighters.

Kincaid had been at war for three years. After his year-long tour in Afghanistan, he'd deployed to Iraq, where he was now on his second tour. In Iraq, he still felt the rush every time he boarded a Black Hawk to go on a raid, but he was growing weary. Afghanistan, for him, had entailed forward movement and provided Kincaid with a sense of accomplishment. Iraq, however, was becoming a stalemate. JSOC captured scores of insurgents every day and interrogated them to gather more intelligence, which led to more raids. The Special Operations soldiers went out almost every night, but inertia had set in; the more insurgents they captured, the more sprouted up.

Maybe, he thought, he was just getting old. At twenty-six, the five-mile runs were requiring more effort, and his body didn't seem to rebound as quickly. He was still young enough, however, to start a new career. He had considered law enforcement, back in the States. He wanted to meet a woman and have a normal life, if such a thing existed. In Fayetteville, there was no shortage of young women willing to marry a Special Forces soldier, but he was particular. Or maybe just too cautious after his failed marriage.

Two hours out from base, the Black Hawks descended to a hundred feet and moved up the Tigris River, heading into the southern outskirts of Mosul, a city of over a million people. Although occupied by US Army and Iraqi army units, the city had experienced a wave of violence. A few months earlier, a car bomb had killed over six hundred people, mainly innocent civilians. Attacks by criminals and terrorists had led to deterioration of the city's infrastructure. Many scientists, professors, doctors, engineers, lawyers, journalists, clergy, as well as professionals and artists in all walks of life, had been either killed or forced to leave the city under the threat of being shot by Al Qaeda. Mosul was a growing stronghold for the terrorist organization.

Kincaid's helicopter hovered over the target, a single-story house built with brown bricks. The exact location had been pinpointed on maps by another Al Qaeda detainee during interrogation the previous night. Kincaid, wearing heavy leather gloves, slid rapidly down the rope about twenty-five meters before gripping it tightly and forcing a stop just a few feet off the ground. He flipped off the safety on his HK and quickly moved aside, scanning the area for hostiles with his night-vision goggles. He had landed just fifty meters from the house where intelligence said Khalid Hamza resided.

Hamza was reportedly a chief manufacturer of Improvised Explosive Devices (IEDs) for Al Qaeda—devices that were ripping apart Humvees carrying American soldiers on patrol throughout Iraq. Intelligence also said Hamza was in touch with Osama bin Laden and might know his whereabouts. Hamza was last seen in Afghanistan, but intelligence indicated that he was now coordinating Al Qaeda's efforts in northern Iraq.

After the remaining soldiers in his squad were on the ground, Kincaid signaled for two men to cover the rear of the house, while he prepared to assault the front. One soldier kicked in the front door, then stood aside as another tossed in a flash bang grenade, which produced a blinding flash of light and a loud noise that caused a momentary loss of hearing.

Kincaid quickly led the way inside, where Hamza's wife was screaming, covering her ears. Accompanying Kincaid was Hamid al-Jabari, his Iraqi-American interpreter. Very few American soldiers were fluent in Arabic, and every unit was accompanied by an interpreter, or "terp." Most of them were Arab-American immigrants from Detroit and other large cities.

In a nearby bedroom, the soldiers found a boy and a girl. The six-year-old girl was crying and screaming; the boy, twelve, was glaring at the soldiers and cursing in Arabic. The soldiers brought them into the living room to join their mother. Kincaid flipped up his night-vision goggles and turned on a lamp. The living room contained a small dining room table with chairs and a large sofa.

"No sign of Hamza," one soldier said.

Kincaid turned to al-Jabari and said, "Ask her where Khalid is."

Al-Jabari turned to the woman and talked to her in Arabic. She shook her head, still crying, and responded with shouts. The girl continued to scream, and lights were coming on in nearby houses.

"She says he has been gone for several days," al-Jabari said. "She doesn't know where."

Kincaid moved closer to the woman and stared at her for a long moment without talking. She became nervous and looked down at the couch. Kincaid followed her eyes, then turned to his soldiers.

"Turn over that couch," he said.

As the soldiers began to lift the couch, one of them said, "Fucking thing's heavy!"

Kincaid motioned for them to drop the couch, and he kneeled in front of it, found a strap, and pulled out the bottom section. Inside, Khalid Hamza was hiding.

"Don't shoot," he said in English.

"You motherfucker!" said one of the soldiers, as he yanked Hamza to his feet and tied his hands with plastic flexicuffs.

Hamza's wife and daughter screamed and tried to prevent the soldiers from taking him. They tugged on Hamza's arms and legs, but soldiers dragged them back. The boy moved aside, edging toward a cabinet on one side of the room.

"Get him on the chopper," Kincaid said. "We're out of here."

Two soldiers provided security on either side of the Black Hawk, which had landed in an adjacent empty lot, while another two dragged Hamza aboard. A black hood was placed over his head, and he was strapped into a canvas seat. Once his team was on the Black Hawk, Kincaid backed toward it, his HK at the ready, probing for hostiles.

As Kincaid was about to board the helicopter, Hamza's son stepped to the front door with an AK-47. He aimed the rifle at Kincaid and fired a shot, which hit the fuselage of the Black Hawk, only inches from Kincaid, who immediately fired three rounds into the boy's chest. As the boy fell to the ground, Hamza's wife came out and kneeled beside her son, screaming at Kincaid, who froze for a moment in the doorway of the Black Hawk. Half a dozen neighbors poured into the compound, shouting at the Americans. More lights came on in other homes.

"Let's get the hell out of here, Wayne," said a member of his team, who pulled him back inside as the Black Hawk quickly ascended.

Kincaid slumped back against the edge of the door. In his three years of combat, he had never shot a child, or a woman.

There had been no time to think about it. He saw the AK-47, and he reacted. He knew there was nothing else he could have done, but he felt a cold emptiness inside. He stared at Hamza, who was struggling with his handcuffs and trying to talk to the interpreter through his hood. Did he know that his son had just died? How would he react if he knew? The Black Hawk flew low over the river until it was out of the city, then gradually rose to 5,000 feet.

When they landed back at Balad, they were met by a black cargo van driven by US Marine guards. They quickly shoved Hamza into the van and strapped him in, while Kincaid and al-Jabari sat next to him. The other Delta soldiers returned to the operations center for debriefing. The van drove past one guard post surrounded by sandbags and entered another part of the compound that held prisoners in a long, two-story wooden building resembling a warehouse. It had no windows, numbers, or signs. The van pulled up in the rear of the building, where another Marine guard opened a door concealed by a wall of sandbags.

The guards, followed by Kincaid and al-Jabari, marched Hamza inside. He was taken into a side room, where the guards stripped off his clothes and dressed him in an orange jumpsuit without removing his black hood. His flexicuffs were replaced with metal Smith and Wesson police handcuffs, and he was led into an eight-by-six-foot metal cell that had a single light bulb encased in a metal cage in the ceiling. There was no toilet or sink. A narrow metal bunk, without a mattress or pillow, extended from one wall.

Kincaid, accompanied by al-Jabari, entered the cell and used a key to unlock Hamza's handcuffs, then jerked off his hood. Hamza squinted against the bright light, then looked at Kincaid and al-Jabari. They stood over him as Hamza sat on the metal bunk.

"You speak English?" Kincaid asked.

"Yes," Hamza said. "Who are you? Why am I here?"

"Your name's Khalid Hamza?" Kincaid asked.

"Yes," Hamza said.

"And you make bombs for Al Qaeda?" Kincaid asked.

Caught off guard by Kincaid's accusation, Hamza looked puzzled and glanced down. He then began to shake his head no. "I know nothing about that," he said.

"Look around you," Kincaid said. "Do you think you will like living here?"

Hamza glanced around the room, then looked back at Kincaid. "I want to see a lawyer," he said.

"That's not going to happen," Kincaid said. "Terrorists who make bombs that kill American soldiers don't have any rights. If you don't cooperate with me, you will spend the rest of your life here, or in Guantanamo. Or maybe they'll just hang you."

"Who are you?" Hamza asked. "What is this place?"

"Think of this as your new home," Kincaid said. "Only, your wife won't be joining you. Or your kids. In fact, if you don't cooperate with me, they may never see you again."

Hamza glared at Kincaid, who stared back at him for half a minute.

"I saw your wife," Kincaid said. "She's a good-looking woman. Shouldn't take her too long to figure out you won't be coming home. She will need somebody to support her and the kids. Then she may have to find another husband. Am I right?"

Hamza, in a fit of rage, tried to stand, but Kincaid pushed him back onto the bunk.

"How do you think I found you, hiding in that couch?" Kincaid asked. He leaned closer to Hamza and said, "Your wife turned you in. She looked at where you were hiding, and she nodded her head."

"You are lying!" Hamza shouted.

"Maybe she already has a lover," Kincaid said. "You were too busy making bombs for Al Qaeda to notice."

Hamza screamed in anger and despair. Kincaid knew from experience that the first twenty-four hours of captivity often produced the most useful intelligence because the detainee was disoriented, confused, and scared. He brought in a chair, sat across from Hamza, and waited until he calmed down.

"Tell me about your relationship with Osama bin Laden," Kincaid said. "When did you see him last?"

"I've never met him," Hamza said.

"We know that's not true," Kincaid said. "We've talked to five other members of Al Qaeda who say you're his main liaison officer in Mosul. We have other witnesses who saw you with bin Laden in Afghanistan."

"Your witnesses are mistaken," Hamza said, looking down and away from Kincaid. "They are confusing me with somebody else."

Kincaid stared at Hamza for more than a minute, saying nothing else. He revealed no emotion, because he had learned that displays of anger by the interrogator usually were unproductive on experienced Al Qaeda operatives. Al Qaeda members received their own counterinterrogation training and looked for ways to push the buttons of the interrogator. When he resumed talking to Hamza, he was calm and displayed no emotion.

"My younger brother was killed at the Pentagon, during the 9/11 attacks," Kincaid said. "For a long time, I was angry, and I swore I was going to kill every one of you Al Qaeda bastards. And that's what I've been doing for three years. Only, I don't feel anger anymore. I really don't feel much of anything. It's like killing a cockroach. I see one, I just kill it."

"The cockroach has survived for millions of years!" Hamza shouted. "Al Qaeda will also survive! But you will not! The sheikh will destroy America!"

Kincaid smiled and leaned forward. "So you now admit that you know bin Laden?" he asked.

Hamza leaned back, with a slight smile emerging. He stared at Kincaid and considered his options. Hamza had graduated from the University of Mosul with a degree in engineering. Until the Americans invaded Iraq, he had a promising future with the Iraqi government. His father had been a member of the Baath Party and had excellent connections with Saddam Hussein. But that was all in the past. Hamza decided he had very few options left. And not long to live. He assumed that the Americans would eventually execute him.

"Everything that happens on this earth was written in the stars millions of years ago," Hamza said. "Nothing that you do can change it. You can save yourself by converting to Islam, or you can burn in hell with the other infidels."

"I'll take my chances in hell," Kincaid said. "Tell me about bin Laden's plans for America."

"America will pay a great price for what it has done to our people," Hamza said. "The sheikh will purify your country with fire."

"You don't understand how powerful America is," Kincaid said. "If Al Qaeda attacks us, we will destroy you, and whatever country helps you."

"It is you who do not understand," Hamza said. "Allah is on our side."

Hamza lay down on the metal bunk and turned his back to Kincaid. "I will not talk anymore," he said.

Kincaid stood and nodded to al-Jabari that he was ready to leave. He would leave Hamza alone for a few days. In his cell, the light never went out. Because the warehouse had no windows, the detainees could not tell day from night. A week could seem like a month. And all around him, other prisoners were screaming. Some screamed because they were angry and frustrated, others because they were on the verge of insanity. Hamza would reach his breaking point. They all did.

Kincaid left the detention center and walked through the dark toward his cubicle in a mobile home, one of several hundred in a sea of trailers inside the compound. He carried a small flashlight with a red lens, which allowed him to see the ground without becoming a target. Almost every night, insurgents in pickup trucks would stop in fields outside the airfield, launch one or two mortars, then take off. They did minor damage, but the attacks served to remind the JSOC soldiers that they were living in a war zone. Balad was known as "Mortaritaville" because of the frequency of mortar attacks.

Kincaid thought about his younger brother, Sam, who had been commissioned a second lieutenant in the US Army infantry after graduating from Texas A&M University. Sam had been on active duty only six months when Al Qaeda flew a jet into the Pentagon, where he was stationed. Kincaid recalled attending Sam's graduation, when the butter bars were pinned on his shoulders. Wearing his Green Beret and Class A uniform, Kincaid had saluted his brother, then embraced him.

When Sam was killed, Kincaid had been consumed by a cold fury. He had immediately volunteered for the first mission to Afghanistan, then for Iraq. For years, he had dedicated his life to killing terrorists. His intense focus did not allow time for relationships, or even to make plans for his future. Until lately. As he unlocked the door to his trailer, he looked around the small cubicle, not much bigger than Hamza's prison cell. It was an irony that did not escape Kincaid, as he sat on his narrow bunk and began to unlace his boots. Eight years in the army. Could he do twenty? And then what?

Kincaid tried to sleep, but the image of Hamza's son

holding the AK-47 would not go away. He should have told his men to thoroughly search the house. They should have found the weapon; Iraqis were allowed to have an AK-47 for personal defense. If the boy had been older, they would have handcuffed him for security. But he was just a boy.

The next day, Hamza was photographed and fingerprinted by an FBI agent who maintained a system known by its acronym, BATS, the Biometric Automated Tool Set. The twenty-two-pound kit recorded a subject's retina scan, hair and eye color, and weight and age, in addition to the fingerprints and photo. Hamza was examined by an army doctor, then returned to his cell.

Hamza's interrogations were continued by JSOC interrogators, known as "gators," who came from the ranks of Army Intelligence, the Defense Intelligence Agency, and the FBI. They worked in concert with intelligence analysts, who fed fresh information obtained through interrogations into their analytical databanks. The intelligence resulted in new raids by the Special Operations soldiers, often within twenty-four hours.

When Hamza needed to use the bathroom, he had to pound on the cell door, hoping that one of the guards heard him. Before leaving the cell for any reason, the guard would put Hamza's hood back on. Hamza was never allowed to see anything outside his cell, or anyone except for the guards and interrogators. He knew there were other prisoners because he could hear them screaming and pounding on their cell doors. The isolation and the frequent interruptions for interrogations at all hours during the day and night drove the detainees to the verge of exhaustion. Once a week, they were allowed a shower. The prisoners lost track of time, and they couldn't tell day from night, because the single light bulb never went out.

After Hamza had been detained for a week, Kincaid decided it was time for another visit. He had Hamza escorted to a spacious room with a table, couch, and chairs, and he set up a video camera in one corner of the room. Before Hamza entered the room, Kincaid placed a small pot of chai tea and two cups on the table. When the guard took off Hamza's hood, he stared around him in disbelief, then settled his gaze on Kincaid.

"Would you like some chai?" Kincaid asked.

Hamza, bewildered, nodded and sat down in a chair as Kincaid poured him a cup of chai. Hamza cautiously sipped the tea, as though it were some unknown elixir. Kincaid poured himself a cup of tea and sat in a chair next to Hamza, facing him.

"Do you remember me?" Kincaid asked, leaning closer to Hamza.

"You brought me here," Hamza said. "How long has it been?" he asked.

"A long time," Kincaid said. "I want to talk about your situation. I know that you have a degree from the College of Engineering in Mosul. You speak English. You are an intelligent man."

Kincaid paused to let his words sink in. His partners in Military Intelligence had used a combination of interrogation approaches designed to make him fear prison and to worry about losing his family. If used properly, the detainee would begin to feel that argument was futile, that only cooperation could lead to any positive outcome. Kincaid had undergone thirteen weeks of interrogation training at Fort Bragg. Most of his interrogations had been on the battlefield, shortly after capturing an insurgent. Hamza, however, was a high-value target, and he could provide information that could save American lives. JSOC was already receiving requests from the

Defense Intelligence Agency to allow their IED specialists from Washington, DC, to take part in the interrogations. Kincaid pointed to a thick file lying on the table next to him.

"In that file are transcripts of over a dozen interrogations of Al Qaeda operatives," Kincaid said. "Every one of them said you are a bomb maker for Al Qaeda. There is no use in denying what you have done. You have not been cooperative with our interrogators. So this is your last chance. If you don't start talking, I'm going to send you before an Iraqi judge. With the evidence we have, he doesn't need your confession. He will hang you based on what others have said about you. This will all happen within a few days. Within a week, you will be dead."

Hamza looked at the file, then back at Kincaid. He sat back in his chair, sipping his chai and looking away from Kincaid. Hamza was exhausted and weak from his stay at the detention center. The daily interrogations had confused him, and he had provided different accounts of what he had done and whom he knew. It was hard to think clearly. He was, in fact, Al Qaeda's chief bomb maker in Mosul and for most of northern Iraq. The IEDs he had made had killed scores of American and Iraqi soldiers.

"What will you do for me if I cooperate?" Hamza asked.

Kincaid tried to maintain a poker face. He was on the verge of smiling, because he knew that Hamza was broken. "I can't promise you anything for sure, but I will make a report for the judge, saying that you cooperated," Kincaid said. "It could mean the difference between a death sentence and spending only a few years in prison."

Hamza nodded, weighing his chances. The chai had boosted his spirits and removed some of the cobwebs from his mind. Hamza wanted to survive. He drank more tea, then looked directly at Kincaid.

"May I ask your name?" Hamza asked.

"Jack," Kincaid said.

"Perhaps someday I will interrogate you, Jack," Hamza said.

"Only if we're both in hell," Kincaid said.

"*Inshallah*," Hamza said. He put down his tea and leaned back in his chair. He looked down, then raised his eyes to look directly at Kincaid.

"I can give you some information about Al Qaeda," Hamza said. "If you promise not to execute me."

"I believe we have a deal," Kincaid said, as he took out a pen and a notepad and gave them to Hamza. "I want the names of all of your associates and the locations of your weapons."

Kincaid had decided not to tell Hamza that his son was dead. Getting the information on the IEDs was crucial, and that news likely would have ended any chance of obtaining his cooperation. At any rate, Kincaid figured Hamza would end up getting hanged by the Iraqi courts or sentenced to life in prison, regardless of what Kincaid recommended.

Several hours later, Kincaid walked out of the interrogation center and across the compound toward the gym. Hamza had given up half a dozen locations of weapons caches and Al Qaeda safe houses, along with the names of a dozen Al Qaeda operatives. His loyalty to Al Qaeda, Kincaid thought, was subordinate to his need to save his own ass.

JSOC was located on the edge of the US airfield in Balad, in a place known as the Compound. The well-guarded site consisted of more than forty acres filled with mobile homes that housed the army's Delta Force, Navy SEALs, Army Rangers, and British Special Operations soldiers, along with teams of American case officers, interrogators, intelligence analysts, and other support people.

The JSOC troops had an air-conditioned gym with a weight room and a dozen elliptical machines, next to a mess hall that served four meals a day for operators who worked around the clock. On one side of the compound was a shooting range, used primarily by soldiers firing their 9mm Berettas, Sig Sauers, and Glocks. The entire compound was surrounded by high concrete walls, with soldiers manning machine guns in guard towers. Interspersed around the living quarters were fifteen-foot-tall Jersey cement blocks, designed to deflect mortar and rifle fire.

As Kincaid walked into the gym, he noticed a tall blond female army interrogator who worked for JSOC. She was running on a treadmill, her long hair waving back and forth. He'd met her before; she had the body of a goddess but the personality of a drill sergeant. She had not accepted his offer to join him for a cup of tea. He was near the end of a year-long tour in Iraq, and he still had not found a girlfriend. There were only a handful of women at Balad, and the competition was furious. He got on the elliptical machine and tried not to look at the blonde. He was looking forward to leaving Iraq before Christmas.

CHAPTER 16

*The principle of reciprocation is almost always employed
at the beginning of a recruitment cycle. One of the easiest
ways for a case officer to initiate and develop a relationship
with a potential agent is to fill some small need the agent
has revealed.*
—*Studies in Intelligence*, vol. 57, no. 1, March 2013

Islamabad, Pakistan
June 1, 2004

As Rauf Jawad stepped off a Pakistani airline 757 at Benazir
Bhutto International Airport, he inhaled the air of his native
country and reflected on the past four years. Jawad had
graduated from the University of New Mexico with a BA in
international relations, but his years at the university had been
lonely and frustrating. He had been distracted by the hundreds
of young women who wore shorts that barely concealed their
private parts and skimpy tops that revealed the top half of their
breasts. He'd fantasized about having sex with them, but he had
been rejected by every girl he had approached.

From conversations with other young men, Jawad knew
about the "hookup" culture that was prevalent at the university.
Young students had sex with no strings attached. It seemed
everyone was doing it. Except him. Jawad worried about his
appearance; he was short and slender, with thick glasses and
dark skin. He was a virgin. And he was a Muslim.

Jawad lived at home with his parents, devout Sunni Muslims who had emigrated from Pakistan when he was only two years old. His father, a physician, had imposed a strict moral code on Jawad: no drinking, no drugs, and no sex before marriage. Jawad was not allowed to attend parties, where girls tried to match the boys in drinking bouts. A girl who was drunk was easy to seduce, he had heard. Of course, he would never consider drinking alcohol. His religion prohibited it. But he couldn't stop thinking about having sex with the girls. Although it was a sin, Jawad masturbated two or three times a day in university restrooms, to avoid losing his sanity.

And then he had met Hasan Rahim, an imam who had visited the Islamic Center at the University of New Mexico. Rahim had expressed sympathy to Jawad. He understood his sexual needs and his frustration. Rahim had then shown Jawad a photo of his niece, Ayisha Fadil, a student in Pakistan. Ayisha was beautiful, and Jawad instantly fell in love with the girl in the photo. Rahim told Jawad that Ayisha was eager to get married and move to America. But first, Jawad needed to have a career, to show that he was capable of supporting a wife.

As a Muslim, Rahim had said, Jawad must try to change America and make it better. Some of the most corrupt elements of the American government were its foreign affairs agencies. Like the State Department. Or the FBI. These organizations had excellent careers for analysts, who look at current events and try to determine what is happening in the world. Had he considered such a path?

Jawad had thought only about following his father into medicine. Rahim pointed out that Jawad had fluency in Urdu and a cultural knowledge of Islam. Such skills would be in demand with the FBI or the State Department.

After his initial meeting with Rahim four years earlier, Jawad had flown to Islamabad with his parents and met Ayisha briefly;

then they had exchanged letters and phone calls. Jawad wanted to marry her immediately, but Ayisha told him she would first complete her own studies at the Islamic International University in Islamabad. In reality, both Ayisha and Rahim wanted to ensure that Jawad obtained useful employment with the US government before she sacrificed herself on the marriage altar.

As Jawad walked through the airport, he looked at the photo he carried of Ayisha and fantasized about their wedding night. He was about to lose his virginity, and it couldn't be soon enough.

Jawad took a taxi to an upscale neighborhood in northern Islamabad. The taxi stopped in front of a palatial home. Two stories high, its entrance was flanked by tall pillars of marble. The house was surrounded by a lush lawn, with mango, lime, and olive trees. In the background to the north were the Margalla Hills, topped by low-hanging clouds. Located in the most exclusive area of Islamabad, the home was the residence of Hasan Rahim, a colonel with the Inter-Services Intelligence agency of Pakistan.

Inside, Jawad was greeted by Rahim, who embraced him.

"Welcome home, brother," Rahim said.

"It is my pleasure, sir," Jawad said, looking around. "I thought Ayisha would be here to greet me."

Rahim smiled as he took Jawad by the arm and led him to a small chamber. "Are you ready for marriage?"

Jawad smiled and nodded. "I am looking forward to it," he said. "When will I see Ayisha?"

Rahim opened the door to a small antechamber, where Jawad's parents were waiting. They hugged their son and exchanged greetings.

"By my authority, I am prepared to conduct your wedding, if you will permit me," Rahim said. "Your bride and her parents are in the next room."

"Yes, of course," Jawad said.

"Then I must ask you, are you entering this marriage on your own free will?" Rahim asked.

"Yes," Jawad said.

Rahim went through a door to another room and asked the same questions of Ayisha. He returned with her. She was dressed in a traditional Pakistani wedding gown, a red anarkali frock laden with gold sequins. Ayisha smiled at Jawad, who felt light-headed with anticipation and excitement.

Rahim produced a marriage license and instructed the bride and groom to sign it.

"We shall now proceed with the ceremony," he said.

After an evening of dancing, eating, and talking to relatives, Jawad and Ayisha took a taxi to the Islamabad Marriott. As they entered the room, Ayisha could see that Jawad trembled and avoided her gaze. She took his hand and sat with him on the edge of the bed.

"Don't worry, Rauf," she said. "I'm also a virgin. We both have much to learn."

She leaned over and kissed him, and he responded with intense passion. Ayisha slowly, sensually slipped off her dress, revealing burgundy panties and bra trimmed with black lace. She began to unbutton his shirt, while he sat still, barely breathing. As she unbuckled his pants, he seemed unable to even lift his arms.

Ayisha was not a virgin, and she knew how to seduce a man. Jawad, to her, was still a boy. She did not love him, but she felt affection for him, as she would a younger cousin or family friend. She would teach him what he needed to know to satisfy her own needs.

<CO>

The next morning, Jawad went to answer a knock at the door and found Rahim standing in the hallway.

"May I talk with you for a few minutes?" Rahim asked.

"Yes, of course," said Jawad, wondering why Rahim felt the need to intrude on them so soon after the wedding.

Rahim sat in an easy chair across from Jawad, with Ayisha on the couch, next to Jawad.

"I want to say how pleased I am with your marriage," Rahim said. "Although I am a little sad that Ayisha will be leaving us for America."

"I will take good care of her, sir," Jawad said.

Rahim smiled and waved his hand. "We are all family now," he said. "Please call me Hasan."

"Very well, Hasan," Jawad said.

"I want to ask you about your career plans," Rahim said. "Ayisha tells me you have been offered a job as an analyst with the FBI."

"That is true," Jawad said. "If I pass the security background check. I took the polygraph test last week, and they said I passed. I believe I will get the job. After I complete training at Quantico, there is an opening for me in the Albuquerque office."

"Excellent," Rahim said. "That will be a good career for you."

Rahim exchanged a brief look with Ayisha, and she nodded. Jawad would never know that they had been planning all along to make the recruitment pitch now, in Pakistan. If they tried to recruit Jawad in the United States and he declined, or turned them in to the FBI, they would be in jeopardy. If Jawad turned them down here, he would likely end up in a fatal accident, run over by a car. An unfortunate way to end a marriage but safer for them.

"I would like to ask you a philosophical question," said

Rahim. "Do you consider yourself a Muslim first, or an American? How do you identify yourself?"

Jawad sat back, puzzled. He turned to Ayisha, and she squeezed his hand in encouragement.

"I've never really thought about it, Hasan," Jawad said. "My religion has always been important to me, but I have grown up in America."

"When I first met you, Rauf, you were very unhappy attending the university in Albuquerque," Rahim said. "You told me you felt you did not belong there, that the women acted like whores. Do you feel any different now?"

Jawad blushed as he looked at Ayisha. "After I met Ayisha, I no longer paid attention to the girls on campus," Jawad said. "But yes, I still feel out of place in America. People there do not seem willing to accept us Muslims. We will always be seen as foreigners."

"If there was something you could do to change things in America, would you be willing to help bring about that change, to make it a better country?" Rahim asked.

"Yes, I suppose. What do you have in mind?" Jawad asked.

"I have many friends in the government of Pakistan who believe that the United States is engaged in a war against Islam," Rahim said. "Living here, so far away, we have a hard time knowing what is really going on in America, especially within the government. What we need is information. Would you be willing to help us obtain information, in order to protect our religion, and the Pakistani people?" Rahim asked.

"Wouldn't that be dangerous?" Jawad asked. "If the FBI learned I was providing you with information, they would arrest me and put me in prison."

Ayisha put her hand on his inner thigh, sending tremors through Jawad. "Rauf, Hasan and I will do everything to protect you. We can teach you how to be safe."

Stunned, Jawad turned to Ayisha. "Are you also involved in this?" he asked, incredulous.

"I was afraid you would not want to marry me if you knew about my government activities," Ayisha said. "I love you, Rauf, but I also love Allah. I am a Muslim, and a Pakistani."

As Ayisha looked at Jawad, pleading with her eyes, she continued to slowly move her hand along his thigh. He began to get an erection. Jawad suddenly stood up and walked back and forth across the room. He looked at Rahim, then back at Ayisha, shaking his head in disbelief. Slowly, he began to realize the gravity of his situation.

"You're an intelligence agent for the Pakistani government!" he shouted at Rahim.

Rahim motioned for him to quiet down. "Calm yourself," Rahim said. "Yes, my friend. I am an intelligence officer for the government of Pakistan. I am also a devout Muslim. I wish no harm to America. I only want to prevent America from doing harm to Pakistan."

Jawad slowly sat down next to Ayisha, but keeping some distance from her. Was she just using him? Was their marriage based on a lie?

"Forgive me, Hasan," he said. "This comes as a great surprise. I don't know what to say."

Rahim walked over to the couch and put his arm around Jawad, comforting him.

"I know this is not easy," Rahim said. "And if you do not want to do this, I will understand. I will leave this room, and you may forget everything that was said."

Jawad looked at Ayisha, who smiled and looked at him warmly. He had just had the most amazing sexual experience, and he did not want it to end.

"What would I have to do?" he asked.

Rahim exhaled slowly, trying not to show his relief. For

years, he had cultivated Jawad, and he did not want to see his efforts wasted. "You would not have to do anything," he said. "Just observe and listen, and occasionally report back to me."

"I hear the US National Security Agency intercepts and reads emails that are sent to places like Pakistan and countries in the Middle East," Jawad said.

Rahim nodded and said, "You will not use any electronic communication with me. I will contact you in person from time to time, or one of my associates will visit you. No one in the US government will know."

Rahim could sense that Jawad's resolve was weakening, and he decided to push him into a commitment. "I must now reach an understanding with you, Jawad," he said. "Are you willing to work with us, to protect Pakistan and the religion of Islam?"

Jawad extended his hand to Rahim, who shook it.

CHAPTER 17

It's no use going back to yesterday, because I was a different person then.
—Lewis Carroll, *Alice's Adventures in Wonderland*

The Duck Pond
University of New Mexico
June 2, 2016

Bill Roberts parked his Chevy behind Popejoy Hall on the University of New Mexico campus and walked toward the student union building, then up to the second-floor lounge, where he sat facing a glass window, pretending to read the student newspaper, and watched the plaza. He observed scores of students walking across the campus, but nobody who appeared to be conducting surveillance. Roberts waited another ten minutes, then walked north along the second floor, past student government offices, downstairs, and out a side door.

Roberts walked through campus toward the Duck Pond. It was almost sundown, so only a few people were around the pond that sat just west of the Zimmerman Library. Roberts walked across a wooden bridge, heading for a small peninsula that featured clumps of oak and mesquite trees. Several dozen mallard ducks swam near a fountain in the pond around the peninsula. He walked to a wooden bench surrounded by oak trees, where Jawad waited for him.

"I hope you have something important," Jawad said.

"I do not want to be seen talking to you unless it is absolutely necessary."

Roberts sat next to him on the bench. After Sanchez had established ties with Al Qaeda and the ISI a year earlier, Hamza had made it clear to Sanchez that, as an infidel, he would take orders from any Muslim in the chain. Subsequently, Sanchez had introduced Roberts to Jawad, telling Roberts that Jawad was the liaison between Al Qaeda and the Zeta cartel. Roberts, consequently, was at the bottom of the chain, and he knew it. But he didn't like it. Roberts pulled out his photo of Kincaid and handed it to Jawad.

"Who is this?" Jawad asked.

"His name's Wayne Kincaid," said Roberts. "He's been hanging out with the Bandidos, but I think he may be DEA."

Jawad studied the photo, then returned it to Roberts. "How do you know him?"

"I got his photo from a Navajo cop on the reservation," Roberts said. "He thinks Kincaid is a Bandido. I'm not so sure."

"Why do you think he is with the DEA?" Jawad asked.

"Too much damned coincidence," Roberts said. "We have a big operation going on, and this guy just shows up and hangs with the Bandidos?"

"Do you think the DEA suspects you?" Jawad asked.

"Maybe. I don't know," Roberts said. "I just got this feeling. Maybe it's time I get out of here."

Jawad stared at Roberts for a long moment before replying. "You may be right. You've been careless and unproductive on your job," Jawad said. "You have a very bad reputation."

"What the hell are you talking about?" Roberts asked.

"You forget that I work with the FBI Joint Terrorism Task Force," Jawad said. "The state police and the FBI know you, and they talk about you in unflattering terms. They say you are lazy, and that you have a gambling problem."

162

Roberts glared at Jawad, imagining how good it would feel to smash his fist into Jawad's scrawny face, breaking his glasses. Then throwing him into the duck pond. The little bastard loved giving him orders, Roberts thought as he struggled to control his temper.

"I'm not the problem," Roberts said. "We gotta do some damage control. And that means taking Kincaid out."

"How do you propose we do that?" Jawad asked.

"We let Al Qaeda take care of him," Roberts said. "You need to get in touch with Sanchez and let him know about Kincaid."

"What if you are wrong? What if Kincaid is not DEA?" Jawad asked.

"Then all we've done is got rid of another biker," Roberts said.

As Roberts walked back across the bridge of the Duck Pond, Jawad thought about his best course of action. He knew he was obligated to tell Sanchez about Kincaid. If he did, however, Sanchez would likely try to hunt down Kincaid and kill him. The death of a federal agent could bring massive, unwanted attention and in turn jeopardize the mission. As for the Al Qaeda operatives, they must be protected. Kincaid could be a problem, however, and he must be investigated.

None of this could interfere with Jawad's cover. Hasan Rahim's instructions had been clear: Jawad must continue his advance into the upper ranks of the FBI. Soon, he would have an opportunity to transfer to FBI headquarters in Washington, DC. He would be in the lion's den, where it would be easier to gather information and, ultimately, influence policy decisions. His wife, Ayisha, could find a job as a translator for FBI headquarters, in the document exploitation division.

The timing could not be better, since the FBI had orders

from the White House to become more inclusive and hire more ethnic people; he knew from his own experience that FBI supervisors were all concerned about not being viewed as racist. Such a reputation was a career killer for a white male FBI supervisor. Jawad had a top-secret security clearance, and nothing in his background would raise a red flag. He did not drink or use drugs, and with Rahim's training, he had been able to pass the FBI's polygraph, which was administered every five years. The main question he had feared was: Have you ever been contacted by a foreign intelligence agency?

The FBI and other federal law enforcement agencies throughout the United States were enamored with the polygraph, even though it was not viewed as reliable by scientists and was not allowed as evidence in American courts. Lie detection by the polygraph is based on the premise that telling a lie causes specific physiological responses based on blood pressure, pulse, and respiration. Rahim taught Jawad to manage his body's unconscious and conscious responses, such as remaining calm and regulating breathing and responses in order to pass the test, thus making the polygraph-machine results inconclusive.

Rahim had assured Jawad that, in reality, most polygraph results were inconclusive. The FBI agents relied more on the pre-polygraph interview for truth detection. They watched for body language and looked for inconsistencies in answers to the same question asked in different ways. Especially the eye movements, which were more reliable than the machine.

Jawad's results were always inconclusive because he was so nervous during the polygraph exam, but the FBI needed people with his background, so the inconsistencies were over-looked because no other red flags showed up during his back-ground investigations. His credibility was also enhanced by his marriage. The FBI viewed married employees as more stable.

Jawad smiled as he recalled Ayisha's revelation to him after they had been married in Islamabad. He had felt betrayed at first, but Ayisha had cushioned him against the shock by making love to him in ways he could never have imagined. She had been patient and gentle with him at first, then unleashed her passion, discarding all her inhibitions. She wore a hijab in public, but she was a tiger in bed. Although submissive in the eyes of the outside world, she had quietly assumed control of their relationship. Her sexual prowess quickly overshadowed his concerns, and she never let him know that Rahim was not her uncle, nor that she had not been a virgin when they married. Jawad, of course, did not know the difference.

Ayisha was not only his wife and lover; she was his case officer. She trained him in all aspects of clandestine activity, including use of secure communications. They never had any direct communication with ISI headquarters. After their initial contact with Rahim, he had turned them over to a Pakistani agent posing as a businessman in Paris, using code words and phrases that were sent in letters through the Pakistani embassy in Washington. Once a year, they traveled on a vacation to Europe or Mexico, where they met their handler at parks and hotel rooms for debriefings. Never the same country, never the same meeting place. Jawad never wrote down any classified information; the ISI was more interested in the FBI's tactics and procedures, and it continued to groom Jawad for a deeper penetration of the bureau.

So much to gain, Jawad thought, and so much to lose if he was exposed. He decided he had no choice but to contact Sanchez. Jawad opened his cell phone and dialed.

"Sanchez, we have a problem."

CHAPTER 18

> *The inherent inflexibility of the FBI bureaucracy conflicts
> with the very heart of the intelligence mission. Intelligence
> officers must be imaginative to intuit patterns that might
> signal an unconventional attack on the order of 9/11. They
> need to act more quickly and decisively than traditional
> law enforcement officers. The FBI moves slowly, managing
> its employees by command and control.*
> —John Yoo, former deputy assistant attorney general,
> *Los Angeles Times*, March 21, 2007

Albuquerque
June 3, 2016

Kincaid took the Montgomery Boulevard exit off I-25 and
rode his Harley east down the busy commercial street, then
turned onto San Pedro Drive, a two-lane street that meandered
through residential neighborhoods. He was now looking not
only for the Bandidos and Zeta cartel operatives operating in
New Mexico—but also Al Qaeda.

Before leaving his apartment in Santa Fe, Kincaid had
downloaded the digital images of the Lybrook safe house and
made eight-by-ten-inch prints of Hamza, Sanchez, and the
other operatives. He normally would have emailed the images
to Jackson, but he still didn't know if there were more leaks at
the Albuquerque DEA office.

In any case, he thought, the FBI should take over the case

and send a dozen agents to raid the reservation safe house. In Kincaid's experience, however, the FBI was cautious and slow to react. It was too full of bureaucrats who were reluctant to take chances.

Kincaid parked his Harley in the Uptown Mall, in front of the Eddie Bauer store. He walked in, pretending to shop for clothes. If he had missed surveillance, this was his final chance to spot it. After a few minutes, he left the store and walked west along Fountain Plaza.

He came to a downstairs walkway next to the Elephant Bar Restaurant and walked down one flight, to the mall's underground parking garage. As he walked through the garage, he looked around for cameras in the ceiling and for people who looked out of place. He was in America, not a foreign country, so he wasn't too concerned about being seen on camera, but he did not want to be seen getting into a car with Jackson, who appeared from behind, slowing down.

"Need a ride?" Jackson asked as he lowered the window on his Chevrolet Tahoe.

Kincaid nodded and quickly got into the front passenger seat. The car pickup was the usual method for DEA agents to conduct meetings. The underground garage was not an ideal pickup site because there was only one way in and out, but it did offer good concealment and a logical cover for being in the shopping area.

Jackson continued around the lot and drove out of the exit. A few miles later, he turned right on Comanche Road, a two-lane street that went through a residential area. Jackson pulled over to the right into Holiday Park, a small patch of green just past Juan Tabo Boulevard. They could hunker down in the parking lot for about fifteen minutes before attracting attention from locals. Retired people walking their dogs or mothers pushing strollers could be very curious and sometimes called police if they saw two men sitting too long in a parked car.

Kincaid reached inside his shirt and withdrew the photos he had taken of Henry, Hamza, and Sanchez. He handed them to Jackson, who looked them over.

"I recognize Sanchez and Henry, but who the hell is that with them?" Jackson asked.

"Khalid Hamza," Kincaid said. "He's Al Qaeda. Or maybe he's with the Islamic State of the Levant, or ISIS, or whatever the hell they call themselves. They're all the same. Jihadist bastards who want to take civilization back to the dark ages."

"How do you know him?" Jackson asked.

"I was in Delta Force, back in Iraq in 2004," Kincaid said. "I captured this son of a bitch in Mosul. He was a bomb maker for Al Qaeda back then. I guess they let him go after we pulled out of Iraq."

The telephoto lens did not bring Hamza into focus as sharp as Kincaid would have liked, but Kincaid was sure it was him. Would it be good enough for a facial recognition match through the FBI's BATS system? Maybe, maybe not.

"Did you take this on the res?" Jackson asked.

"Yeah," Kincaid said. "I followed John Henry up there from Las Cruces. He brought five of these guys up from a house down in Mesilla."

"How did you get on to Henry?" Jackson asked.

"I saw him take a phone call at a bar in Pecos," Kincaid said. "So I followed him down to Las Cruces two nights ago, to this house. I kept after him the next morning, up to a house on the res. I took these photos just before sundown."

"I'm fucking impressed," Jackson said. "And he never made you?"

"Don't think so," Kincaid said.

Jackson continued looking over the dozen photos that

Kincaid had handed him. Henry was clearly visible, talking to Sanchez. Several of the photos showed the Al Qaeda operatives taking weapons out of Sanchez's truck. He also noted something else.

"What's this?" Jackson asked.

"I think it's an RPG," Kincaid said.

"Fuck me!" Jackson shouted. "You think the Al Qaeda guys are supplying Sanchez with the heroin?"

"I'd bet a lot of money on that," Kincaid said. "But I think the heroin is the least of our problems. Hamza wouldn't risk coming to New Mexico just to supply the cartel with heroin. He's planning an attack."

Jackson thought for a few moments, then said, "We've got to go to the FBI with this, Wayne."

"Will they do anything about it?" Kincaid asked. "Or sit around and jerk off while the bureaucrats in Washington hold a bunch of meetings?"

"I don't know," Jackson said. "But the FBI's got jurisdiction on the reservation. We have to bring them in on this."

"If we go there, my cover's blown," Kincaid said.

"We have to take that chance," Jackson said. "I need you to explain this to the FBI."

Jackson picked up his phone and made a call to the FBI special agent in charge of the Albuquerque office, Scott Holman, who told him to come to FBI headquarters. At the gate, Jackson showed his identification to the guard, then parked in front of the three-story brown brick building and went inside with Kincaid.

They secured their weapons in a locker, went through the security screening checkpoint, and took the elevator to the third floor. As they headed to the terrorism task force at the end of the hall, several agents stared at them. Most FBI agents were clean-cut, and Jackson and Kincaid stood out with their beards and casual clothes. They walked into Holman's office, where he was just ending a phone call.

"Hello, George," Holman said. "I just got off the phone with headquarters in Washington. They want to know what the hell is going on here."

"Scott, I want you to meet Wayne Kincaid," Jackson said, as he shook Holman's hand. "He's one of our agents. Wayne has some photos we want to show you."

"Okay," Holman said. "Let's go in the briefing room. We have some other people I want in on this."

Holman had been in the FBI for twenty years. He was a devout Mormon, part of a growing Mormon cadre that had expanded during the latter years of the Carter administration. Jimmy Carter had issued orders to both the CIA and FBI to recruit more trustworthy individuals who did not drink to excess or use marijuana. Most young Mormon men went on a two-year overseas stint as a missionary; consequently, they had language skills, and they did not smoke, drink, or use drugs. On the downside, they often had trouble blending in with undercover operations because they were so straight. It was like sending Mitt Romney undercover.

Holman led them around the corner to a room filled by a long cherrywood table with fourteen padded leather chairs around it. On a wall overlooking the room were photos of President Obama and FBI Director James Comey. Holman took his seat at the head of the table, which was already occupied by several FBI agents and representatives from the Albuquerque police and the New Mexico state police.

Jawad sat on one side. When he recognized Kincaid from the photo Roberts had shown him, he quickly looked down at his notepad and tried to compose himself. He was trembling inside. Everything he had worked for the past decade was in jeopardy, and he could end up in prison. He had to fight an impulse to run out of the conference room.

"Gentlemen," Holman began, "this is George Jackson, special agent in charge of the DEA in Albuquerque. I think most of you know him. With him is Wayne Kincaid, one of his agents. George, what do you have for us?"

Jackson took the photos from Kincaid and passed them to Holman. "Wayne took these yesterday on the Navajo reservation, near an old ranch house off State Road 7900, just north of Lybrook. The photos show Arturo Sanchez, who is a major player with the Zeta cartel. He is meeting with Khalid Hamza, whom we believe to be a member of Al Qaeda. Also present was John Henry, president of the New Mexico Bandidos. We suspect that Al Qaeda may have formed some kind of partnership with the Zetas. This is also further evidence that the cartels are working with the Bandidos."

Jawad had to find a way around this; he had to stall the task force.

Holman, on the other hand, felt threatened. The reservation was his turf. If Al Qaeda terrorists were meeting a member of the cartel without his knowledge and were planning a terrorist attack, this could end up destroying his career. He had to find a way to take credit but avoid any blame.

"The FBI has jurisdiction on the reservation," Holman said. "Why didn't you inform me about this, George?"

Jackson stared at Holman for a moment. "Wayne just took these photos late yesterday. I only saw them a few minutes ago," Jackson said.

"Why were you on the reservation to begin with, Kincaid?" Holman asked.

"I was following John Henry from Las Cruces," Kincaid said. "He picked up these five guys from Al Qaeda and drove them right to the res."

"How do you know this guy is Al Qaeda?" Holman asked, pointing to the photo of Hamza.

"I captured him back in 2004, in Mosul," Kincaid said. "When I was with the Joint Special Operations Command. He confessed to being a bomb maker for Al Qaeda."

"So why is he on the street?" Holman asked.

"The Iraqi government let a lot of the jihadis go after we left Iraq in 2011," Kincaid said. "I guess he was one of those released."

"You should have notified me the minute you recognized this guy from Al Qaeda," Holman said. "The FBI is responsible for counterterrorism in America."

Jawad lifted his hand. "Excuse me, Mr. Holman, may I speak on this matter?" he asked.

"Go ahead, Rauf," Holman said. He turned to Jackson and Kincaid and added, "Rauf Jawad is one of our top counterterrorism analysts."

Jawad picked up the photo of Hamza and looked at it, then said, "How far away were you when you took this photo?"

"Maybe a hundred yards," Kincaid said. "With a 300-millimeter telephoto."

"This photo seems a little fuzzy, and there are shadows," Jawad said. "Are you sure this is Hamza? If you captured him in 2004, he is now more than a decade older."

"Not a hundred percent," Kincaid said. "But it's better to assume I'm right, in case it is him. If we have Al Qaeda operatives here in New Mexico, we need to do something about it."

Holman could see that Kincaid was annoyed by Jawad, who came across as condescending. Many times in his career,

Holman himself had had his share of disputes with analysts, most of whom never saw the outside of an office. Like many agents, Holman viewed analysts as glorified clerks. Jawad, however, was his analyst, and he felt obliged to support him. And, he didn't like the DEA, who, in his mind, were mostly cowboys who went around the rules.

"Perhaps, sir, we should send this photo to Quantico for analysis," Jawad said. "They can run it against their BATS records and see if there is a match."

"Sounds like a good idea to me," Holman said, looking at Jackson and Kincaid. "Any objections?"

"Yeah," Kincaid said. "While we all sit around debating the authenticity of this photo, these Al Qaeda people may be carrying out a terrorist attack."

"Sir," Jawad said, "how do we even know that these are people from the Middle East? They may be from South America, and this meeting with Sanchez could have something to do with narcotics, not terrorism. We shouldn't start racially profiling these people until we know more."

Jawad's last sentence was enough to send a cold chill through Holman, who was being considered for a new job in Washington as a deputy assistant director. A complaint of racism from Jawad, or even a doubt raised in a report, could bring that process to a screeching halt. All it took was one Equal Opportunity Commission complaint to derail a career. Since the 9/11 attacks, the FBI had been heavily criticized by American Muslim activists for racial profiling. After Barack Obama became president, the White House prohibited the FBI and other members of the US Intelligence Community from even using the term "War on Terror" or "Islamic terrorists" in their intelligence reports. Terrorist attacks, such as the 2009 Fort Hood massacre, were labeled by the federal government as "workplace violence." The FBI had become, in effect, a politically correct organization, and Holman was a team player.

"Rauf is right," Holman said. "We need more information. We'll run this photo through BATS, and if this is Khalid Hamza, I promise you the full resources of this office."

"How long will that take?" Jackson asked.

"Shouldn't be more than a few days," Holman said. "But the Quantico lab is pretty busy."

As Jackson and Kincaid prepared to leave, Holman took them aside and said, "I think you had better stay away from the reservation until we figure this out."

"We'll be in touch," Jackson said, without replying to Holman's demand.

Kincaid turned to Jackson as they walked toward the Tahoe. "Fucking FBI! What's with Holman?"

"Holman's a devout Mormon," Jackson said. "He doesn't smoke, drink, or chase women. And he doesn't want anything to jeopardize his career. Like being accused of discrimination against Muslims."

"I'm worried about this, George," Kincaid said. "People are going to die because the goddamned FBI is so politically correct."

"How sure are you about Hamza?" Jackson asked as he climbed into the Tahoe.

"That photo wasn't great, but I'm sure it was him," Kincaid said.

Jackson was in a legal bind, because the FBI did have jurisdiction over felony crimes on the reservation, and it was in charge of counterterrorism operations in the United States. If he ignored Holman's demand, he would be putting his own career in jeopardy. But if he ignored the activities of Al Qaeda terrorist operatives and they launched an attack on American soil, he would also be blamed, the FBI order notwithstanding.

To hell with FBI politics; he was not about to let terrorists kill innocent Americans.

"Wayne, can you get back out there and find out what these bastards are doing?" Jackson asked.

"I was hoping you'd say that," Kincaid said, as he strapped on his seat belt. "I have a hunch about that analyst. Let's wait a few minutes and see if I'm right."

As Kincaid suspected, it was not long at all before Jawad quietly left the building. He got into his car, a nondescript Honda Accord, and drove north up the frontage road to Montgomery. Jackson pulled out behind him, keeping two or three cars between them.

"Looks like he's in a hurry to go somewhere," Jackson said. "Think he's dirty?"

Kincaid nodded. "I was watching him, back at the briefing room. He looked real nervous when he saw me come in. And when you told Holman about Sanchez and Hamza and passed around those photos, I thought he was going to faint."

Jawad turned right onto Carlisle Boulevard, drove a few blocks south, and then turned left on Menaul Street. As Jackson followed Jawad down Cutler Avenue, two men in a Hyundai Elantra parked in the Pavilions shopping center observed him drive by. The man in the passenger seat picked up his cell phone.

"He's running an SDR," Kincaid said. "No other reason to go around in a loop."

"Yeah," Jackson said. "But he doesn't know what the hell he's doing. He should have stopped at the Walmart."

Jawad had made a mistake that alerted Kincaid and Jackson. If he had stopped at the plaza and entered the Walmart or some other store to make a purchase, it would have justified his route. By driving out of the way of a normal route to the university, he had confirmed their suspicions.

Countersurveillance was a tactic that both Jackson and Kincaid frequently used. With only one car, however, it was a challenge if the target being followed was trained in SDRs. Jawad, however, gave no indication that he was even looking for surveillance. At Yale Boulevard, Jawad turned left and drove south past the Fairview Park and into the parking lot of the Islamic Center. As Jackson drove past the center, they saw Jawad rushing inside the front entrance. They continued without stopping.

"Looks like he's in a big hurry," Kincaid said.

"The bastard's up to something," Jackson said. "Why else would he run the SDR?"

"What do you plan to do?" Kincaid asked, as Jackson turned left on Gibson Boulevard and headed east.

"I think you're right: Jawad's dirty," Jackson said. "We just have to prove it."

Jawad was relieved to see Ayisha. She motioned him inside her office and locked the door.

"What is happening, Rauf?" she asked.

"I just came from work," he said. "The DEA has photographs of Hamza and Sanchez meeting on the reservation!"

"Sit down and have some chai," Ayisha said. "Tell me everything."

After Jawad recounted the details of the meeting, she said, "Rahim is here. We need to tell him about this."

"Rahim! What is he doing here?" Jawad asked.

Ayisha stared at him with annoyance. "This is his operation. Did you forget?" she asked. "I will go find him."

After Ayisha left the room to get Rahim, Jawad began to lose his composure. He wondered if he should leave the country. What would he do in Pakistan? Where else could he go? How could he support himself? He could not go to prison;

he had heard stories about what happened to men in prison. He shuddered at the thought of being raped by infidels.

Ayisha returned with Rahim, who did not seem pleased to see Jawad. Rahim briefly shook his hand and motioned for Jawad to sit; then he leaned against a desk, looking down at Jawad. Ayisha sat in a chair, watching Jawad, who clasped his hands to keep them from trembling.

"I am surprised to see you, Hasan," Jawad said. "You didn't tell me you were coming to Albuquerque."

"Were you followed here from the FBI?" Rahim asked.

"No, of course not," Jawad said. "I took the route I usually take."

Rahim folded his arms and stared at Jawad. "I have several ISI agents running countersurveillance," he said. "You were followed from the FBI to here by two men in a black Tahoe."

"I'm sorry I did not see them," Jawad said, looking down at the floor.

"Did you stop at the Walmart and make a purchase, like I trained you?" Ayisha asked. "And did you look for surveillance after walking out of the Walmart?"

Jawad shook his head no. "I wasn't thinking clearly. I was worried."

"It seems the FBI has suspicions about our operations," Rahim said. "What has happened to attract their attention?"

"This agent from the DEA, Kincaid, has photos of Sanchez and Hamza, and John Henry, out at the safe house on the reservation," Jawad said. "He knows Hamza, said he captured him in Mosul years ago. He tried to convince the FBI to open an investigation, so I had to object. I told them his photo of Hamza was unclear, that he may have just been another drug dealer from Mexico."

"That was a good move," Rahim said, nodding his head. "What is the FBI going to do?"

"We are sending the photo to Quantico, for comparison with the FBI's photo database of Al Qaeda detainees from Iraq," Jawad said. "This may take several days."

"Then we have to accelerate our timetable," Rahim said.

"Hasan, do you think I should make plans to leave the United States? Is my cover in jeopardy?" Jawad asked.

"And give up everything we have worked for?" Ayisha asked. "When we are on the verge of a new career in Washington? You would have us run away?"

"I was thinking of you," Jawad said. "Of what would happen if we are caught and sent to prison."

Ayisha moved closer to Rauf and placed her hand on his inner thigh, which was both reassuring and sensual.

"Is Kincaid a serious threat?" she asked.

"Yes. He knows too much," Jawad said. "I have bought us some time, but we have to get rid of him."

Rahim looked at Jawad for a few moments, trying to assess his state of mind. Was he reliable? Could he still be trusted to protect the interests of Pakistan? After nearly ten years with the FBI, did he still believe in the cause? Jawad had always appeared too nervous. He truly was not cut out to be a field agent. He had to go.

"You need to get back to work," Rahim said. "And keep me informed about what the FBI is doing."

Jawad stood up, nodding as he opened the door. As he left, Ayisha did not stand but smiled from her chair. After he walked out, Rahim checked the hallway to ensure Jawad was gone, then quietly closed the door, locked it, and turned to Ayisha.

"Do you trust your husband?" Rahim asked, sitting next to her.

"He has always been weak," she said. "I'm concerned he will not be able to withstand an interrogation by the FBI."

Rahim nodded in agreement and picked up her hand, kissing it. "You still have a magical effect on me. Every time I see you, I feel like a young man."

She softly kissed his hand in return and said, "You know how to please a woman. In ways that Rauf has never learned. It's still like having sex with a boy."

"I know it has been difficult for you," he said. "You have been a true patriot, marrying a man you do not love."

Ayisha, during her first year of marriage, had shocked Jawad when she'd told him she had a medical condition that would prevent her having children. He'd been disappointed but accepted the news. She never told him she had an IUD.

Rahim went to the desk and opened his briefcase; he withdrew a Pakistani passport and handed it to Ayisha. "This is a diplomatic passport," he said. "In two days, you will fly to New York, and from there to Paris and Islamabad."

Ayisha looked over the passport and asked, "Isn't there one for Rauf?"

"We need him here to complete the mission," Rahim said. "He will assist Khalid. After the mission is complete, he will join you in Islamabad."

"I must confess, I am puzzled," she said. "I thought it was important that Rauf go to Washington, and continue his career with the FBI."

"That was our intention," Rahim said. "Unfortunately, Rauf has not progressed as we had hoped. He lacks the natural instincts for this work. And, as you just said, he is a weak man. We too are concerned he would not hold up under interrogation."

Ayisha knew that Rauf would not be joining her in Islamabad, but if Rahim wanted to maintain that polite fiction, who was she to argue? For years, the ISI had paid the couple's salaries into a numbered Dubai banking account that had steadily accrued interest. She would not have to work, although she likely would be able to continue her career as a senior ISI agent. Good female agents were uncommon in the ISI, and she had a promising future in Islamabad. They owed her.

"Will you be coming with me?" she asked.

"Yes. My work here is almost done," he said.

CHAPTER 19

If atomic bombs are to be added as new weapons to the arsenals of a warring world, or to the arsenals of nations preparing for war, then the time will come when mankind will curse the names of Los Alamos and Hiroshima.
—J. Robert Oppenheimer, speech at Los Alamos, October 16, 1945

Los Alamos National Laboratory
June 3, 2016

Hamza set out to drive the shortest route to Los Alamos from the safe house near Lybrook. Adnan Kadar sat next to him in the front seat of his Honda Accord. They had rented the car with a driver's license and credit card supplied by Sanchez, so if they had to deal with police, the car could not be traced to them. Beneath his seat, Kadar had stowed a Glock 9mm.

Hamza took Highway 550 south to Cuba, then followed State Road 126 east through the Jemez Mountains to Highway 4, which led directly into the west side of the Los Alamos labs. The map, however, didn't indicate that State Road 126 was torn up and under construction for forty miles. It was dangerous to drive more than twenty miles per hour through the narrow, winding road that was now little more than a dirt path filled with ruts. The road was closely bordered by pine and spruce trees that rose over one hundred feet high. It was a world of shadows and hairpin turns, and Hamza began to feel claustrophobic.

After nearly an hour of driving, Hamza stopped at the side of the road, which overlooked Valles Caldera National Preserve, a former eighty-nine-thousand-acre ranch nestled inside a volcanic caldera. The view was breathtaking, with lush green meadows and yellow wildflowers. It was still a working ranch, with cattle scattered over the grasslands, sharing space with elk and deer. Radiation from a nuclear explosion in Los Alamos would likely ruin the area for wildlife and people, he thought.

"A very beautiful place," Hamza said. "We may be the last visitors to see it in this lifetime."

"It's very sad," Kadar said. "America is such a magnificent country."

"If we must destroy this place, it is the will of Allah," Hamza said.

One of their missions today was to determine whether the route was passable for the rental truck carrying the bomb, which would arrive in a few days. The truck might have gotten through the narrow dirt road, but the real problem came in arriving at the back side of Los Alamos. They approached a sign that said all vehicles were subject to search, and they narrowly avoided driving into a security checkpoint manned by armed guards.

"Pick up the Glock and prepare yourself," Hamza said as he pulled over on the shoulder and began to turn the car around. A sedan with several passengers passed them and stopped at the security checkpoint, only two hundred yards down the road.

Trying not to panic, Hamza turned the car around and drove back to an intersection. He took an alternative route to the east that ran through White Rock and circled back around to the Highway 502, which led directly to the city of Los Alamos. Hamza concluded that a rental truck going through the area might attract unwanted attention, because it would be illogical for anyone to use Highway 4 through the mountains.

He decided he would have to drive the truck to Bernalillo and up through Santa Fe to Los Alamos. Once again, Hamza thought, he had proven the need for area familiarization. He silently thanked his Al Qaeda trainers who had taught him this tactic. Maps could be misleading, and sometimes they were out of date. And the Internet was sometimes lacking in detail in remote areas.

Highway 502 became Trinity Drive, which led them directly to the center of downtown Los Alamos. Hamza stopped in the parking lot of the Chamber of Commerce visitors' center.

"I still find it hard to believe that you can just drive into Los Alamos," Kadar said. "Don't they have any other checkpoints, besides the one on the west side?"

Hamza shook his head and smiled at Kadar. "Americans are very lax on their security," he said. "They are so arrogant they think they cannot be attacked in their own country."

"I thought the attacks on the World Trade Center taught them that lesson," Kadar said.

"Americans have short memories," Hamza said. "They are more concerned with making money."

As he got out of the car, Hamza told Kadar to remain in the Honda while he went into the center. A courteous employee gave him a map of the city and pointed out the various local museums, most of which were located only a few blocks from the visitors' center.

"Is it possible to tour the labs?" Hamza asked.

"Yes, but you have to make a reservation," she said. "They have to clear you through security."

"Of course," Hamza said.

Back in the car, he opened the map and showed it to Kadar. The tourist guide said the Los Alamos labs employed about eleven thousand people and operated more than 2,100 facilities over thirty-eight square miles. The city's population was about twelve thousand. Hamza looked around the parking lot and smiled.

"This is where we bring the truck," he said. "We are only a few hundred meters from the labs. They will not pay any attention to a small cargo truck in the parking lot."

"I don't understand why we are setting off the bomb here," Kadar said. "Why not a big city, like Los Angeles, or even Albuquerque?"

"Los Alamos is where the Americans created the bomb during World War Two," Hamza said. "This place has one of the highest concentrations of PhDs on earth. Scientists, engineers, technicians. All of them looking for better ways to kill Muslims."

Hamza drove out of the parking lot and continued west on Trinity Drive. He looked at the gray metal sheds that lay behind the chain-link fence. Behind the fence, guards carrying M-4 rifles patrolled the area. They seemed ominous in their black boots and khaki uniforms.

"You see why our leaders want to destroy this place?" Hamza asked. "It has enormous symbolic value. We will be striking at the center of the American war machine. All it takes is one atomic bomb, and this place will be uninhabitable for years."

"And Americans will no longer feel safe," Kadar said. "What kind of damage can we do here?" he asked.

"I anticipate an explosion the size of the Hiroshima blast, which was about sixteen kilotons. It will destroy the labs and the entire city. It will kill more than twenty thousand people and lead to the evacuation of hundreds of square miles of radioactively contaminated land," Hamza said. "That would probably affect Santa Fe, the state capital, which has a much larger population than Los Alamos. They may even have to evacuate the capital, and it will ruin their tourism industry."

The commuting distance from Santa Fe to Los Alamos is thirty-six miles. The flight distance, however, is only twenty-five miles, and winds would likely carry radiation directly into Santa Fe, a city of more than a hundred thousand.

"That would be devastating," Kadar said, amazed at the potential consequences of such an attack. "May Allah provide us with this opportunity."

"You want to know something very ironic?" Hamza asked. "Los Alamos National Laboratory is responsible for nuclear crime forensics. Their scientists are supposed to help detect and prevent acts of nuclear terrorism."

Hamza and Kadar both burst out laughing, as Hamza turned right on Diamond Drive, then right again on Canyon Road.

"This will be a very easy drive," Hamza said. "I have not seen any checkpoints, and only a few police officers in the city itself."

"The police will not bother you as long as you do not speed," Kadar said. "Will you be driving the truck? Or shall I?"

"Jabril and Ahmed will drive the truck," Hamza said. "They have volunteered to stay with the truck, as martyrs. We will follow in this car, to provide security. I will set the timer, but they will ignite the bomb if the police discover them. After we ensure the truck is parked in the right place, we will leave the area and drive to Texas, with Mohammed. Sanchez has made arrangements for us to cross the border back into Mexico at Laredo, Texas."

Kadar was hesitant to raise the topic, but it had always been on his mind. "Do you really believe that martyrs are rewarded in heaven with seventy-two virgins?" he asked.

Hamza burst out laughing. "That's what we tell the ignorant young men. Jabril and Ahmed are the ones Vladimir Lenin would have called useful idiots." He turned to Kadar and asked, "Surely you don't believe in that nonsense?"

"Of course not," he said. Kadar had enough intelligence to be skeptical of that promise, but it was an issue that he dared not raise with the imams. At the same time, he was a little disappointed. He liked the idea of having seventy-two virgins for all of eternity.

As Hamza drove by the Los Alamos High School, he observed several dozen young men in green football uniforms practicing their skills. It was a pity they were going to die, he reflected, but quickly dismissed his guilt as he thought of all the Muslim children killed by American bombs in Iraq and Afghanistan.

CHAPTER 20

A man's very highest moment is, I have no doubt at all,
when he kneels in the dust, and beats his breast, and tells
all the sins of his life.
—Oscar Wilde, *De Profundis*

Bataan Memorial
Santa Fe
June 3, 2016

Sundown was approaching as Kincaid walked up to the Bataan
Memorial, a half-moon shaped white granite memorial that
paid tribute to the eighteen hundred New Mexico National
Guardsmen who participated in the infamous Bataan Death
March, after the Japanese defeated American forces in the
Philippines at the outset of World War II. Japanese troops
would frequently beat and bayonet prisoners who fell behind
or were unable to walk. Only half of the New Mexico soldiers
survived.

Kincaid watched as Linda Benally left the Bataan Memorial
Building. Kincaid had called her office, posing as a state government employee, and found out her location. She had been to a
meeting with public health officials to discuss how to better share
information between the Indian Health Service and the State of
New Mexico. As she walked west toward the parking lot, Kincaid
stepped from behind the Bataan Memorial and approached her.
Benally stopped and grew tense as Kincaid walked up.

"I told you I don't want to see you anymore," she said.

"If you'll just give me a minute, there's something I need to say," Kincaid said.

Benally was still angry and disappointed with Kincaid, but she was torn with conflicting emotions. She still liked him, even though she didn't trust him. She nodded and walked with him to a bench next to the memorial. Kincaid sat a few feet away her.

"I'm not who you think I am," he said. "I'm not a drug dealer, and I didn't join the Bandidos."

"Then who are you?" she asked.

"I'm an agent for the Drug Enforcement Agency," he said, taking his credentials out of his jacket and showing them to her. By doing so, he knew he was putting his life in jeopardy and also risking his entire operation. He was also violating DEA regulations that prohibited him from disclosing his identity to anyone without a need to know it.

Benally looked at his credentials, then shoved them back at him. "What's this all about?" she asked.

"I was sent to New Mexico to investigate the Bandidos, and their connections to the Mexican cartels."

"So, you've been *using* me to get in with the Bandidos?" she asked.

Kincaid sighed, then looked at her. "I didn't plan on doing it that way, but it happened," he said. "I was attracted to you, and I like you."

"Damn you, Wayne," she said. "I thought you were for real, and I liked you. I haven't trusted a man for a long time, and now it looks like I never will."

Benally started to get up to leave, but Kincaid placed a hand on her arm. "When I went with you to your uncle's place, and we went to that pond and made love, it meant something to me," he said.

Benally stopped and turned to him, still suspicious but also interested. "I'm listening," she said.

"It's like I've had this dark cloud following me around," he said. "For a few hours that day, it went away."

"What do you mean?" she asked.

"My life's complicated, and most women don't want to be with someone who lives the way I do," he said. "I figured I was doing them a favor, moving on. I didn't think I was ever going to meet a woman I could get involved with again. But I'd like to spend time with you, and see if we can work something out."

She looked at his eyes, barely visible in the fading light. What she saw was truth. Or at least what he believed to be true. Could she trust a man who had lied to her, who apparently lied for a living?

She leaned over and started to kiss him, then backed away.

"What's wrong?" he asked.

"What kind of life could we have?" she asked. "You go around pretending to be somebody you're not. Hanging out with drug dealers. I would worry about you all the time."

Kincaid nodded. "I can understand why you wouldn't want to get involved with me," he said. "It would be difficult."

Benally stared at Kincaid, trying to make up her mind. She was still suspicious.

"Are you investigating my cousin Danny?" she asked.

"He's not our target," Kincaid said. "But he may end up doing prison time, being involved with these people."

"Aren't you afraid I'll tell him?" she asked.

"Look, I'm breaking federal law just telling you who I am," Kincaid said. "If you tell anyone, I could end up dead. But I decided I have to take a chance. I have to trust you."

"Tell me about Danny," she said. "What's he gotten himself into?"

Kincaid pondered how much to tell her. This was not

something he could postpone and check with Jackson about, or anybody else. How much could he trust her?

"Danny's involved with some dangerous people," he said. "He's working for a Mexican drug cartel, and the Bandidos."

"Damn it," she said, looking down. "What can we do?"

"If he's willing to testify against the Bandidos and the Mexicans, I might be able to get him a deal with the US Attorney," Kincaid said.

"Wouldn't that be dangerous?' she asked. "If one gang didn't come after him, the other one would."

Kincaid nodded. "We could try to get him into witness relocation," he said. "Give him a new identity, move him somewhere else in the country."

"That would really upset my uncle."

"Wouldn't he be more upset if Danny ends up dead, or in prison?"

"Do you want me to talk to Danny?" she asked.

"No. I'll do that," he said. "Try to get him over to your place sometime tomorrow night, and I'll meet him."

They both stood up and walked toward her Jeep. She unlocked the door and turned to Kincaid. "Can I really trust you?"

Kincaid brushed back a strand of hair from her face and said, "I've just put my life in your hands."

He leaned over and gently kissed her on the lips, then walked to his Harley. Kincaid watched as Benally got into her Jeep and drove away. He was not satisfied with what he had said. Talking to a woman about his feelings was not his strong point, but he wanted Benally. Maybe he really could have a life with her. He got on his Harley and kicked the starter.

CHAPTER 21

*Do you understand, sir, do you understand what it means
when you have absolutely nowhere to turn?*
—Fyodor Dostoyevsky, *Crime and Punishment*

Safe house
Lybrook, New Mexico
June 4, 2016

As Roberts turned off Highway 550 and headed down State
Road 7900, he pondered his options. The call from Sanchez
had unnerved him. Why did he want to meet him at the safe
house? Roberts was already on edge with the possibility that
Kincaid could be investigating the cartel's operations—and
him. After receiving the call from Sanchez last night, Roberts
packed for his flight, which would leave Albuquerque at 5:30
this evening. He had his passport in his glove compartment
and a suitcase full of clothes in the trunk of his car, which
he would leave at the airport after he met with Sanchez this
morning. He would take a flight to Mexico City, then head for
Belize. Roberts had enough money in his Belize bank account
to live comfortably, thanks to his work for the Zetas.

Money truly would solve his problems, he thought.
Growing up in a blue-collar family in Los Angeles, Roberts had
never had enough. After a stint as a military policeman in the
US Army, he'd joined the DEA and ended up in Albuquerque,

partly because personnel assumed that he could speak Spanish and blend in with the local population.

He'd married Gloria Rodriguez, a beautiful woman he'd met in the Pecos Casino, where she worked as a cocktail waitress. Roberts had just ended a rare lucky streak, in which he had won five thousand dollars at the craps tables. Gloria, who was tired of working, thought he was a good catch. She soon became disenchanted, however, after he continued to lose money while gambling and could barely afford the mortgage on their modest home in southeast Albuquerque. Bills piled up because Gloria couldn't control her spending, and Roberts couldn't stop gambling.

Roberts became delusional, thinking that he could make enough in the casinos to solve their financial problems. Gloria, however, realized that he was a loser and asked for a divorce. She convinced a judge that she deserved alimony equal to half of Roberts's income. That was when Arturo Sanchez had come to the rescue. He hoped he would never see Sanchez again, after today.

Roberts arrived at the safe house as Sanchez walked out the front door.

"Good morning, Bill," Sanchez said, as Roberts got out of his car.

Roberts walked around his car and approached Sanchez, who did not offer to shake his hand. "Morning, Arturo," he said. "What's up?"

Five men carrying AK-47s walked out from behind the house. Roberts slowly began to comprehend what was happening. He was afraid, then angry. "Who are these guys? What the hell's going on?" he demanded.

Sanchez walked closer to Roberts. "You have become a liability, my friend."

Roberts panicked and tried to run back to his car. Two of

the men intercepted him and grabbed his arms while another searched him, finding a Sig Sauer 9mm in a holster behind his back. The assailant also found the photo of Kincaid inside Roberts's jacket pocket. He handed it to Sanchez.

"Who is this?" Sanchez asked. He immediately recognized Kincaid from their encounter in Red River.

"That's Wayne Kincaid," Roberts said. "He rides with the Bandidos."

"Why do you have it?" Sanchez demanded.

"I think he may be a narc for the DEA," Roberts said.

Sanchez handed the photo of Kincaid to one of the men, who also recognized him. He scowled at the photo, looking as if he wanted to crush it in his hands.

"This man was in Army Special Forces, in Iraq," the man said.

"How do you know that?" Sanchez asked.

"He captured me, and he interrogated me. And he shot my son. We need to kill him."

Sanchez walked up to Roberts and said, "I never really trusted you. In part, because you are a DEA agent, and you betrayed your own people. What kind of man would do that?"

Roberts trembled with fear as he looked at Sanchez and the other men. "I can leave New Mexico tonight. I already have a ticket. You'll never see me again!"

Sanchez shook his head. "The DEA would track you down. And you would talk. You would say anything to save your skin and make a deal to avoid prison."

"Please, Arturo! I'll do anything you want!" he begged. "Please don't do this!"

Sanchez pointed toward the badlands. "I'm going to give you a ten-minute head start, in that direction," he said. "Then, these men will come after you. If you can get away, you will be free."

The men released Roberts, who staggered slowly toward the badlands. He looked back at Sanchez, then turned and began to run. After a few hundred yards, he was already out of breath and slowing down. Roberts was overweight and out of condition. As he staggered into the desert, four of the men began to saddle the horses in the corral. Roberts looked back, saw what was happening, and started running again as his adrenaline kicked in.

The men mounted their horses and lined up near Sanchez, who looked at his watch. When ten minutes had passed, he waved them on. The riders took their time, trotting the horses and spreading out. Roberts had just crossed a ridge when he turned and saw the riders moving. He dropped down into an arroyo and began jogging to the right, through deep sand. He stumbled and fell, got up, and continued running through the sand.

Two of the riders crossed the arroyo and followed it on one side, while the other two followed the closer side. The rifles hung by straps across their chests, locked and loaded. The man who had searched Roberts carried an RPG. As they walked along the arroyo, they could see Roberts's footprints.

In desperation, Roberts found a washed-out crevice on one side of the arroyo. It was not quite a cave, but it offered some concealment. Unfortunately, he had no way to hide his footprints leading to it. Roberts crawled inside and lay down, hoping the riders would overlook him. They did not. All four riders moved down into the arroyo and formed a semicircle around the crevice. Roberts looked up, terrified. The men opened fire simultaneously, each emptying a thirty-round magazine into Roberts. The RPG round hit the canyon wall just above Roberts's body, causing an explosion that buried him in dirt.

∞

As the riders followed Roberts, Sanchez turned to Hamza and said, "You said your men needed some target practice."

"An excellent training opportunity," Hamza said. "Although it would have been more challenging if you had let him keep his weapon."

Sanchez walked with Hamza to Roberts's Chevrolet and opened the door.

"What will you do with his car?" Hamza asked.

"I will drive it to downtown Albuquerque," he said. In Albuquerque, he would leave the keys in the ignition with the windows open. He knew it would be stolen within a few hours and likely driven across the border into Juarez by one of the seven thousand gang members in Albuquerque. "Some of the city's gangsters may need transportation."

"What about Kincaid?" Hamza asked.

"I will take care of him," Sanchez said, and got into the car.

CHAPTER 22

There's only one way of escaping trouble; and that's killing things.
—George Bernard Shaw, *Pygmalion*

Safe house
Lybrook, New Mexico
June 4, 2016
2:00 p.m.

After two days on the road from Houston, Dowdy was near the end of his journey with the rental truck. He turned off Highway 550 and drove west on State Road 7900. *Just a few more miles*, he thought, anxious to be done with the trip. He was too damned old to be driving across country in a truck; his back was killing him. Just a few years ago, he could have made the trip in one day. Hell, he had just applied for social security. He didn't have to worry about medical costs since Congress had provided all Vietnam veterans with free care at any VA hospital. It might not be the best care, but it was good enough for him.

Dowdy arrived at the safe house, where several of the men were riding horses around the old ranch. Hamza and Henry were sitting on the porch, under an overhang, smoking cigarettes. Dowdy stopped the truck, got out, and walked over to the porch, where he handed the keys to Hamza.

"Thank you," Hamza said. "Did you have any problems?"

"Nah," Dowdy said. "Got a sore ass from driving two days, that's all."

Henry walked around the truck, noting the padlock on the rear door. He turned to Hamza, who was walking next to him.

"What's in the truck?" Henry asked.

"You don't need to know," Hamza said.

Henry leaned against the truck and folded his arms, looking at Hamza. "I figure you boys are going to attack something here in New Mexico," he said. "I'd just like to know when and where, so we can stay the hell away."

"I'm sorry, my friend," Hamza said. "I cannot discuss our plans."

"Might be a good time to go on vacation, out of state," Dowdy said.

Henry shrugged and started walking to his van. "C'mon, Harry," he said. "We've got things to do."

As Henry drove his van away from the safe house, he said, "Those fuckers are crazy, Harry. What was in that box?"

"Some big fucking metal crate," Dowdy said. "Prob'ly weighed a thousand pounds."

"Did you look inside?" Henry asked.

"Couldn't. It had some fancy electronic lock," Dowdy said.

"I got a bad feeling about this, man," Henry said.

Fort Marcy Monument
Santa Fe
7:00 p.m.

Sanchez turned right off Bishops Lodge Road and headed up to the monument for Fort Marcy. He parked at the end of a loop and walked down a footpath that led past several benches, casually looking for signs of surveillance. The sun was on its way down, and shadows were spreading across the monument grounds. Sanchez reflected on the history of the place. As a citizen of Mexico, he still viewed Santa Fe as captured territory, which had belonged to Mexico until 1846, when US Army General Stephen Kearney took it over and built the fort.

As a soldier, Sanchez could appreciate Kearney's choice for the fort's location. The ground was flat but elevated, overlooking the Santa Fe plaza, only six hundred meters away. Ironic, he thought, that the fort had never been used to defend the city but was ultimately destroyed by American gold hunters, who were so destructive that they tore down the walls of the fort. Now it was a park where tourists could view the city—and where Sanchez could meet the Bandidos.

Henry and Dowdy arrived a few minutes later, walking up a steep path. They found Sanchez sitting at a metal picnic table enshrouded by cedar trees.

"Got your message, Arturo," Henry said. "What's up?"

Sanchez showed Kincaid's photo to Henry and Dowdy, illuminating it with a small flashlight.

"I met this guy in Red River, at the rally. Remember him?" Sanchez asked.

"Yeah," Henry said. "That's Wayne Kincaid. He's been hanging with us a few weeks."

"What do you know about him?" Sanchez asked.

"He said he just retired from the army," Dowdy said. "I checked him out with the people at Fort Bragg. He seems legit."

Sanchez nodded, smiling. "He would seem that way. The Drug Enforcement Agency is very good at preparing cover backgrounds for their agents."

"That son of a bitch!" Henry shouted. "He's a narc?"

"Yes. And I am sure he has targeted the Bandidos," Sanchez said. "And it is likely he has made the connection between us."

"What about your DEA source?" Dowdy asked. "Maybe he knows something about Kincaid."

198

"Agent Roberts is no longer with us," Sanchez said.

"Glad to hear it," Henry said. "I never trusted that fat, sleazy bastard. But what're we gonna do about Kincaid?"

"Roberts's disappearance will bring us a lot of unwanted attention from the federal government," Sanchez said. "Killing Kincaid will make things even worse. But it has to be done, because he can identify our friends from Iraq. Only, we are going to make it seem as though the Iraqis did it. The police will blame both killings on Al Qaeda."

Sanchez handed Henry a plastic bag containing a card with words from the battle cry of the Muslim Brotherhood, the Egyptian organization that inspired Al Qaeda:

Allah is our objective.
The Prophet is our leader.
The Koran is our law.
Jihad is our way.
Dying in the way of Allah is our highest hope.
Allahu-Akbar! Allahu-Akbar!

"After you kill Kincaid, leave this card tucked inside his shirt," Sanchez said. "And be careful not to get your fingerprints on it."

Henry nodded and put the bag in his pocket. He pulled out his knife and examined the edge to see if it was still sharp. "You mind if I cut his nuts off?" Henry asked.

"I don't care what you do with his nuts," Sanchez said. "But I want you to cut off his head, and place it on his chest."

Linda Benally's home
Santa Fe
8:00 p.m.

Kincaid parked his Harley in front of Benally's place and knocked on the door. This time she was glad to see him, although hesitant when she embraced him.

"Do I get to come in?" he asked.

Benally smiled and motioned him inside. "I don't know if I should be seeing you," she said, turning to him. "I'm not really sure who you are. Is Wayne your real name?"

"Yeah," he said. "Last time I checked."

"You're a pretty damned good liar, Wayne," she said, as she took his jacket and hung it on a peg. She sat down on the couch, and he sat across from her. "So tell me, how do I know when you're lying to me?"

"I don't lie to my friends," he said. "It's just something I have to do on the job. Kinda like being an actor. They give you lines, and you follow a script."

"So you're not going to lie to me anymore?" she asked.

"No," he said.

Benally leaned forward and smiled at Kincaid. She placed a hand on his thigh. "Do you still think you can handle a purely sexual relationship with me?" she asked.

"No," he said, taking her hand and holding it. "That's not enough."

"I'm not sure I want to take that kind of chance," she said, letting go of his hand. "I don't want to get hurt again."

Kincaid nodded in understanding. He took a deep breath and slowly let it out. "When I caught my wife in bed with another man, I was only eighteen," he said. "That was twenty years ago, and I don't think I ever really got over it, until now."

"I'm still not sure I can trust you," she said. "But I may give you one more chance."

They were interrupted by a knock on the door, and she rose to answer it. Haskie was standing on the porch.

"Come in, Danny," she said.

As Haskie walked in, he was surprised to see Kincaid, who stood up.

"What's he doing here?" Danny asked.

"Sit down, Danny," she said. "Wayne wants to talk to you."

Haskie pulled a chair from the kitchen table and cautiously sat on it, with the chair back facing Kincaid, who walked closer. Kincaid pulled his identification from his hip pocket and showed it to him.

"I'm a federal agent, Danny," Kincaid said. "I saw you out near Bisti a few days ago, with Arturo Sanchez, John Henry, and their Iraqi friends."

Haskie glared at Kincaid as he stood up and backed away. "So you're a narc," Haskie said. "You got nothing on me."

"How about conspiracy to transport narcotics for sale?" Kincaid said. "Sanchez is wanted by the DEA, and your association with him is all we need to put you away, because you already have a record as a drug dealer. But it gets a lot worse, Danny. Those guys with Sanchez are Al Qaeda, and I'm pretty damn sure they aren't here sightseeing. You can also be charged with conspiracy to commit acts of terrorism, and that's a whole lot of time in federal prison. You'd be an old man before you got out. If you ever got out."

The information about Al Qaeda startled Benally, who moved closer to Haskie. "Jesus, Danny! Terrorists?"

Haskie's jaw dropped as he backed up against the wall. "I don't know who these guys are," he said. "Some friends of Sanchez, who helped him bring in some dope from Afghanistan."

Benally turned to Kincaid. "What the hell is going on here?"

"I'm not sure yet," Kincaid said. "But I know their leader. His name's Khalid Hamza, and I captured him in Iraq twelve years ago. He made bombs for Al Qaeda. You're hanging around with some very dangerous people, Danny."

Benally grabbed Haskie by the shoulders and shook him. "You better tell us what's going on," she said. "Wayne said if you help him, he can make a deal for you with the US Attorney."

"That won't do me no good if Sanchez tells his people to cut my head off," Haskie said, moving toward the front door. "I won't be safe anywhere. Sure as hell not in prison."

"If you testify against Sanchez, Danny, I'll get you in the witness protection program," Kincaid said. "We'll take care of you. Sanchez is the guy we're after, not you."

Haskie suddenly bolted out of the front door, ran to his pickup truck, and drove away.

"Can't you stop him?" Benally asked, turning to Kincaid.

"Let him think it over," Kincaid said, as he reached for his jacket. He put it on and moved toward the door.

"Where are you going?" Linda asked.

"Gotta check out things on the res, before Danny tells his friends who I am," Kincaid said. "We have to find out what these people are doing."

Benally embraced him, then looked in his eyes. "Be careful," she said.

CHAPTER 23

If you don't hunt it down and kill it, it will hunt you
down and kill you.
—Flannery O'Connor, *Wise Blood*

Highway 550
June 4, 2016
9:00 p.m.

After Kincaid got on his Harley, he reached down and transferred his Kahr 9mm from his boot to the inside of his jacket. His cover was blown, and he figured he no longer needed to be discreet. He started the bike and left.

As he rode onto Airport Road, Henry and Dowdy pulled out of a nearby parking lot and followed Kincaid, with their lights off. They had staked out Benally's home, looking for Kincaid. When Kincaid turned south to the access ramp for I-25, they turned on their lights and followed, merging into the flow of traffic.

At the Bernalillo exit, Kincaid headed west on Highway 550, toward the reservation. Henry and Dowdy stayed close through the heavy traffic in Bernalillo, then pulled back as Kincaid left the city limits. He continued past the Santa Ana and Zia Indian reservations, and the highway narrowed to two lanes.

☙

As the traffic thinned out, Kincaid noticed the motorcycle headlights behind him. Too spaced out and irregular for a car or truck, and they stayed back at the same distance. He sped up, and they increased their speed. Who the hell was following him?

Kincaid didn't think Haskie had had time to phone anybody. But a lot of people had seen him at the FBI headquarters the day before, including that analyst, Rauf Jawad. He was sure Jawad was dirty, but did Al Qaeda really have a man inside the FBI? It seemed unlikely, but stranger things had happened. He cursed himself for not carrying more firepower. His Kahr had seven rounds, and he had only one spare magazine.

About fifty miles from Bernalillo, Kincaid rounded a bend in the highway and turned right onto a narrow dirt service road that led up to an oil derrick. He followed the road for about a hundred yards, then killed his light and quickly pulled off the road, stopping his Harley behind some cedar shrubs. The two motorcycles pulled off the same exit, and as they got closer, Kincaid recognized Henry and Dowdy. They slowed down, looking for him, and he stepped out on the road in front of them, Kahr in hand. Both Bandidos swerved to the left, nearly crashing their bikes. Dowdy jumped off his Harley and ran behind some brush, but Henry had spilled his bike and struggled to upright it as Kincaid walked up.

"Looking for me?" Kincaid asked.

"Fucking narc!" Henry shouted as he dropped his bike and began to pull his .357 Smith & Wesson. Before Henry could raise his weapon, Kincaid shot him twice in the chest. Henry fired his revolver once as he fell; the round struck the pavement. Kincaid quickly moved to one side, away from the glare of the bike's headlight, as Dowdy fired a round from his 9mm Beretta. The round passed inches from Kincaid's head.

Kincaid fired one round toward the flash of gunfire and

ran to his right, across the ditch, looking for cover behind some cedar shrubs. He didn't fire again because he couldn't see Dowdy, and he wanted to conserve his limited ammo. He could hear Dowdy moving away from the road, farther into the brush. Dowdy was careless at first, then began to move quietly. Kincaid tried to control his breathing, while also moving slowly, listening for Dowdy.

He remembered that Dowdy had been a grunt in Vietnam with the 101st. How much did Dowdy recall from his time in the jungles of Vietnam nearly a half century ago? Kincaid would try to move to Dowdy's left flank, but what would Dowdy do? Would he anticipate Kincaid's move and set up an ambush, waiting for him? Or would he keep moving and listening?

For several minutes, the area became quiet, as both Dowdy and Kincaid stayed silent, each listening for the other. Dowdy, crouched behind a cedar shrub, rose and slowly began to move to his left, toward Kincaid. Although his instincts were good, Dowdy was sixty-six years old, and his coordination and eyesight were not as good as they once had been. As Dowdy moved from behind the shrub he stepped on a fallen branch, and it snapped.

"Drop your weapon, Harry," Kincaid said, as he walked up slowly behind Dowdy.

"I can't do that, Kincaid," Dowdy said. "I'm not going back to prison. Too damned old for that."

Kincaid moved closer, to within ten feet of Dowdy. "I don't want to shoot you, Harry," he said. "You've fucked up, but you're still a Vietnam vet. I can help you, if you'll let me."

Dowdy took a deep breath and slowly let it out. "I've had a pretty good ride, Kincaid," he said. "I never really wanted to end up in some damned old veteran's home, sitting in a wheelchair."

Dowdy turned and pointed his Beretta toward Kincaid,

who shot him twice in the chest. Kincaid walked up to Dowdy, whose already dead eyes were staring up at the moonlight. Kincaid felt no remorse for killing Henry, but he had not wanted to shoot Dowdy, a fellow combat veteran.

Kincaid walked back to the road and got on his Harley. He started it and continued up Highway 550. He didn't call in the shooting because he didn't want to spend all night talking to the cops while Al Qaeda could be making plans to kill Americans. Since the Bandidos obviously were out to kill him, his cover was definitely blown. It was likely that Hamza knew he was coming.

Santa Fe River
10:00 p.m.

Haskie drove his Ford south on Don Gaspar Avenue in Santa Fe to Vargas Avenue, where he parked and walked along the sidewalk bordering the Santa Fe River, a narrow creek that was usually dry. Sanchez drove up from behind and motioned for Haskie to get in his Chevrolet.

"I'm glad to see that you remembered your training for the pickup," Sanchez said, checking his side mirrors as he drove. "What is so urgent that you had to meet with me?"

"I just came from my cousin's," Haskie said. "Wayne Kincaid was there. He showed me his credentials. He's a narc for the DEA."

"I know," Sanchez said. "He's being taken care of as we speak."

"How?" Haskie asked.

"Our Bandido friends are handling it for me," Sanchez said. "They do not like narcs."

Haskie was quiet for a moment, as he thought about the implications of killing Kincaid. The Feds would be crawling all over New Mexico, looking for anyone involved—including him.

"I'm sure Kincaid told his superiors about us," Haskie said. "He has photos of you meeting with the Al Qaeda guys. They probably have warrants out for our arrest by now."

Sanchez nodded as he looked at Haskie, who hoped he didn't look as nervous as he felt.

"What did Kincaid talk about with you?" Sanchez asked.

"He offered me a deal, if I cooperated," Haskie said. "Told me I could go into witness protection."

"What did you say?" Sanchez asked.

"I told him I'd take my chances, and I left," Haskie said.

"What's your next move, Danny?" Sanchez asked.

"I think I'll head over to the res in Arizona," Haskie said. "I got some friends over there. I may hide out for a while."

Sanchez nodded and wondered how susceptible Haskie was to interrogation. He knew Haskie was close to Benally and his uncle. Then there was John Clearwater, the Navajo cop. Together, Clearwater and the old man might convince Haskie to make a deal with the cops and testify against Sanchez. Haskie was young, and he was scared. And he was expendable. As they crossed Paseo de Peralta, Sanchez pointed to his right, to the Rosario Cemetery, located on the south end of the Santa Fe National Cemetery.

"We can talk there for a while," Sanchez said. "We need to figure this out."

He drove up a narrow road lined with headstones and monuments, stopping between the chapel and a well-lit twenty-foot monument with a cross at the top. Sanchez made a decision. It was time to cut his losses and go back to Mexico. Too many loose ends here, and too much going on with the Al Qaeda lunatics. He could later resume his dealings with Hasan Rahim, to continue importing the heroin from Afghanistan.

Sanchez got out of the car, and Haskie opened the passenger door. As they walked to the rear of the car, Haskie heard Sanchez unsnap his holster. Haskie quickly pulled a Woolrich elite tactical knife from a sheath in his right front pants pocket.

As Sanchez drew his Glock, Haskie stabbed him in the throat. Sanchez dropped the gun and reached for Haskie's knife, but Haskie grabbed his arm and twisted the knife, cutting off Sanchez's airway and causing him to lose consciousness. Haskie shoved him onto the pavement, beneath the statue with the cross. As Haskie withdrew his knife, blood poured from Sanchez, spreading across the pavement under the cross.

Haskie opened the trunk of the Chevrolet and found a cache of weapons, including an AK-47. He drove back to Vargas Avenue, where his truck was parked, and quickly transferred the weapons to his F-150.

As he drove toward Bernalillo, Haskie reviewed his options. He could drive to Arizona and hide out indefinitely with some friends. Or he could do something to help Kincaid. He didn't care about Kincaid, but Linda did. She was his family, and the only person he really cared about. So if Kincaid mattered to her, Haskie had to help him. If Kincaid was still alive.

CHAPTER 24

For they have sown the wind, and they shall reap the whirlwind.
—Hosea, 8:7, King James Bible

Safe house
Lybrook, New Mexico
June 5, 2016
1:00 a.m.

Kincaid stopped his Harley about half a mile from the house. Any closer and they could hear the loud noise made by the bike's exhaust. He parked the Harley off the road behind a clump of piñon trees and began walking toward the house, staying off the road and using cedar shrubs and terrain as concealment. The lack of moonlight helped conceal his approach but also made it more difficult to see what lay ahead. Were sentries posted around the home? Would the horses make noise as he got closer?

Kincaid crouched behind a piñon tree and checked his cell phone, which had no signal. He began to regret his decision not to call Jackson, but he still needed more information to satisfy the FBI. Kincaid turned off his phone and took the Kahr 9mm from his pocket. About fifty meters from the site, Kincaid moved to the ground and began to low crawl, snaking his way through the cedar shrubs and sagebrush. He saw lights on in the house, and he slowly made his way to a window on the back, always staying in the shadows. The window was open, and he could hear voices.

Inside, Hamza had a three-foot-wide whiteboard on a pedestal. He pointed with a stick to the board, while the Al Qaeda operatives sat in chairs, watching. Pasted on the board was a Google satellite map of Los Alamos. Fortunately, Hamza was speaking in English.

"Adnan, Mohammed, and I will drive to this parking lot," he said. "Jabril and Ahmed will follow in the truck and park across the lot, away from us. I will then enter the back of the truck and set the timer. Jabril and Ahmed will remain with the truck. We will then have two hours to get out of the area before the bomb explodes."

Kincaid slowly raised his head to the bottom level of the window, where he was able to see the whiteboard.

"How much damage will the bomb do?" one of the men asked.

"This is a sixteen-kiloton enriched uranium bomb," Hamza said. "It is the same size the Americans used on Hiroshima, Japan, in 1945. It will kill everyone in the city and the surrounding area. Perhaps twenty thousand people, at least."

Kincaid's heart began to pound, and he gripped his Kahr, deliberating whether he would be able to kill all five men. He couldn't see everyone, only Hamza and the backs of two others. Where were the rest? How many rounds did he have left? He had used five on Henry and Dowdy. He had replaced that clip with another one containing seven rounds, and still had two rounds from the other clip. That was nine rounds for five terrorists. If they were lined up as targets. But they weren't.

"We should be able to reach the Pecos Casino before the bomb goes off," Hamza said. "We will change cars there and drive east into Texas. In two days, we will drive across the border at Laredo into Mexico."

Kincaid had seen and heard enough. He knew he had to leave and alert the FBI. As he turned to move away, an outside light came on and a man stepped out with an AK-47 pointed straight at him. Hamza and the others rushed out the side door and aimed at Kincaid, who dropped his weapon. Hamza slowly approached Kincaid, then smiled as he recognized him.

"Well, it's my old friend Jack," Hamza said. "You should have called and let me know you were coming."

"Hello, Khalid," Kincaid said. "I see you're still playing with bombs."

Hamza smiled at Kincaid, then hit him in the gut with his rifle butt. Kincaid sank to his knees, gasping for breath. Hamza searched Kincaid and found his cell phone, which he took.

"Now it is my turn to interrogate you, Jack," Hamza said. "Kadar, handcuff him and take him inside."

Kadar clapped a pair of Smith & Wesson metal handcuffs on Kincaid, while another man held his hands behind his back. They shoved him through the door into the kitchen and placed him in a chair against a wall. Kincaid looked at the whiteboard, trying to collect his thoughts. How in hell did these bastards get their hands on a nuclear bomb? How did they get it into New Mexico? And how was he going to get out of here alive?

Hamza pulled up a chair, its back toward Kincaid. He sat down and smiled at Kincaid. "Who else knows you are here?"

"The FBI, the DEA, and Homeland Security," Kincaid said. "So you might as well forget about your plans. You'll never make it to Los Alamos."

"I think you are alone," Hamza said. "If the federal government knew what we were planning, there would be helicopters flying overhead and a hundred cops outside."

Kincaid shrugged. "They'll be along."

As Kincaid talked, he moved his fingers inside his belt, behind his back. Inside his leather belt, he had glued a small

211

pouch, just large enough to hold a handcuff key. Fortunately, they had cuffed his hands palms inward, so he was able to move his fingers. American law enforcement officers were trained to cuff the hands back to back, to prevent what Kincaid was attempting. He felt the key and slowly began to extract it.

"We don't have time to waste on you, Jack," Hamza said as he opened the wallet they had found in Kincaid's back pocket. "Or, it seems, Wayne Kincaid. Is that your real name?"

Kincaid nodded. "I guess it'll do for now," he said. Kincaid very slowly began to feel for the key hole on his left wrist handcuff, as he held the key with his right fingers. His chair was up against the wall, so none of the terrorists had a direct view of his hands. He concentrated on not dropping the key.

"I spent many years in prison because of you," Hamza said. "I lost my wife, my children, and my home. And you killed my only son."

"He was shooting at me," Kincaid said. "I didn't have any choice."

Hamza stared at Kincaid with an intense hatred. Then he smiled. "You will not die so quickly," he said.

"How did you get out of prison?" Kincaid asked.

"After you Americans left Iraq, the government wanted to show how generous they were to the Sunni leaders in Anbar province," he said. "So they let me go. After seven years in prison. I think you should pay for that."

Hamza walked to the kitchen and poured himself a cup of tea from a pot. He sipped it as he studied Kincaid.

"Back in Iraq, I asked how you became involved with Al Qaeda," Kincaid said. "Before I die, would you like to tell me how it all began?" He was stalling, but he hoped Hamza's vanity would distract him from that fact.

Hamza smiled and returned to his chair. "I will grant you a dying wish. I had just begun to work on my graduate degree in engineering in Mosul when you Americans invaded. At first, I thought it was a good thing, that you got rid of Saddam Hussein. But one day, your warplanes bombed my family home in Mosul. You killed my parents, and my brother, and my sister."

Hamza sighed and sipped the chai. He was silent for almost a minute. Kincaid said nothing.

"I went to my mosque to pray and seek guidance from my imam," Hamza said. "He encouraged me to come back, and we began to talk about our religion, and the need to protect our country from the Americans. Eventually, he told me he belonged to Al Qaeda, and he offered to train me on how to make bombs. When I was ready, we drove to a road used by American soldiers. We placed one IED by the side of the road, and the imam drove the car a block away to wait for me. He had another IED in the trunk of the car, and we were going to drive to another part of the city and explode it, after the first one. I had two cell phones, one for each IED."

Hamza smiled as he recalled the incident. He put down his cup of chai and leaned back in his chair, rubbing his eyes. He looked directly at Kincaid. "As the American convoy arrived next to the IED, I dialed the cell phone to ignite it," he said. "Unfortunately, it was the wrong cell phone. I blew up the imam, in his car a block away."

Hamza started laughing, softly at first, then louder, tears pouring from his eyes. "I killed the imam!"

Kincaid joined him in the laughter. "No shit? You really killed your own imam?" he asked.

"Yes, yes! I blew him and his car to hell!" Hamza shouted.

The other men joined in the laughter. They had all heard the story.

"What did the other Al Qaeda members do when you told them?" Kincaid asked.

213

"I told them the Americans killed him," Hamza said. "When I went to his funeral, I cried real tears, to convince the others. Many of them hugged me, in consolation."

Kincaid finally found the keyhole in his left handcuff and slowly inserted the key and turned it. The serrated edge fell open, and he transferred the key to his left hand and searched for the right cuff keyhole. He tried not to move his arms, to avoid detection.

"Maybe we should put him in an orange suit," Hamza said to the other operatives, who laughed. "And put him in a small cell with a single light bulb that never goes out." Hamza turned to face Kincaid. "But we don't have time for that. I need some answers, and you are going to give them to me."

Hamza walked over to the kitchen counter and opened a drawer, then pulled out a Black and Decker portable drill. He squeezed the trigger, making sure it was charged, and turned toward Kincaid.

"You Americans make nice toys," Hamza said as he walked toward Kincaid, who found the hole to his right cuff and turned the key as Hamza leaned over with the drill.

As Hamza smiled and moved the drill within inches of his knee, Kincaid swung the handcuffs with his right hand, hitting Hamza across the jaw. He kicked Hamza in the knee and shoved him toward the other men, then bolted out the side door and ran around the corner of the house, into the dark.

"Kill him!" Hamza screamed, as he lay on the floor, clutching his knee. The others were stunned and scrambled for their weapons, which were lying around the room. Nobody had imagined that Kincaid had a chance at escape, and they had relaxed. Three found their AK-47s and ran after Kincaid, while the other man went out the front door, to guard the truck and seal off escape in that direction.

Kincaid was running west, in the opposite direction from

his Harley, but he couldn't chance running into the operatives, who were spreading out and firing random bursts from their AK-47s into the night. He paused behind a piñon tree and tried to control his breathing. He had to move, but in what direction? Was there any place he could get help? Kincaid considered lying in wait to overpower one of the operatives and take his weapon. Too risky, he decided, and too much at stake. He had to warn the police. Kincaid decided to head for the Bisti Badlands. It would be impossible to follow him there in a pickup truck. In the worst-case scenario, he was about thirty-five miles from Farmington. He would have to walk, or run.

Inside the safe house, Hamza sat in a chair, massaging his knee and grimacing in pain. He was bleeding from a cut on his jaw. The other operatives returned, shaking their heads.

"We couldn't find him," Kadar said. "You want us to use the horses?"

"Yes, and get moving," Hamza said. "If he gets to a phone, we are dead. Sanchez says he rides a motorcycle. Go back up the road and shoot holes in it, in case he tries to circle back."

Kadar and the other three operatives went to the corral and began saddling the horses, which were nervous because of the gunfire and noise. When Kadar had his horse ready, he walked to the front door of the house, where Hamza handed him the RPG.

"When you find Kincaid, I want you to blow him to pieces with this," he said. "I want to make sure the bastard is dead!"

Kadar nodded and looped the RPG over his shoulder as he mounted the horse. He carried his AK-47 in his right hand and guided the reins with his left. Jabril rode back up the road to find Kincaid's motorcycle, while the other riders used flashlights to find Kincaid's footprints and began to follow him into the badlands.

∞

From behind the horse corral, Haskie quietly moved away on foot. He had arrived just after Kincaid and had watched Kincaid's capture and escape. Haskie had parked his pickup off the road and walked to the safe house, using back trails. If they were about to launch an attack, he needed to know when and where so he could be as far away as possible. After Kincaid was captured and taken inside the house, Haskie had moved from behind the corral up to the site, listening through a window on the opposite side of Kincaid. Since all the operatives were inside, he was not overly concerned about being seen, until Kincaid made his break.

Haskie had hidden under a cedar shrub when Kincaid leaped out the side door. He crawled to the corral after the men rode away. Haskie walked to his pickup and drove to another corral a few miles away, where he kept several other horses. He grabbed the AK-47 he'd taken from Sanchez, saddled a horse, and quietly rode west, trying to guess which direction Kincaid was headed.

Haskie was now determined to help stop the Al Qaeda attack. If a nuclear bomb went off in Los Alamos, the radiation would affect the surrounding areas, including parts of Navajo country. His own people would suffer. He thought about calling the police, but who would believe him? He headed toward the old Bisti Trading Post, which had been deserted for years. Next to it was an abandoned warehouse and the ruins of a Baptist church. Haskie hoped Kincaid would find the place.

Kincaid descended into an arroyo, alternately jogging and walking through the sandy wash in his boots, which were made for riding a motorcycle, not for hiking through the desert. It was difficult going, but he wanted to avoid the skyline. The wash wound through the desert, moving in a northwesterly direction. Kincaid was thirsty and fatigued from the stress of being captured, and he was overwhelmed with anxiety about the pending nuclear attack on Los Alamos. He had to stop it. He had to put aside the fatigue and the thirst and push on.

Kincaid had endured far worse in Ranger school at Fort Benning, and in the Special Forces Qualifications course at Fort Bragg. Beyond the physical endurance demands, he knew this was a mental challenge that he had to overcome. He had to take the pain. If he quit, thousands of innocent Americans would die. Kincaid envisioned the children in elementary schools at Los Alamos being incinerated. Entire families wiped out of existence. Radiation poisoning would eventually kill thousands more in the area. It would be a tremendous victory for Al Qaeda to kill so many Americans, deep within the territory of America.

After a few miles, the wash led to the deserted Bisti Trading Post, a one-story relic of the past. Kincaid ran from the arroyo to the trading post, went inside, and looked for anything he could use as a weapon. Finding nothing, he went through the back door and ran to an old church. Nearly exhausted and thirsty, Kincaid sat down next to the church wall. In the moonlight, he could just make out a message written on the wall: *Jesus Loves All the Little Children of the World.*

If not for the risk of being heard by his pursuers, Kincaid would have burst out laughing. Because his ex-wife, Robyn, was a Baptist preacher's daughter, he had been to church every Sunday for his last two years of high school. Since leaving his wife, however, Kincaid had become agnostic in his religious views. He hoped that God existed, but he wasn't convinced. Jesus had told his followers to turn the other cheek. Kincaid didn't think that would work very well with Al Qaeda. He needed a weapon.

Kincaid's thoughts were interrupted by a slight noise behind the church. He quietly stood and walked around the corner, where he saw a shadow moving a few yards away. He looked down and saw an AK-47 and a canteen of water leaned against the wall. Kincaid picked up the rifle and found it was loaded with a full thirty-round magazine. He carried the rifle and canteen into the shadows away from the church. After looking around once more, Kincaid drank, then looked in the direction of the shadow and smiled. He could hear the faint sound of a horse leaving the area. Nobody but Haskie could have left the rifle.

Kincaid walked to the edge of the service road, which led west. He decided it was too open, with too little cover against armed men on horseback. He turned north toward the badlands and began a slow jog across the desert, holding the rifle at port arms—left hand on the stock near the barrel, right hand on the stock near the trigger guard. Now, he had a chance to survive. But he had to find a good killing ground.

CHAPTER 25

All warfare is based on deception.
—Sun Tzu, *Art of War*

Safe house
Lybrook, New Mexico
June 5, 2016
5:00 a.m.

An hour before dawn, Jawad arrived at the safe house in his Honda Civic. He still did not understand why Rahim had ordered him to take part in the mission. Jawad lacked the skills for such activities. Rahim said that the Al Qaeda men were going to conduct a terrorist attack using explosives against the Four Corners power plant at Farmington. The plant supplied electricity to Phoenix and Los Angeles, and the attack would disrupt the economy in both areas. Rahim said he would not have to actually participate in the attack, just observe how it was carried out. To be a leader of men, Rahim said, Jawad would need operational knowledge.

As Jawad got out of his car, Hamza opened the front door. He pointed his AK-47 toward Jawad, then a flashlight. After verifying Jawad's identity, he extinguished the light. No lights were on in the house.

"Come inside, quickly," Hamza said.

Alarmed and frightened, Jawad went inside, and Hamza shut and locked the door.

"Sit down," Hamza said, motioning Jawad to a chair.

"Is something wrong?" Jawad asked as he looked around the darkened house. A night-light provided dim illumination in the room.

Hamza laid the rifle on the table and sat next to Jawad.

"Keep your voice low," Hamza said.

"I don't understand," Jawad said. "Where are your men?"

"We had a visitor tonight," he said. "The DEA agent, Wayne Kincaid. We caught him listening at the window."

"Where is he now?" Jawad asked.

"Unfortunately, he escaped," Hamza said. "My men are out looking for him. He has no weapons, and he is on foot, so we will find him."

Jawad's fear turned to anger as he stood up. "What if he calls the authorities?"

Hamza laid Kincaid's cell phone on the table. "Not without a phone," he said.

Jawad slowly returned to his seat and sighed. "He may have told his superiors he was coming here," he said. "We should postpone the mission."

Hamza moved his chair closer to Jawad and stared at him, the dim light giving his face a slightly demonic look. Jawad began to fear that Hamza was not entirely sane.

"I don't think you understand what is at stake with this operation," Hamza said. "We are now in a holy war, and this attack will prove that America is vulnerable. The infidels have invaded our lands and killed millions of our men, women, and children. Allah commands that we seek retribution."

"How does bombing a single power plant accomplish that?" Jawad asked.

"Is that what Rahim told you? That we are going to bomb a power plant?" Hamza asked.

Jawad sighed and looked away as he began to realize that he

220

was not in the loop. Arrogant by nature, he found it difficult to comprehend that he had been a fool.

"We are not bombing the power plant, are we?" Jawad quietly asked.

"No, my friend," Hamza said. "We are going to cut off the head of the snake. You are no doubt familiar with the Manhattan Project, when America created the atomic bomb used on Japan? We are going to destroy that installation, and Los Alamos, the city around it."

"You are going to use an atomic bomb?" Jawad asked, incredulous. "Where did you get it? And how did you get it into this country?"

"The details need not concern you," Hamza said. "The weapon is outside, in the truck. All we have to do is drive it to Los Alamos. We had planned to set the timer and leave before it went off. But now things have changed. We must assume that the FBI will be looking for us. So we will set off the bomb together. We will become martyrs."

Jawad abruptly stood and paced back and forth across the room. He felt trapped and desperate. He approved of conventional terrorist attacks. They were necessary to make a point, that America was vulnerable. But an atomic bomb? That would result in retaliation against Muslims everywhere. America would launch a war against Islam. Jawad briefly glanced at the AK-47 lying on the table and wondered if he could grab it and force Hamza to abandon his plan. He quickly rejected the notion, realizing that he had never fired a rifle and also lacked the courage to use it.

"Does Rahim know about this?" Jawad asked.

Hamza stared at Jawad with pity. How could such an intelligent man be so naïve? "It was Rahim's idea," he said. "He has planned this operation for years, ever since he met Osama bin Laden."

"This was bin Laden's plan?" Jawad asked. "He's dead! This is crazy!"

Hamza turned on a small lamp so that he could better scrutinize Jawad's face. "I would be more careful with my choice of words if I were you," Hamza said. "Bin Laden never expected to live forever. Al Qaeda, as I'm sure you know, means the base, or the foundation of a movement that will restore the caliphate and move the world to embrace Islam as the only true religion. Our lives here on earth mean nothing compared to what awaits true believers in paradise."

Jawad slowly backed away from Hamza, as he wondered if he could get out of the room and make it to his car before Hamza shot him. He had no desire to be a martyr.

"Don't you realize that the Americans have an enormous nuclear arsenal? If they find out who is behind this, they will incinerate you, and any Islamic country involved in this," Jawad said.

"It is you who does not understand," Hamza said, as he stood and moved closer to Jawad. "It does not matter how many nuclear weapons America, or the West, has. Allah is on our side, and we will prevail."

As Hamza talked, Jawad had slowly moved closer to the door. Suddenly, he bolted, running toward his car. While Jawad struggled to extract his car keys from his pocket and to open the car door, Hamza placed a hand on his shoulder and spun him around. Hamza hit him in the stomach with his fist, and Jawad collapsed on the ground, sobbing.

Bisti Badlands
5:30 a.m.

Sunrise was only minutes away, and Kincaid was desperately searching for a killing zone, where he could set up an ambush for his pursuers. He could not chance a running gun battle with four armed horsemen, nor could he risk being trapped in a desert fortress with no means of communication. His water was gone, he was hungry, and he had only one magazine for the AK-47. He had walked and run for nearly ten miles, and he needed to rest. Despite all of his special operations training and experience, he was thirty-eight years old, Kincaid reminded himself, and he was feeling every year of it. His legs felt like lead, and his lungs were on fire. He was becoming light-headed from dehydration.

As the shadows faded, Kincaid could see ahead about a quarter mile, where an ancient floodplain narrowed into a thirty-foot-wide arroyo bordered by high cliffs. He had been walking through a multicolored eroded landscape of small clayish hills, shallow ravines, and strange rock formations called Hoodoos, giant pillars of yellow-and-white sandstone that were topped by what appeared to be hats, or in some cases, large beaks. It was almost like being on an alien planet.

Suddenly, he heard hoofbeats approaching. With the increasing light, the Al Qaeda operatives were more easily able to follow his footprints. His adrenaline kicked in, and Kincaid began jogging toward the arroyo. The riders would have to follow him into it. He made no attempt to conceal his footprints. The riders were coming from the southwest, so the sun would be hitting their eyes as they approached. If he could make it in time, before he was seen.

Just inside the mouth of the arroyo, Kincaid spotted a slight depression, only about twenty inches below the lip of a wedge of sandstone. It was not visible from a distance, and it offered only bare concealment, not cover from gunfire. It would have to do. Kincaid lay on his back in the depression, with the AK-47 across his chest. He flipped off the safety and waited.

Kincaid could hear the horses approaching. He peeked

over the wedge of sandstone and saw Kadar arriving on the floodplain with his fellow operatives. They all carried their weapons looped over their shoulders, locked and loaded. Kadar raised his right hand, a signal to halt, and looked down at Kincaid's footprints leading into the arroyo. As far as Kadar knew, Kincaid was not armed. He motioned his team to unsling their weapons and move onward at a slow walk. The sun was appearing before them over the horizon.

Kincaid lowered himself back down and took a few deep breaths. He knew how vulnerable his position was. If they saw him, he would be killed. There was no place to run. He was mostly concerned about the horses. What if they smelled him and started to neigh? He stared straight up at the morning sky, as the gray turned to blue, with streaks of orange coloring the cumulus clouds. A vulture soared overhead, looking for his morning meal.

A good day to die, Kincaid thought. *For them, not for me.* He gripped his rifle more tightly as the horses came closer. He could feel his heart pounding, and he struggled to control his breathing. Two shots, center mass, for each man, he thought. And shoot the horses, if they are used as shields.

Kadar and another rider came within a few meters of Kincaid, and Kadar's horse neighed and moved aside as he smelled Kincaid.

Kincaid rose to one knee and quickly shot the two men fifteen meters to the rear. He then shot Kadar, who was flipping off his safety and trying to aim his rifle. The sun in his eyes cost him several seconds. Kadar fell from his saddle as the horse reared in terror at the noise of the gun. The man next to Kadar struggled to control his horse, and Kincaid shot him before he could bring his rifle around. The battle lasted seven seconds.

Kincaid slowly stood, his ears ringing from the gunshots. He could barely hear the horses screaming. He had walked through the valley of death and survived. The sun emerged over the horizon, its rays illuminating the landscape and giving him hope. Kincaid took a deep breath and tried to calm himself. His heart was pounding. The world around him seemed surreal. He checked himself to ensure he was not wounded.

Kincaid slowly walked over to Kadar, who was bleeding from wounds in his chest and abdomen. Although he was dying, Kadar struggled to find his rifle, lying just out of his reach. Kincaid shot him in the head. He felt no remorse for a man who had planned to kill tens of thousands of innocent people. Kincaid turned and walked toward Kadar's horse, which had run about fifty meters and stopped, with the reins trailing on the ground. The other three horses had run away and would be difficult to catch.

He had to reassure this horse and ride him back to the safe house. Everything depended on it. If he couldn't, Hamza could still carry out the attack on his own. Kincaid breathed in deeply and exhaled slowly. He looped his rifle over his back and slowly approached the horse, which backed up several feet. The noise of the rifle and the smell of blood had terrified the horse, an Appaloosa.

"Easy, boy. Easy," Kincaid said. He placed a hand on his neck, rubbing it. He knew that a horse would react to a man according to its intuition. If the man was nervous or afraid, the horse would be afraid. A horse looked for confidence and safety in a man. Kincaid found a canteen on the saddle and poured some into his hand, letting the horse sip it. If he was thirsty, the horse would be too.

After giving the horse a few more sips, Kincaid drank from the canteen. He then picked up the reins and led the horse back through the entrance of the arroyo, past the dead operatives. He stopped next to Kadar and picked up the RPG. Outside the entrance to the arroyo, Kincaid mounted the horse and headed back toward the safe house at a slow trot. He had to stop the truck, and he was going to kill Khalid Hamza.

Safe house
7:30 a.m.

Hamza stepped onto the porch and looked down at Jawad, whom he had handcuffed to the porch rail. Jawad cowered, trying to curl himself into a ball, then thought about Ayisha and found enough courage to stand and face Hamza.

"Are you willing to become a martyr today?" Hamza asked. "Are you ready to leave this world for paradise?"

Jawad was now convinced that Hamza was irrational but still believed there was a way to reach him. "Rahim has invested a great deal of money and time to help me find a place in the FBI," he said. "He would be very upset if he knew you were putting me in jeopardy."

Hamza laughed and shook his head. "You still don't understand, do you?" he asked.

"What do you mean?" Jawad asked.

"Rahim is disappointed in you," Hamza said. "You have failed to meet his expectations, and he decided that you should become a martyr."

"You are lying!" Jawad shouted, as he shook his handcuffs and tried to break free. "I have to go home! I have a wife!"

Hamza shook his head and walked closer to Jawad. "Your wife will be leaving soon for Pakistan. Rahim is with her. He will take good care of her."

"No! This can't be true!" Jawad screamed as he fell back to his knees, sobbing.

Hamza stepped back into the house and returned with two prayer rugs, which he laid on the ground outside the house, facing east, toward Mecca, Saudi Arabia. He turned back to Jawad.

"Will you join me in prayers?" Hamza asked.

Jawad shook his head no and continued to cry. Hamza returned to his prayer rug and kneeled, then leaned over so that his head touched the ground. He prayed:

Praise and glory be to You, O Allah.
Blessed be Your Name, exalted be Your Majesty and Glory.
There is no god but You.
I seek Allah's shelter from Satan, the condemned.

Jawad stopped crying and examined his handcuffs, looking for a way to get them off. He began to shake the porch frame, desperate to get free.

May peace be upon us and on the devout servants of Allah.
I testify that there is no god but Allah.
And I testify that Muhammad is His servant and messenger.

Hamza stood and carefully folded his prayer rug, which he placed inside the truck. He looked at his watch, concerned that his men had not returned. Hamza went back inside and emerged with his rifle and a backpack, which he also placed in the truck. Two hours had passed since sunrise. He wanted to reach Los Alamos well before noon, the hour he intended to explode the bomb; it was a three-hour drive. He would no longer be going to Laredo. Hamza walked over to Jawad and uncuffed him from the rail. He then cuffed his hands behind his back and walked him back to the prayer spot, facing the morning sun.

"What are you doing?" Jawad asked, as Hamza shoved him to his knees.

"As Allah commands me," said Hamza, and he withdrew a hunting knife from his belt and commenced to saw off Jawad's head. Jawad screamed in pain and passed out. Hamza placed

227

Jawad's severed head on the picnic table, then got into the truck and left.

From half a mile away, Kincaid could see the truck leaving the safe house, heading northeast up the dirt road. He galloped east toward the bluff where the road ascended onto the plateau, weaving his way through piñon trees and around piles of rocks. His horse was almost spent but sensed Kincaid's urgency and found the energy to keep going.

Kincaid stopped behind a clump of rocks overlooking the road and unstrapped the RPG. He walked into the center of the road as Hamza drove over the crest. Kincaid hoped that the RPG would not trigger the atomic bomb, but he was no expert. If that was the case, he thought, better to have a nuclear explosion in a remote area than in Los Alamos. If the bomb did ignite, he would never know about it.

Kincaid could see the astonishment, then fury, in Hamza's eyes, as he recognized Kincaid. The truck's engine roared as it headed straight for him. Kincaid took aim and pulled the trigger from less than fifty yards away. The grenade went through the engine block and exploded, tearing apart the front end of the truck and sending the steering column through Hamza's chest. Shards of glass from the windshield decapitated him, and the truck turned over into the ditch. Kincaid walked to the truck and yanked open the passenger door. He pulled out Hamza's backpack and found his cell phone inside. He was able to get a signal at this elevation, and he dialed George Jackson's cell phone.

"Where the hell are you, Wayne?" Jackson asked.

"On the res. You can tell the FBI we have some evidence about Al Qaeda," he said. "Tell Holman to bring some body bags."

Kincaid waited half an hour until John Clearwater, the Navajo police detective, arrived on the scene. As he walked from his patrol SUV to the overturned truck, Clearwater recognized Kincaid from the photo Roberts had shown him.

"You must be the Bandido," Clearwater said, smiling.

Kincaid stood up from the rock he had been sitting on and showed his DEA ID to Clearwater. "I was for a while," Kincaid said. "Until they shot up my motorcycle."

Clearwater looked inside the truck at Hamza's body, then turned back to Kincaid. "What's in the back of the truck?"

"I haven't looked inside yet," Kincaid said, "but I'm pretty sure it's a uranium bomb. I think we better let the experts from Los Alamos check it out."

Kincaid slowly mounted his horse and rode next to Clearwater. "Tell the FBI I'll drop by later and make my report."

"Where you going?" Clearwater asked.

"I need to see an old friend," Kincaid said, and rode away.

CHAPTER 26

War is hard on soldiers. They see death and destruction. They see comrades injured or killed—and sometimes they must kill others. Some endure the horrors of being a prisoner of war. Returning to a normal life after these kinds of experiences can be very difficult. American Indian cultures have special traditions that help their warriors return home.
—National Museum of the American Indian

Benally Ranch
Navajo Reservation
June 5, 2016
9:30 a.m.

Linda Benally parked her Jeep in front of Herman's home, got out, and knocked on the front door. She started to go inside, then noticed smoke coming from the hogan. She walked over and opened the door. Herman, dressed in his traditional Navajo ceremonial clothes, was making a sand painting. It was a figure of the Encircling Guardian, a square with the east side opened to face the sun. The figure had three crooked arrows in his headdress and carried several arrows beneath his wings. A pot with juniper leaves was brewing over a fire built within a ring of stones; the smoke drifted toward the hole in the ceiling.

"What's going on, Herman?" she asked.

Herman smiled and said, "I'm preparing an Enemy Way ceremony."

Linda sat on a cougar pelt and watched him. "Who is it for?"

"Your friend Wayne," he said.

Linda looked around, puzzled. "Where is he?"

Herman placed a few more sticks on the fire. "He'll be along soon."

Kincaid stopped his horse on a bluff overlooking Herman's place. He could see the smoke coming from the hogan, and he saw Linda's Jeep. He was tired. More tired than he had ever been. He cantered down the hill and up to the corral. Linda came out of the hogan to meet him as he dismounted gingerly.

"Are you okay?" she asked as she approached him, noticing the AK-47, which he laid against the corral fence.

Kincaid was exhausted but relieved. The stress of the fight had drained him of emotion. Without a word, he embraced Linda and held her for a long moment.

"Did you see Danny?" she asked.

"He's somewhere on the res," Kincaid said. "Last time I saw him was at the old Bisti church."

"What?" she asked.

"It's a long story. Is Herman in there?" he asked, pointing toward the hogan.

"Yes," she said. "He's waiting for you."

Kincaid moved toward the hogan, as though in a trance. He could see the faces of Hamza and the boy he had killed in Mosul. He heard the screams of the boy's mother. He saw the faces of Al Qaeda insurgents he had killed, too many to remember. He recalled the sound of the Black Hawk's rotor blades and smelled the orange dust of Iraq. He remembered riding across the mountains of Afghanistan and living in caves.

And the Taliban he had killed. Too many to remember. He had been a soldier for so long. Was he really walking toward the hogan? Or was he watching somebody else? He pulled back the entrance door and walked inside, where Herman motioned for him to kneel in front of the sand painting. It was hot, and Kincaid was already sweating.

"It's time to expel your demons," Herman said.

Kincaid kneeled on the edge of the sand painting and watched Herman. Smoke filtered up through the hole in the ceiling as Herman began to chant:

Happily may their roads back home be on the trail of pollen.
Happily may they all get back.
In beauty I walk.
With beauty before me, I walk.
With beauty behind me, I walk.
With beauty below me, I walk.
With beauty above me, I walk.
With beauty all around me, I walk.

Kincaid began to sweat profusely. He was mesmerized by the singing, and he could feel the tension leave his body. He could see the faces of the men he had just shot. He could hear the screams of the horses. He could see the truck explode.

Herman continued to sing:

It is finished in beauty,
It is finished in beauty,
It is finished in beauty,
It is finished in beauty.

The images of battle began to fade, and Kincaid felt a sense of peace. His war was finally over, and he was coming home.

Acknowledgments

I wish to thank Maya Myers, a superb editor whose skills elevated my novel, and the very supportive staff at IngramElliott publishing.

About the Author

John Young decided he would become a novelist when he was a teenager growing up on a farm in eastern New Mexico. He took Ernest Hemingway's advice to go out into the world and experience it, then write. In 1969, he joined the US Army and served one year in Vietnam with the Army Security Agency.

After leaving the army in 1972, he studied journalism at the University of Arizona and became a reporter at the *Arizona Daily Star*, covering the police beat. During the 1980s, he was a reporter for the Voice of America in Washington, DC, and a writer for the US Information Agency.

He moved to Los Angeles in 1988 to study screenwriting and worked as a private investigator to support himself—and for the experience. He was also a police officer and a private investigator in New Mexico.

After the 9/11 attacks, he joined the FBI as a counter-terrorism analyst, working at the National Counterterrorism Center from 2002 through 2004. Not content to sit behind a desk, he joined the Defense Intelligence Agency and became an operations officer, after lengthy training in human intelligence collection. He served in Iraq with the Joint Special Operations Command in 2006 and 2008, and subsequently worked as an instructor for US Army Intelligence at Ft. Huachuca, Arizona. He lives in Tucson, Arizona.

We delight in publishing the nontraditional,
unconventional, and alternative including:

Fiction
Metaphysical
Professional and Nonfiction
Romance
Young Adult
Book Snaps

Review our list of themes and topics, and perhaps
they will inspire you to consider writing for
original genres and audiences.

www.ingramelliott.com

CPSIA information can be obtained
at www.ICGtesting.com
Printed in the USA
FFOW04n1602061017
40764FF